MAGICIANS

A Novel of Transformation and Co-Creation

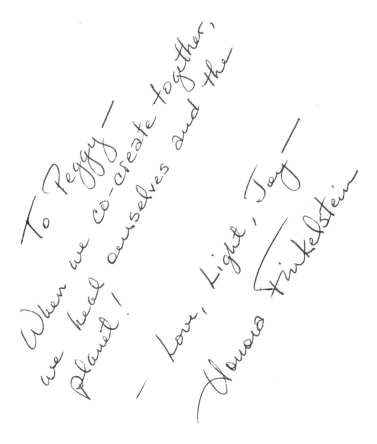

To Peggy —
When we co-create together,
we heal ourselves and the
planet!

Love, Light, Joy —
Norma Finkelstein

MAGICIANS

A Novel of Transformation and Co-Creation

by
Honora Finkelstein

Seraph Press
SUNWEAVERS, Inc.
Reston, Virginia

MAGICIANS
A Novel of Transformation and Co-Creation

© 1994 by Honora Finkelstein.

Published July 1994 by Seraph Press, Reston, VA.

ISBN: 1-885776-00-4

Cover art by Nathan MacDicken.
Book design by Homer Mensch.

HOW TO ORDER:
Please submit all orders and correspondence to
SUNWEAVERS, Inc., 2104 Twin Mill Lane, Oakton, VA 22124;
Telephone: (703) 264-5033.

DEDICATION

This book is dedicated to all the ordinary citizens of the world who are beginning to trust themselves enough to open, reach, risk, love, and act--they are the miracle workers who truly will heal the planet.

FOREWORD

Magicians is a work of fiction. No character in it is intended to bear any resemblance to any real person, either living or dead. However, some real people who have made contributions to planetary healing are named in the book, because I believe it's important even in a work of fiction to give credit where it's due!

I am indebted to the late Frank Capra for having instilled in me at a very early age a faith in the goodness of human beings, and a respect for the magic of life, wherever it may be found.

I also wish to acknowledge my many teachers, whose influence led to the writing of this book: P.M.H. Atwater for her work on the well-documented phenomenon of the near death experience; Dr. Elisabeth Kübler-Ross for graciously giving me information on AIDS, as well as George Melton and the late Wil Garcia for information about AIDS survivors; Drs. Scott Jones and Jan Northup for sharing information on all of their psychic experiments with dolphins; Danaan Parry for creating the Earthstewards Network; the late Jean Eek, whose "Consciousness Frontiers" classes have been for years an inspiration for spiritual growth and development; Barbara Carpenter, whose vision of a Network of Light becomes a reality in this book; Edward Winchester, whose work with the Pentagon Meditation Club, the Peace Shield Meditation Campaign, and the Government Employees Meditation Service have contributed to "peacemongering" in countless ways; Dennis Weaver, Valerie Harper and others for creating the L.I.F.E. program for feeding the hungry in Los Angeles; Tolly Burkan for bringing firewalking to the United States; Gerri Wells for developing the Pink Panthers (which to my knowledge have never actually operated outside of New York City but which I have taken the liberty of expanding to Washington, D.C.); Machaelle Small Wright for her work with nature spirits and devas at Perelandra Nature Center; Hannelore Hahn for empowering women around the world through the International Women's Writing Guild; Barbara Marx Hubbard for asking the question: "What is the purpose of our power?" and all the work she has done to answer that question; Steve Morgan for information on green businesses; my sister Pat Carr for inspiration on many levels for many decades; my husband Jay for all the support he has contributed to my growth; my children

Aileen McCulloch, Kathleen Lynch, Bridget Ingram, and Michael Finkelstein for teaching me so much about relationships and co-creativity; my partner Susan Smily for telling me it really was time to publish and making sure it happened; all the friends who read the manuscript and critiqued it for me; and Dr. Win Wenger for first inspiring me to write this book.

And finally, I want to acknowledge Bugs Bunny and Merlin the Magician for letting me *know* there are other dimensions of being, and Veetkarm and Prem Deben for helping me and lots of others get there. Thanks, guys!

PROLOGUE

Cassie dreamed.

She and Timmy were in the backseat; Mom and Daddy were in the front, and Daddy was driving because they were all really tired of this trip, and Daddy drove faster than Mom did so they could get it over with sooner.

They had been to visit Aunt Georgie in Virginia during Christmas vacation, and had "done" Washington, D.C. Days and days of museums and the zoo and a movie and a musical play that Timmy had slept through both of. Then they had gone down and "done" Williamsburg for three days. Now they were heading back to Akron, Ohio, on I-70, and Mom had patiently told them at least three times in the last five minutes that they were about halfway across Pennsylvania.

Cassie and Timmy were playing one of those endless "look-for-the" games Mom always made up when long car trips got very boring, like finding words that started with letters of the alphabet on road signs—in alphabetical order. Cassie always had an advantage over Timmy in that game because he was only 5 and though, thanks to "Sesame Street," he'd known the alphabet since he was less than 2, had in fact spoken some letters before he'd even said her name or his own, he still sometimes got the letters out of order.

This time the game they were playing gave Timmy an advantage. They were counting U-Haul trucks, trailers, and hamburger boxes on top of cars versus Ryder ones, and Timmy had been given the U-Haul stuff to count. Cassie had four Ryder trucks to Timmy's 11; she was convinced that unless they could pass a Ryder rental lot, she was going to lose miserably.

"There's another U-Haul!" Timmy shrieked, and wriggled out of his seat belt for the forty-leventh time on this trip.

"*Put* your seatbelt back on this *minute*, Timmy!" Mom demanded. "Cassie, are *you* in your seatbelt?"

"Yes, ma'am," Cassie answered, and reached to poke Timmy back into his belt.

That was when the accident happened. She didn't see it, but it was like she knew inside her head how it happened. Daddy was

1

going about 75 mph, and he was in the passing lane, but somebody wanted to go even faster and was on Daddy's rear bumper, pushing him to move over to the right. Except there wasn't any place to move to because there was a big truck in the way, but the person behind kept pushing them anyway, and then Daddy got ahead of the truck and pulled in front of it, but he didn't have quite enough room, and they got clipped from behind and spun off the road to the right, and she was trying to hold on to Timmy, and Daddy was braking except they were now moving along the shoulder of the highway, and then they smashed through a guardrail, and Timmy flew out from under her hands and in between Mom and Daddy and his head went through the windshield.

That was the only part of the accident she actually saw. Except that then they were all four out of the car, floating up, and up, and she could see their crashed car from above twisted partway through the guardrail with the front part all squashed in sort of like a mangled accordion. Looking at the car, she didn't understand how Mom and Daddy and Timmy could still be alive, but then the reason didn't seem to matter much because it felt so good to be out and floating.

Then it got very dark, as if a storm cloud were covering the whole sky or maybe the sun had just disappeared, and she couldn't see the car anymore, but they all four joined hands and started whishing up fast, like fizzy bubbles in a glass of gingerale. And then they were heading out of the darkness toward a lighted place, and the air around them was like gingerale, clear but golden, then growing brighter and brighter as they rose higher and higher. Cassie giggled. It was *fun* to float up fast like this, like gingerale bubbles in a crystal clear glass.

And she didn't know quite how to say it, but the sense of being *loved* was growing brighter and brighter, too. Minute by minute she was filling up with an immense joy, a rapture that was taking over her whole being.

Until abruptly they came to a stop, and she heard a tiny voice in her ear, shouting, but from a long distance away, "Live, dammit! Live!" and she felt a sudden congestion in her chest that was pulling at her. She didn't want to stop, she wanted to continue moving up into that glorious lovelight, but she felt the pressure in her chest trying to draw her downward, back toward the car.

Mom bent forward to kiss her, and Timmy released Mom's hand so he could hug Cassie round the waist. And Daddy kissed her on top of the head like he often did, and though his lips didn't move, she heard him say, "See ya later, kiddo," and then the congestion in her chest happened again, and she was being pulled backward, away from them very fast. Like Daddy's metal tape measure when it was pulled out and then released, she was whooshing backward toward her box. No, the tape measure was around her chest and every few seconds it would tighten up hard, but she continued to whoosh backward.

And her eyes flew open as a paramedic in a blue long-sleeved shirt thumped her one more time on the chest and demanded of her, "Live, dammit! Live!" and she knew she hadn't been dreaming after all.

When Cassandra Allman was 10 years, four months, three weeks, two days, nine hours, and 17 minutes old, she died of cardiac arrest resulting from the shock of a car accident. Seven minutes later she was brought back to life.

And life would never be the same again.

PART I
The Drawing of the Circle

"I believe that the Godhead is broken up, like the bread at the Last Supper, and that we are the pieces."

—Herman Melville, in a letter
to Nathaniel Hawthorne

Lucy Whitefeather didn't like cocktail parties, and this New Year's Eve gathering was no exception. Such affairs were noisy, with lots of people who didn't know each other making polite, superficial conversation. And for Lucy, who commonly experienced synesthesia, seeing sounds and hearing color vibrations, as well as seeing auras around people, a large party could be both emotionally jangling and physically draining.

And why was it that at cocktail parties people who really shouldn't always drank too much, as if there would never be another party or another drink? It looked as if it was going to prove true even at this party, although the only thing being served was white wine.

At least this time it was good white wine. Joel Miner, who owned the gallery in downtown Dallas where Lucy showed her work, was the host of this open house, and he'd ordered several cases of both domestic dry and German sweet wines.

But Lucy had for years maintained a strict limit of two glasses per evening regardless of the festivity. So far she had accepted only one glass and had taken only one sip, just enough to get the full flavor of the rich Mosel. That sip had been about an hour before when she'd arrived, and still the person Joel had invited her here to meet hadn't shown up.

She pulled open the little hand-crocheted evening bag which held her Mickey Mouse watch. She'd crocheted the bag herself this afternoon to hold her driver's license, keys, business cards, and the watch, which she'd decided wasn't quite dressy enough to go with the filmy silver-white Indian cotton dress she'd chosen to wear this evening.

5

Mickey's little hand was on the 10 and his big hand was on the 12. Where the heck was this guy Joel was trying to fix her up with? If the Ancestors hadn't told her this morning that the man Joel was introducing her to tonight was an unawakened rainbow warrior, and that she would have the option of helping him attain his purpose and his potential, she'd pay polite respect to Joel and leave. But then again, if the Ancestors hadn't insisted she come, she wouldn't even *be* at this party. She'd be home with her dog and a good book.

She'd already made the rounds of Joel's large main floor once, moving from room to room, speaking to clients and art patrons, paying her social respects to a couple of critics from the Dallas newspapers, and talking with other artists from the gallery. Fortunately, Joel was playing classical music on his compact disc player, so the waves she was picking up were fairly synchronous and easy to tune out. But she was afraid her party smile might flake off soon, like dried poster paint applied too thickly to a child's art project.

Joel must have sensed her discomfort as he came up moments later and laid a fatherly hand on her shoulder. He was a big, burly, huggy bear, and as he stood behind her, he rested his chin on the top of her head.

"I know how you feel about parties," he whispered, "though you're being a game girl. I do think it would be good if you could meet Adam, though probably better for him than for you. If he hasn't shown up in about 30 minutes, I'm willing to write him off as an utter clod and let you escape."

She turned around and offered Joel a genuine smile, then she puckered her lips for a little kiss, which he returned.

"Thanks, sweetie," she said. "I hate to be antisocial, but sometimes these affairs create a little too much input for me, and I find it hard to have to process so much all at once."

Joel, who was fully aware of Lucy's unusual ability to experience mixed senses and see color around people, said, "Is the music okay? This Bach's for you."

She laughed. "It's fine," she said.

"So," he continued, stepping back a pace and striking a pose for her, "how's *my* color tonight?"

She grinned. "Not bad! I can tell your heart chakra's in the right place," she said jokingly.

6

He opened his arms, and she stepped into them for a friendly hug, cuddling into the warmth as she felt his heart energy penetrate her throat area, making her body tingle all the way down to her toes. For a gallery owner and dealer in a competitive business like the art trade, Joel was incredibly open and loving. The least judgmental person Lucy had ever encountered, he really lived from his heart, which generally appeared to her as bright, pulsating, rosy-pink hibiscus blossoms continuously unfolding. A hug from Joel was like getting presents from Santa Claus, whether you deserved them or not.

"Um," she purred when they finally stopped hugging and separated, "that got my endorphins flowing. Put me back in the game, coach!"

Joel smiled and gently turned her around as he said softly, "Good news! While we were basking in each other's glow, the fellow I asked you here to meet arrived."

She looked toward the door where a man of medium height, about 35 years of age, was taking off his top coat with the assistance of the butler Joel had hired for the evening. Divested of his outer wear, he then turned his attention to the crowd in the room. Joel raised his hand and waved to him, and the man smiled slightly and made his way to where they were standing.

"Lucy," said Joel, "I want you to meet my friend Adam Loveless. Adam, this is Lucy Whitefeather, the young artist I've been raving to you about. You two are a study in contrasts, and I've been most eager to see what kind of mixed media projects you may contrive together."

Adam looked at Lucy myopically; she extended her hand and looked him in the eyes. She was immediately aware that he'd already been ringing in the New Year without moderation before he'd gotten to this party. His eyes were glassy, and the nimbus around his head was pulsating erratically. She tried not to be put off, but his lack of discipline was disconcerting to her.

"Be peaceful," her inner voices cut in. "All you need do tonight is make the contact with him, and extend an offer of help, should he need it. Do not invest anything personal in this meeting."

She relaxed then and smiled. "Hello, Adam," she said, ignoring the jangle she picked up when she smelled the whiskey on his breath.

He focused on her briefly, but then let his attention drift over the rest of the crowd as he answered a perfunctory, "Nice to meet you."

His lack of grace wasn't lost on Joel, who said, "Well, I'll leave you two to get acquainted while I go take care of my other guests. I know you have to leave soon, Lucy."

Adam reached for a glass of wine from the tray being carried through the crowd by the butler, then said to Lucy, still without giving her his full attention, "So, you're an artist. What do you paint?"

She watched his face as he looked everywhere but at her and answered in a most ordinary voice, "Oh, you know, the usual—devas, elementals, nature spirits, totem animals—that sort of thing." She knew if he weren't listening, he'd simply nod politely at her tone without registering her meaning.

He nodded politely. "Interesting," he said.

He chugged down the glass of wine and reached for another as the butler made a return circuit.

"So. . ." he said, finally looking at her, letting his eyes sweep her from head to toe and back again, "Joel has been trying to get us together for a long time."

She could tell he had taken her measure and wasn't in the least impressed. She waited for him to continue the conversational gambit, but he just stood there looking at her in a noncommittal way, as if she were a bowl of Brussels sprouts.

Finally she observed him make what she perceived as a tiny acquiescent shrug, and he said, "So. . . I guess you're my date for tonight?"

The laugh started somewhere down around her solar plexus. She tried to suppress it, putting her hand over her mouth, but it gushed around the edges in an outrageous yawking deluge that caused those nearest her and Adam to turn and stare momentarily.

Adam, in his partially inebriated state, wasn't sure why she was laughing, but he drew himself up defensively.

"Noop," she said, shaking her head, as she began to get control of her convulsive mirth. She crooked her finger and gestured for him to incline his ear so only he could hear. "Sorry," she said, "but I guess Joel misled you. I'm not dessert, to be stopped by for after you've had dinner elsewhere. Also, I'm afraid I don't go out with adolescents."

Adam drew back as if he'd been slapped, and Lucy continued, "Now that I have your attention, let me explain that I'm here because Joel and some others of my acquaintance think highly enough of you to believe you may need my help. So I'm offering it. If a crisis comes for you, and you don't know how to handle it, you may give me a call. Or not. Your choice. I'm in touch with those who know how to heal and make whole both people and situations, but neither they nor I will do so unless invited."

Adam started to say something, but she put a finger on his lips and continued, "If I've offended you, I really didn't mean to. But I needed for you to listen to me, if only for a few seconds. I'm not here to make judgments. But please remember me when your crisis comes. And remember also, whatever happens, the negatives we experience are our opportunities for growth."

Then, very quickly, and obviously much to his surprise, she kissed him.

"Happy New Year, Adam Loveless," she said, and handed him her wine glass. Then she whirled and strode to the coat closet, where she extracted a wool poncho, wrapped herself in it, opened the front door, and escaped without even saying a farewell or thank you to Joel.

Adam stood with a dazed expression, watching her go. But as soon as the door was closed behind her, he put down the wine glass she had thrust at him and followed her out.

The street was dark, and there was no way to see clearly the direction she'd taken. Then an engine caught, and a black truck pulled out from the curb half a block down and headed off around the corner.

"A truck," he groused to himself. "She's a crazy girl who drives a friggin' truck!"

*****

"Poor little thing, orphaned at such a young age. And me her only living relative," said Georgia Allman to her friend Sophie Nussbaum. They were having lunch at the American Cafe in Tyson's Corner.

"She keeps wanting to talk about the accident," Georgia mumbled around a bite of her chicken and walnut salad croissant, "and how she thinks she died and went with her parents and Timmy to heaven, but was then pulled back again by the paramedic who dragged her out of the car. I've told her it was just a dream, but she insists it wasn't, and she won't stop trying to talk about it. Do you think I should take her to a psychiatrist?"

"Absolutely not!" Sophie snorted. "The child isn't psychotic."

"Well, what do you think I should do? I mean, I don't *believe* in heaven. Carl Sagan says all that stuff people claim they experience when they supposedly die and are brought back, like being in a tunnel and then going toward a light, is just a memory from birth—you know, going down the birth canal and then popping out."

"That theory seems to me to be seriously flawed," said Sophie. "For instance, how many babies have their eyes open when they're being born and can see the light at the end of the birth canal?"

Georgia ignored the question and sighed heavily. "Well, anyway, you wouldn't believe the paperwork I've had to handle as the executrix of my brother's estate. He and his wife did leave a will, but there was no provision for putting anything in a trust fund, so Cassie can use everything she inherits now if she wants to. Which I guess in one way is nice, because I won't have to be out of pocket for her upkeep for a while, but then again there probably won't be a whole lot left for her to go to college with when the time comes."

Georgia dropped her voice to an almost conspiratorial whisper. "But I guess the worst part for me is that here I am, at my advanced age, looking forward to some prime time traveling around the world before it's too late for me to really have fun, and I'm suddenly catapulted into motherhood. As her legal guardian, I'll end up being responsible for her until I'm nearly 70. And I was just beginning to enjoy my retirement from the government. Why, I was going to the Bahamas next month, and now I've had to cancel my plans!"

Georgia paused for dramatic effect, so that the awfulness of her plight could sink in to Sophie. When Sophie did nothing but raise her eyebrows, Georgia continued her monologue, "Well, in any case, I'm really tired of listening to her try to describe what she thinks happened to her. I mean, my brother and I weren't especially close because he was so much younger, and frankly I never got along very well with his wife. But I'm *trying* to do the right thing. And yet every time I want to offer Cassie consolation over the death of her family, she just looks at me sort of pityingly and says they're fine. Now, really, don't you think there's something wrong with her?"

Sophie never stopped being amazed at how perceptually limited and insensitive a well-educated person like Georgia could be. They'd been friends since college, much longer than Sophie liked to remember, nearly 40 years, and she'd probably keep on having lunch with her every three months or so until they were both too old to navigate their own wheelchairs. But Georgia was self-centered, narrow, conservative, and left-brained; and when it came to spiritual matters, the woman was not just a closed door, she was locked, bolted, and safety-chained.

"Georgie," she said patiently, "your niece doesn't just *think* she died. She *did* die. From what you told me the paramedic report said, she was legally dead for several minutes. And the near death experience is a highly documented, thoroughly attested to phenomenon, despite Carl Sagan's quasi-scientific explanation. It's so well documented it has its own acronym, NDE. Millions of people have had NDEs. There have been at least eight *million* cases of reported NDEs in the United States. And that doesn't include the cases that *aren't* reported. And it doesn't include children, many more of whom have also had near death experiences. There are even cases of tiny babies having NDEs and remembering them long enough so that when they learn to talk, they describe the experience.

"In any case," Sophie added emphatically, stabbing a forkful of quiche, "your niece Cassandra is a bright, loving little girl. Remember, I'm the one who toured the Smithsonian with your brother's family for three days straight in December, so I got to know the kid pretty well. She's a sweetie. And she's lost her whole family, which would be pretty traumatic under normal circumstances, except that because of her NDE she really believes they're in fine shape, but *elsewhere*. Is that essentially correct?"

"Yes," said Georgia.

"Then, instead of turning her off when she tries to tell you about the experience, you might ask her some questions, like whether she thinks she'll see her family again. Try to find out how she feels about that blissful state in which she last saw them. A lot of people who've had positive near death experiences feel that giving up that state of unconditional love and beauty is the worst part about coming back."

"But, see," protested Georgia, "the whole situation just makes me horribly uncomfortable. I mean, I'm not a psychologist, and I *don't* like having to draw people out. And I'm an atheist, for Pete's sake. I don't *believe* in all that afterlife crap."

"Well, I do," said Sophie softly. "Maybe you should let Cassie move in with me for a while."

Georgia's eyes widened. "Are you serious?" she asked.

"I'm always serious, except when I'm joking," said Sophie. "In this case, I'm dead serious. Or perhaps I should say *near dead*."

Georgia's whole face relaxed into a smile as if she'd just been given a lovely present.

"How long do you want her to stay?" she asked.

And that was how Cassandra Allman, age 10, and Sophie Nussbaum, age 59, became housemates.

*****

Sophie Nussbaum considered herself a pragmatist. By that she meant that a theory was good if it worked. More specifically, she meant by it that a theory was good if it worked for *her*.

When she encountered any idea—from the merits of aroma therapy to the study of dream symbols, from playing music to her plants to a belief in the hereafter as reported by near death experiencers—her principal criterion for making use of that idea was *not* whether some expert had given it a seal of approval, but whether it could be said to measurably enhance her own life.

So, with all due respect to Dr. Sagan, who she was sure had lots of other good ideas, his easy dismissal of the tunnel experience of many NDEs did not in any way diminish its credibility so far as she was concerned.

Sophie had come to the conclusion after nearly six decades of living that the opinions of "authorities" in almost any field were too narrow to fit *her* perspective on reality. Part of the problem was that most so-called experts were hard scientists, not philosophers, and thus leaned toward the understanding of the head, usually at the expense of the heart. Or another way of looking at the discrepancy was what Sophie thought of as "half-brained thinking"—refusing to let the left-hemisphere know what the right hemisphere might be doing.

Another part of the problem, she realized, was that there was just too darn much knowledge these days for anybody to know it all. With every new scientific discovery, knowledge kept increasing at what seemed an exponential rate, leading to more discoveries and ever more expansion of knowledge. And so, modern culture had come to respect and even rhapsodize the specialists in all fields, because they at least had a handle on one particular, narrow part of all there was to know.

For example, most doctors didn't treat the whole body anymore—they specialized in a part of the body, or even in one specific organ. Sophie fully expected one of these days to go to a doctor for an ingrown toenail on her left big toe, and hear the doctor say, "I'm sorry, but I specialize only in *right* big toes!"

But Sophie was a generalist. She truly wanted to know everything about everything. If *she'd* been a doctor, she would have been a family practitioner. And possibly even a practitioner of the family of man—people truly fascinated her with their infinitely various inspirations, ideologies, and idiosyncrasies. So fascinating did she find the human mind that she'd actually thought about becoming a psychologist herself earlier in her life. But her college money had been close to running out, with just enough to squeak out a BA and nothing left for the master's degree or Ph.D. she'd have needed even in the '50s in order to establish herself as a legitimate counselor.

She had ended up majoring in English and minoring in psychology and had ultimately spent 35 years as a high school teacher. In many ways this divergence from her first career choice had been a blessing. It had granted her, during her early singlehood, freedom from her parents' domination, and while it couldn't be considered a lucrative profession, it was both comfortable and respectable.

It had allowed her to sublimate her desires for both motherhood and the field of psychoanalysis by supplying her regularly each September with a new crop of students/subjects, many of whom came to her instead of their assigned counselors with their personal problems. At Christmas, even with the cost of stamps having gone into orbit somewhere beyond Pluto, she could still always count on getting a couple of hundred cards and notes from former students, updating her on their present successes.

And through the literature classes she'd been required to teach, she had learned about the history, philosophy, art, architecture, religion, psychology, and general world view of enough individuals and groups to cut a broad swath across the spectrum known as humanity. At the same time, what she had taught had sparked an avid curiosity in her about how the universe really worked and what man's purpose might be in the grand schemata.

This was, in effect, what had made her a generalist instead of a toady to specialization. It was what had made her a pragmatist and an individualist.

And being an English teacher had ultimately given her one other thing as well. At a time when she had just about decided no man was ever going to please her enough to become her permanent breakfast partner, she had met Saul Nussbaum, the high school principal she had married when she was 35. *Her* beloved Saul.

A man of strength and humor, a fair and just disciplinarian, a good administrator, Saul was also in his mid-30s when they'd met and, remarkably, still a bachelor. Sophie thought him extremely shy with women; he had the reputation among their colleagues of never dating.

She had been thrown together with him on the school's self-study committee and had come to admire both his intelligence and integrity. She'd hoped he would eventually invite her out, but he never had. So two weeks before the end of the spring term, with three months of summer vacation looming like a void in front of her and a transfer to another school in the district scheduled for the fall, she had decided to advance on him.

And why not? If the college kids and even some of the high school kids of that era could go around burning their bras and wearing beads and flowers and taking birth control pills and talking about making love not war, why shouldn't a mature woman invite a mature gentleman to dinner at her apartment?

She was absolutely sure he would *be* a gentleman. Secretly, and while she would never have admitted it to anybody, she had her fingers crossed that he wouldn't also be gay. When she thought back, though, she'd had some gay male friends in college, and not one of them was shy around women.

The memory of that first date still brought a tiny smile to her lips. She had invited Saul on the pretext of discussing the demerits of the "new" English. He had accepted after the barest hesitation. When he rang the doorbell, he had a small bouquet of fresh spring flowers in his hand, and she felt a little flutter in her tummy. He seemed a very old-school gentleman, come courting.

Unfortunately, Sophie really didn't like to cook, preferred salads or soup and sandwiches to heavier meals at night when she was eating alone, and seldom prepared meat just for herself. So, though she'd been cooking for herself and occasionally for guests for over a decade, that night she managed to cremate the potroast. When she took it out of the oven and looked at its charred little carcass, she was afraid she might start crying.

Saul had stared at the lump of carbon as she removed it from the roasting pan and without a trace of irony had said, "Ah, a good Jewish potroast. Just like my mother used to make. Funny, you don't look Jewish."

So instead of being embarrassed, Sophie had laughed. "Well, I'm *not* Jewish, so you'll have to tell me what a good Jewish wife does when the potroast becomes a burnt offering."

"In my family we had a tradition," said Saul. "We got Chinese takeout."

"I'd actually be happy to take *you* out for Chinese—my treat!" said Sophie, "—to make up for the potroast."

"No, no," he'd answered, looking at her carefully coutured dining table, complete with gleaming crystal, silver, and wine bottle chilling in an ice bucket. "Everything here is lovely. We'll just call out for some sort of main dish to go with whatever else you have. Trust me, we'll enjoy it."

And they did.

They didn't get around to talking about the "new" English that night. They had enjoyed the takeout with the other side dishes she had prepared and they had talked about Gilbert and Sullivan operettas, which they both loved, grand opera which they both tolerated provided they'd had naps earlier in the day, and Beatles music which they weren't quite sure about. After they'd shared the wine, had had dessert and coffee, and Sophie had carried the dishes into her tiny kitchen to clean up, she had felt Saul behind her, his hands on her shoulders.

Gently turning her around, he had looked into her eyes and said, "I think you should marry me." Then he had kissed her in a way that sent more heat to her groin than anyone else's kiss had done since she'd first played spin-the-bottle in junior high.

To say, "But we hardly know each other," seemed both trite and somehow not true, so she'd just said, "Why?"

"Because," he said, kissing her unprotesting lips in between the words, "you—make—a lousy—potroast—and you need—someone around—who likes—to cook."

"No-o-o," she said, "I don't mean why should I marry you—I can think of plenty of reasons. But why do you want to marry me?"

"Oh, you want *my* reason," he said softly, as he gently brushed a strand of hair back from her cheek. "Well, you are such a buttoned-down lady at school it never occurred to me you might need someone like me. But when you took that piece of charcoal out of the oven, you looked so vulnerable, and this feeling just welled up inside me. I figured it had to be either love or hunger." He shrugged. "Now I've eaten, but I'm still feeling that same feeling. So I guess it's love."

They spent the rest of that first date making love, and when she woke up in the circle of his arms the next morning she stroked his stubbly chin and said, "I mistakenly thought you were shy around women."

"Oh," he responded, "I *am* shy, and I needed help to overcome it." He ran his hand down her back, cupped her buttocks, and gently drew her closer. "Good help is really hard to find."

They were married two days after the end of the term. They were lovers all of their married life. She had hoped they would have a child, but it didn't happen, and Saul was accepting.

"We could adopt," he said, "but neither of us is a spring chicken. Still, we have all the young ones at school to mold. And we have each other, and such a miracle is the one thing for which I would be willing to offer up everlasting gratitude."

Saul was, in fact, a cultural rather than a religious Jew, and not nearly as interested as Sophie in the way the universe worked.

Once, when she was pontificating about some philosophical principle, he had listened very patiently throughout. Then, when she paused for breath, he interjected, "I found a wonderful recipe today for chicken marengo."

She just looked at him for a long moment, totally derailed from her philosophizing, then said, "You know, Saul, you should have been the Jewish mother, and I should have been the rabbi."

Saul shrugged and grinned. "Next life," he said, "if there is one."

Sophie's own background had been nominally Christian but effectively secular, with a tree at Christmas and new patent leather shoes for Easter, and maybe a trip to the nearby Methodist church on one or the other of those occasions. As a consequence, Sophie had not been browbeaten by any dogma, though secretly she had hungered for the meaning and purpose she thought religion was supposed to offer.

And so, during her 14 years as a spinster school teacher, she had shopped around, taking instruction first among the Protestant sects, then at the Catholic church, then at the nearby Reform synagogue. She had frequently visited Buddhist temples wherever she found them, had investigated the Mormons, and had studied American Indian religions and Islamic customs. She was reading up on Hinduism and contemplating a trip to India when she married Saul, and had to admit she found the concepts of karma, dharma, brahma, maya, and transmigration of souls among the most provocative ideas she'd ever encountered.

Saul told her that, although he was rather relaxed about religion, his family in New York would at least say they were not, so she had volunteered to convert to Judaism. He talked her out of it.

"Even with all you know about all these religions," he had said, "you still seem almost like a *tabula rasa*—you can take the good from each of these philosophies, but still be unsullied by the bad. And there are some negatives in every religion. But you have the joy of a true spiritual eclectic, selecting the choicest kernels of truth as you understand them, and letting the dogmas that make fanatics of some people fall away like chaff. So don't even consider tying yourself down to just one religion.

"And besides," he continued with a devilish little smile, "with a name like Sophie Nussbaum, you'll fool most of my relatives into thinking you're Jewish anyway. Believe me, what they don't know won't hurt them. Or us. Of course, if they ask you directly, you should tell the truth."

They had both laughed about the fact that they'd been married nearly 10 years before anybody asked, and then it was his younger cousin Sarah. They had gone to New York for Passover, and at the dinner table, Sarah had mentioned she was dating a nice young man from Boston whom she had met at college.

"Is he Jewish?" asked Saul's mother Anna suspiciously.

"No, he isn't," said Sarah. "But then, Sophie isn't Jewish either, are you Sophie?"

Sophie nearly choked on a bite of gefilte fish. "No, I'm not," she said when she'd recovered, wondering what plague was about to be visited upon her and Saul. She glanced at Saul, who was pursing his lips and trying not to laugh.

Saul's mother's eyes became as round as her special Passover dinner plates, and she said to Saul's father, "Mordachai, did you know Sophie isn't Jewish?"

Saul's father, without looking up from his dinner, answered, "Of course."

And that was that. The subject never came up again until the day Saul died, and then it was Sophie, not Saul's family, who brought it up.

Saul had died of a heart attack, just a month after he and Sophie had retired from the public schools. On the phone to Saul's mother, Sophie realized she was still in shock.

"You'll have to help me get through this, Anna," she said, not even trying to conceal the anguish in her voice. "We hadn't talked much about what he wanted; we really hadn't considered that either of us might go so soon."

Through her own grief, Anna had soothed Sophie, had talked about sitting Shiva, about funeral arrangements, about having someone say Kaddish for Saul when the time came. The family flew down from New York, bringing their own rabbi with them. And so Saul was buried at the King David Cemetery with appropriate Jewish grace.

Saul's unexpected death had caused Sophie to learn all she could about near death experiences. She knew, for example, that a small percentage of people didn't have positive experiences when they died, but she was convinced a good man like Saul would have gone immediately, as the majority of people reported, into the blissful light. She could picture him in that other dimension right now, making gentle jokes and enjoying the fact that he was someplace he'd never really believed in!

What she didn't understand was why he had gone so soon. And why he had left her behind. They had both waited so long before they'd found each other. And they'd had a mere 21 years together, too short, too short.

Sometimes when she walked through the bedroom they had shared all those years, she would glance at the picture they had had taken of the two of them together on their honeymoon, and she would say aloud, "I don't know why I'm still here without you, my love, but there must be a reason. So wait for me, wherever you are. And don't you *dare* come back over here until I get *there!*"

*****

Adam Loveless was feeling ill. He decided about 3 p.m. on the Thursday after New Year's week that he was maybe coming down with the flu, so he knocked off early from work and went home.

When he got there, he took his temperature, but it was normal. Still, he felt out of kilter, off, like things weren't meshing quite right. He decided to go to bed early and poured himself three fingers of Jack Daniels Black Label to help him relax.

He had a date that night with a sports massage therapist he'd met on the weekend. He fished in his briefcase for his address book, looked up her number, and called the office where she worked.

"Hi, Sheila? This is Adam. . . Adam Loveless. Yeah! Hey, I'm sorry to break our date so late, but I think I'm coming down with something. . . Yeah! I've been feeling awful all afternoon and I wouldn't want you to catch it. . . Yeah!. . . No, I don't want to expose you to whatever it is I'm getting. . . Right!. . . Listen, I'm really sorry. . . No, I mean it. . . I know, but I just feel awful. . . Hey! Catch you later, babe! . . . Yeah, sure, maybe next weekend I'll give you a call. If I'm feeling better."

He hung up the phone and took a long swig of the whiskey, savoring the burn as it slipped down his esophagus and hit his empty stomach.

Sheila had sounded disappointed, and maybe just the least bit miffed, like she wasn't sure she believed he was sick. Well, he'd make it up to her on the weekend. She was, he thought, just his type—pretty, seductive, not too pushy, only moderately bright, and though he hadn't tried her out, she sounded as if she'd be very pliable when it came to sex.

Not at all like that crazy artist Joel had tried to fix him up with. He'd really been stung by Lucy's attitude toward him, much more than he'd liked to admit. Being laughed at was the ultimate rebuff. Who did she think she was, anyway? And why had Joel been so hot for Adam to meet her?

She was really sort of plain looking, when you got right down to it, not the type of girl you'd want to show off to friends you'd want to impress. And her clothes were kind of strange, sort of *nouveau* hippie, with lots of filmy Indian cotton, silver and semi-precious stones in her jewelry, thong sandals—in winter, yet!—and feather earrings. She certainly wasn't a fashion model, and she wasn't a business professional. And she drove a pickup, for chrissake!

Joel had said she was a really fine artist. Well, he could see some of her creative bent in the way she dressed. But he couldn't say he'd found her attractive physically. No, she definitely wasn't to his taste. He determined to put her—and her obnoxious laughter—completely out of his mind.

After all, he'd found no lack for company after hours with other young ladies who liked riding in his BMW—he'd been with at least three—or was it four?—since the New Year. And they all dressed well, were good looking, were satisfactory in bed, and didn't criticize him. Or laugh at him. Was she really calling him adolescent?

He took off his shoes and lay down on the couch. Maybe he was just working too hard. He lay back on the couch pillows and closed his eyes.

Adam had been geared toward the fast lane since he was a little kid. The eldest son of a mustang Army colonel in the Air Defense Artillery, he'd been dragged up in various places round the world—Monterrey, the Philippines, the Washington, D.C. area, and Germany, plus lots of his father's duty tours at Ft. Bliss in El Paso, Texas.

Like a lot of Army brats with hardnosed military dads, he'd had maximum pressure put on him to excel. And he'd succumbed to the pressure, making straight A's, going out for sports, and aiming toward a lucrative career for himself in computer technology.

In fact, the only thing his dad had wanted him to do that he hadn't done was join the military himself. But as a child in the post-Vietnam era, he'd seen what that particular war had done to lots of vets, and he'd decided when he was 16 to resist his father's insistence and make his way in business instead, where he could earn a general's salary without having to wait to middle age. Still, parental pressure had become part of his own internal set of tapes, so when he went off to school, he continued to push himself to succeed in all areas of his life.

He'd gone to the University of Texas at Austin, then had acquired the requisite MBA from the University of Houston. And when the oil business had collapsed in Houston, he'd moved on to Dallas where the economy was more active and more stable. And where there was more chance of acquiring the yuppies' signs of success, like a fancy car, an equally fancy apartment full of high-tech electronic equipment, a Rolex, and a fistful of gold credit cards.

Of course, when you had a high paying job, you had a lot of pressure. But, hey! As the exercise gurus said, "No pain, no gain!"

Speaking of which, Adam didn't exercise much, at least not as much as he should. Maybe a tennis game with a friend every other weekend or so. He'd thought about it on New Year's day and resolved to do more. It was now mid-January and he hadn't done much about it yet, but he resolved again as he was drifting off to sleep on the couch to get in a couple of sets of tennis this weekend.

He woke up around midnight with a tingling sensation down his left side. He thought maybe he'd slept wrong, and that his extremities had just gone to sleep. He tried to shake himself to wake them up, get the blood flowing, get the sensation back.

But no, that wasn't helping. As the minutes wore on, the sensation in his left hand and foot became less perceptible. What in hell was going on? He began to panic; he got out his pocket knife and stuck his thumb. He couldn't feel it, though blood welled out of the cut.

He got up, and was grateful to note he could still walk, though it was like walking on a foot that was dead asleep. He went into the bedroom, lay down on the bed, and decided if he wasn't better in two hours, he was calling the hospital.

By 2 a.m. he had virtually no sensation on his left side. He picked up the phone and dialed 911.

*****

Joe Jacobson was tired.

He was tired of writing a twice-weekly column. He was tired of spending 10 hours a day in front of a computer screen. He was tired of the beastly January drizzle outside, tired of not being able to see the sky from his desk, tired of riding the Metro both ways to work, tired of eating bologna sandwiches for lunch, tired of not having the culinary creativity to make something more interesting for lunch. But 99 percent of his creativity went into his writing.

Unfortunately, he was also tired of writing. He was tired of the issues of racism, black education, and the politics of poverty in Washington, D.C. He was tired of facing the realities that existed for poor, undereducated people in the nation's capital city, about which he had been writing for too many years.

And Joe was still suffering from the emotional recoil of events of the previous year, obviously agonizing more than he'd like to admit.

First of all, the suicide of Dave Shumacher, the city's famous black homeless advocate, had left Joe reeling. For all Shumacher's volubility, his volatility, his crazy intensity, Joe had admired him tremendously, had always been inspired to write eloquently after he'd interviewed the man. The man had had dreams. He'd had vision.

In fact, Joe had been inspired enough by Shumacher to actually volunteer at some of the shelters in town, had helped organize food and clothing collection drives—and had written some vibrant, in-depth pieces on the people he'd worked both with and for there.

Even now, months later, Joe shook his head, remembering the shock and the pain the workers for homelessness and hunger had experienced when Shumacher had been found with the back of his head blown out. Joe had actually hoped it had been murder, but an investigation and a suicide note indicated Shumacher had simply given in to despair.

Joe was devastated. He knew the movement to provide for the homeless could ill afford the loss of such a strong, outspoken, and vital leader. Why, this winter, there had already been 14 deaths of streetpeople from exposure, and the season was barely underway!

And Joe had once admitted to his wife Celeste that underlying his pain over Shumacher's death was an element of anger. Hell, a world which still had such a precarious hold on hope needed people like Dave on the front lines, making news people would pay attention to. People with a prominent profile had a responsibility to be models for others.

Damn it! Shumacher was an icon—in Joe's mind, he didn't have the *right* to throw his life away.

Joe nudged the remains of his bologna sandwich off into the trash basket beside his desk, and thought about the other problems besetting this capital city. Though the present local administration really seemed to be trying to make change happen, the government was still an unwieldy bureaucracy that encouraged waste, mediocrity, and empire building, with an accounting system that looked at where money was spent, but not at the results of the spending. In some ways, it was just a smaller version of the bigger, even more monolithic federal bureaucracy. And that didn't make it any easier to dismantle, whenever any forward-thinking public servant might decide to try.

And then there was the negative image the city seemed to project to people around the country. All too often lately, especially with the scandals about members of the government being involved in either graft or drug-related incidents, the national news had often focused on black-versus-white antagonism, and on the highly publicized drug-trafficking problem in the city. As a black newspaperman in the nation's capital, which was itself 80 percent black, Joe was particularly sensitive to the image members of his race in this particular political spotlight presented to the rest of the nation.

First and foremost, Joe was a newspaperman, and as he liked to think of himself, a watchdog for the public interest. And he tried hard to stay unbiased. But he was really burned out on the subjects of racial tension, minority education, hunger, homelessness, drugs, and other negatives.

Unfortunately, Joe thought, as he stuffed his unfinished bag of potato chips into the bottom drawer of his desk, the "city" was really synonymous with the consciousness of the people who lived and worked in it, where all too many of those in positions of power paid lip service to idealism, but ultimately failed to walk their talk. Politicians, whether in city, state, or federal office, would promise just about anything to get elected, but afterward, the bureaucratic monolith often shunted them into the chutes of self-interest and kowtowing to organized constituencies where prior promises were packed up for storage until the next election.

Or maybe it was really a *lack* of consciousness that was the problem. Joe himself had once had the ironic experience of overhearing a fellow in a grocery store make a drug buy, volubly and in front of some young children, while outside two cops were writing up jaywalking tickets to pedestrians.

Such *un*consciousness extended to the blindness which had been at the core of the country's energy policy, or lack of one. If the federal government had been more farsighted in the '80s, when gas was cheap and plentiful again after the throttling in the '70s by the Arab oil cartel, the U.S. could have been energy self-sufficient by 1990.

Joe had recently applied for a position as environmental editor on the paper, and he'd been doing some research on energy alternatives to fossil fuels. To his amazement, he'd learned that if solar energy had received the financial support from the federal government that had been channeled into other energy sources during the last decade, the solar industry could have been supplying over 80 percent of the country's fuel needs at present, including heating, electrical, *and* automobile powering needs! The technology was already there—all that was needed was support of the solar economy by the federal government so the industry could expand enough for its output to become cheap. And the beauty of solar power was that it was completely non-polluting!

Instead, the nearsighted federal administrations of the '80s had cut out the tax credit to those homeowners who had been willing to implement solar heating on their own. With such help from our own government, we had no need of foreign adversaries.

Joe slouched down in his chair morosely.

At the same time, the U.S. could have phased out the use of nuclear energy, that *bete noire* so many people found terrifying even without the threat of nuclear war because of the lack of clear, safe controls on the proliferation of nuclear wastes. The government would have to spend billions just to clean up the messes that had already been made at existing nuclear sites. And a nuclear plant had a life expectancy of a mere 30 years; after that the reactor would have absorbed so much radioactivity that the plant must be shut down and decommissioned—at a cost of $50 million to as much as $3 billion dollars each. By the middle of the next decade, 67 of the nation's nuclear plants would be ready for decommissioning. What a waste!

And then there was the good news—which never made the newspapers—about wind energy, another source of non-polluting renewable energy that didn't get any credit as being a realistic alternative. Yet, in California right now, there were enough windmills operating to supply all the energy needs of a city the size of San Francisco or Washington, D.C., and wind energy was obviously the most realistic way at present for third world countries to supply their energy needs. If he got the job as environmental editor, he was going to do a special series on renewables.

But through successive changes in leadership, the U.S. government still wasn't making energy self-sufficiency a priorty. Joe tended to smolder around the edges whenever he thought about the situation the country was currently in.

He sighed and looked at his watch. So far, the auspices for the new year hadn't been that terrific. He'd recently read a report indicating that the destruction of the world's rain forests had not been curtailed by the initiatives of Earth Summit. Another not very nice thing to think about, especially with the better scientific minds suggesting many of the environmental problems the planet was facing could only be reversed if all the earth's governments worked together. And that still didn't seem to be happening.

Joe kicked himself for indulging in such draining thoughts during lunch; his depressing reveries were guaranteed to kill what appetite the ubiquitous bologna didn't.

He shrugged and wiped the crumbs from his desk straight into the trash. Another lovely lunchtime was over, and his blank computer screen, patiently blipping a single gray space marker on a field of black, awaited the advent of this afternoon's deathless prose.

Still Joe sat listlessly at his desk, staring at the blip on his screen and wondering just what it would take to get governments to really start thinking globally. And what could ordinary people do to make that actually happen? Experience told him most people just didn't believe they had much say in how the future would turn out. And what really bothered him was that on cold, bleak, winter days like today, he felt powerless himself. So he went by turns from being depressed to angry to cynical to scared silly. To just plain too tired to think.

Joe closed his eyes for a minute to rest them. At the moment what he really wanted to do was sleep through the afternoon.

Only those who believed in something higher and better than 9 to 5 appointed rounds, only true visionaries were willing to risk, and reach, and welcome the change that was necessary to bring about a vision of hope others thought impossible. And such visionaries were too often labeled crazy windmill tilters, unless of course they were incredibly rich, powerful, and influential. Then they were just considered "eccentric."

Joe yearned to find someone, anyone, rich and eccentric, poor but honest, or middle class and idealistic like himself who could marshall the masses with a dream of hope. He was running near empty in his hope tank.

Then he heard a voice.

"Hey, Joe!"

He looked at his computer screen and felt the hair on the back of his neck prickle. There, in black and white, as if Joe were looking at a television instead of a monitor, was the face of Dave Shumacher.

Taken aback, Joe rubbed his eyes and squinted.

"Don't start to sweat, Joe," said Shumacher. "This is just a dream, brought on by your exhaustion and sense of powerlessness. But I really do have a message for *you*," Shumacher continued, pointing his finger like Uncle Sam in a military poster.

Joe was pretty unnerved, seeing Shumacher on his viewing screen, and all he could do was stammer a shaky, "O-o-okay."

"Your subconscious picked me to give you the message," said Shumacher, "because of the way you idolized me at one point, and because I'm a good example for you of what can happen when people get really depressed and feel totally ineffectual. What I'm trying to say is, it's not really me who's talking to you. It's you! Do you understand?"

Joe nodded.

"Okay," said Shumacher. "So! You've probably noticed, haven't you, that time seems to have sped up lately?"

Joe nodded again, vigorously this time. His calendar was fuller than it had ever been before—every night of the week, he could count on having an opportunity, and sometimes a requirement, to attend some event, and usually two or three. He felt he was living a year's worth of activities for every month that passed. No wonder he was so tired.

"Well," said Shumacher, "that's because we, the human race, are heading toward the final countdown for our species. If we don't wake everybody up to action pretty damn soon, we're *kaput!*"

Shumacher drew his finger across his throat in the classic cliche.

"I mean, this is nothing new to you. You've thought about it for a long time. But one of the things you haven't recognized yet is that we're all one. I'm you and you're me, and we always were one, even when I really was Dave Shumacher, and not just a figment of your subconscious. But we didn't act like one, and most of us still don't. I was the wild and crazy activist, and you were the idealistic newspaperman, just like everybody else on the planet thought he or she was autonomous. And in the process of each of us doing our own thing, and feeling as if we're going it alone in this insane world, we sooner or later end up suffering burnout.

"So now I'm dead and you're exhausted, and a whole lot of other people are feeling depressed or cynical or hopeless or nuts. And what they don't realize is that we're all connected, so what one does affects the whole. All that time I was trying to make waves and kept thinking the tide was pushing me back, I really was making a difference. I just didn't know it myself."

Joe nodded again.

"Anyway," continued Shumacher, "getting back to that speedup of time. What's going on is that people are experiencing about as much testing right now as they can tolerate. And it's on all levels for each individual—physical, attitudinal, mental, and spiritual. It's happening everywhere, really, and to everybody. If people haven't learned their particular lessons before, they're getting lots of opportunities to learn them quickly now and in a short period of time. And it's happening both for individuals and for groups."

Joe just kept nodding, still too boggled by what he was seeing and hearing on his screen to move or say anything.

"So," said Shumacher, "I'm here to tell you that your role in all this is to wake people up. And you're gonna have a major opportunity to do so soon. And when that happens, you'll need to use all your influence, all your contacts, and all your skill as a writer to reach as many people as possible."

"What do you mean?" asked Joe.

"That you have a lot more power than you think you do. Everybody does, of course. But as a newspaperman, and an idealistic one at that, you'll have a real opportunity not just to report the news but to help shape it. You want to save the world? Well, you can't do it all by your lonesome, as I found out. But you can use everything at your disposal—and working as you do for one of the biggest papers in the country, that's a lot!—to wake it up and teach it how to save itself."

"How?" thought Joe, and realized the figure on the screen answered him without his having voiced his question. But then why not? The figure wasn't supposed to be there anyway.

"By writing about some of the upbeat stuff that happens. In fact, by writing about *all* the upbeat stuff you can find out. That's what'll open the door. It's what will whistle the really big opportunity your way. And *then* you're going to get a chance to spread the word soon about something really major that's going to have an effect not just on this country but on the whole world. It's going to shift the world's consciousness!

"So pay attention. And just keep writing about the upbeat things people are doing to try to salvage the planet. Give 'em some space. Give 'em as much space and as much copy as you can. Give people a reason to think there's hope for the future, and that they can maybe contribute to some of the possible efforts that need to be taken. Let them know they're not alone in wanting a better world. That's the real crusher—when you think you're all alone."

Shumacher winked, and like the Cheshire cat, began to dissolve. But as he was fading out, he offered one last piece of advice.

"And by the way, Joe, you need to lighten up. It's the only way to learn to fly!"

Then his wink became the blip on the monitor.

Joe shook himself and looked around. He'd either fallen asleep and dreamed his conversation with Shumacher, or he'd hypnotized himself watching the blinking blip and had hallucinated the experience.

He promised himself to switch from bologna to something less boring and more palatable. Or maybe he'd start going out for lunch a couple of times a week. But no more lunchtime napping! He hit the menu button that brought his story queue onto the screen.

*****

Since Saul's death Georgia had observed a slight strain of what she considered dottiness about Sophie. For example, Sophie had been taking classes in all sorts of *outre* subjects, like shamanism, astrology, gardening with nature spirits, out of body experiences, and who knew what other kinds of kookiness. Why, she'd even walked on hot coals and gone off to the islands last summer to swim with a pod of dolphins in the company of a psychic who was interested in interspecies communication!

Not that Sophie ever volunteered to talk about any of these pursuits unless asked. And not that her interests in any way diminished Georgia's desire to let Cassie move in with Sophie. If any of Sophie's ideas rubbed off, the child might grow up a little eccentric. But so what?

Nevertheless, Georgia's perception of Sophie as a certifiable flake left her unprepared for Sophie's insistence that all legal, educational, and financial details of the living arrangement be worked out in advance.

For example, Sophie knew from her years of teaching she would need legal guardianship papers in order to register Cassie in the elementary school nearest her home, so she took Georgia by the hand and led her to the county courthouse in Fairfax to execute the paperwork.

The dour official behind the desk wrinkled her brow at Georgia and glared over the top of her half-lens glasses.

"And just why is it, Ms. Allman, that you want to turn custody of your niece over to Ms. Nussbaum?"

Georgia cleared her throat and collected her composure.

"Well," she said, "I'm going to be traveling quite a bit during the next year, and my friend," she nodded in Sophie's direction, "and I felt it would be in the child's best interest to have her placed with someone who can provide a stable—and stationary—home for her so she can continue with her schooling."

"And you believe Ms. Nussbaum is the best person to do this?" asked the official.

"Oh, yes," answered Georgia brightly. "We've been friends for 40 years, and I just know my niece will get along famously with Sophie. She's a schoolteacher, you know. Retired now, but, I mean, what could be better than to have a built-in tutor for a guardian?"

The official turned her scrutiny to Sophie. "Do you intend for this arrangement to be permanent, or just for the period while Ms. Allman is travelling?"

"At this point," said Sophie, "I have a verbal agreement with Miss Allman to take Cassandra until the end of the school year, although frankly, I would be perfectly happy to retain custody until she comes of legal age, should she wish to stay with me that long. I'm widowed, retired, and have a lot of time on my hands."

Without facial expression, the official stared first at Sophie, then at Georgia. Finally, she pushed papers toward them. "Fill out these forms," she said.

On the way out of the courthouse, Georgia asked, "It's a little early. Do you think we should go to lunch now?"

"No," said Sophie. "I think we should go call either your lawyer or mine. As her legal guardian, I believe some arrangement needs to be made so that Cassandra can draw a regular stipend from her parents' estate while you're away. Furthermore, I want you to consider seriously having a will made in which you name Cassie as your heir. She's your only living relative, and before you go batting around the world, you need to be sure she's provided for. As you told me before, there's probably enough money from her parents' estate for her to reach her majority, but not

30

necessarily enough for college. If anything happens to you, and you've provided for her in your will, there *will* be money for college. If nothing happens, and you're still around when she graduates high school, you can provide for her or not, as you see fit."

Georgia looked a little surprised. "When did you turn into such a take-charge person?" she asked.

"Five minutes ago," said Sophie, "when I finally became a mother."

*****

It was strange, thought Adam, not being able to feel things on his left side. With care he could walk, if he hobbled along with a crutch and put most of the pressure on his right leg and arm.

The doctors couldn't really trace the cause. He'd had EEGs and brain, spine, and body scans, plus the whole neurological battery of tests, including a spinal tap for multiple sclerosis.

The good news was that the tests showed nothing. The bad news was that the tests showed nothing. No MS. No scarring of the spinal sheathe. No tumors in brain, spine, or body. Blood pressure on the high side, but still normal. No blood disorders. Zero, zip—*nada*.

The doctors wrote him off as a "crock," having a "neurological disorder of undefined, possibly psychological origin." In layman's terms, a psychosomatic or hysterical illness. All in his head. A mental case.

"You could start working with a psychologist. Or you can just go home and rest. Or take a month off and go sit on the beach," urged his doctor. "Cozumel is nice this time of year. And maybe this problem will just go away on its own."

Thanks, doc. Don't forget to send me your bill.

The day he got out of the hospital was toward the end of January. He hadn't wanted to talk to any of his friends, so he'd had a taxi drive him home.

Sitting alone in his apartment, he saw on the end table by the couch the glass of Jack Daniels he had poured that night three weeks ago, still with about half its contents intact. It triggered a memory of his call to Sheila. Then, by stream-of-consciousness

31

contrast, he thought of Lucy Whitefeather, and her cryptic remarks about a crisis he was going to have.

He labored to his feet, grabbed the glass by two fingers on the rim, and by carefully leaning on pieces of furniture in his path, he made his way to the kitchen where he poured the contents down the drain. Then he struggled to the bedroom, where he could lie on the bed and feel sorry for himself in the dark and silence.

He woke in the middle of the afternoon from a dream of Lucy and debated with himself about calling her.

He didn't call then, but when the same dream kept returning over the course of the next three days, he changed his mind. At worst, she'd just laugh at him again. And maybe the dream would stop if he contacted her.

And so, one morning later in the week, he looked up her number. It wasn't in the phone book, so he called the gallery where she'd had her showing. The receptionist wouldn't give out her number, of course, but he did convince the girl to call Lucy and give her *his* number. Lucy got back to him within 15 minutes, and when he'd told her the details of his crisis, she volunteered to come to his apartment right away.

"Your color is poor," she said when she arrived, looking not at him but off to both sides of his body. "Your aura at the moment is sort of two-toned and very subdued, so I would surmise you are drastically out of balance energetically. If you will go lie down, we will do some breathing exercises."

He started to hobble to the couch, but she said, "No, it would be better if you were to lie on a bed, so I can get to both sides of you. The problem with the left side may actually stem from an energy imbalance on the right."

He gestured toward the bedroom and followed limpingly behind as she led the way. He noticed that she stopped as she entered and looked up to right and left, as if sniffing the air.

"I'm sorry," he began, "I haven't cleaned up since I . . ."

"Don't apologize," she commanded. "I am merely sensing the energies. There are thoughtforms left over from others who have visited here. Maybe you should have it all cleansed when you are better."

She shrugged and glanced at the still unmade bed. Without saying anything, she began to make it up neatly. "Lie crosswise on top of the spread," she directed, "so I can get to your head as well as your feet. Here, let's put a pillow under your knees."

He gingerly lay down crosswise on the big kingsize bed as she'd instructed and waited as she positioned the pillow under his legs.

She watched him for a few moments, then said, "Your breathing is too shallow most of the time. You aren't giving yourself enough oxygen the way you breathe. Here," she urged, "make a circle with your thumb and forefinger on each hand." She helped him hold his left thumb and index finger in a circle. "Good! That'll help you relax a little more and breathe easier. Rest your hands on your thighs, just below your pelvis. Elbows down on the bed. There, are you comfortable? Relaxed? Good. Now follow my lead and breathe with me. In. And out. In. And out. Good, that's better. In. And out."

As she began to soothe him to relax and breathe more deeply, Adam found himself beginning to drift down and down. Soon he was so relaxed he felt he couldn't move an eyelash.

"Just give yourself up totally, and when I begin to touch your body, don't even think of trying to move to help me. And whatever feelings come, just let them flow through you. If you fall asleep, that's okay. Whatever happens, just let it be."

She removed his slippers and socks and began to massage his feet. Though he hadn't felt any real sensation from the left foot for several days, he realized he was feeling heat from her hands as she worked on him. And once she dug so deeply into a point on the bottom of his foot that he actually winced with pain.

"Ho," said Lucy, "so you are not totally without feeling after all! Continue to breathe deeply, and just stay as relaxed as you can."

When she had finished with his feet, she massaged his hands. Then she moved to other places on his body, his legs, his arms, his chest. As she worked, she would sometimes touch, press, or massage points. Other times, he could feel the heat from her hands even through his clothing, but he knew she held her hands an inch or two above his body.

Finally, she moved to his head. Kneeling on the floor behind him, she cradled his head in her hands. He thought the heat she was generating by this time was like an electric heating pad. Then she shifted her position, with one hand under his head and the other on his forehead. He could feel the heat flowing down from his face through his neck and into his shoulders. Then she stroked his cheeks, his ears, and finally shifted again so that one hand was under the back of his neck and the other was sending radiant heat into his throat.

A pressure began to well up in his throat. If he hadn't been so deeply relaxed, he would have felt embarrassed at what happened next, for he began to weep. First the tears were simply seeping out under his eyelids, but Lucy, never moving, whispered, "Release it. Let it go," and he heard himself making muffled moaning noises, then sobs, then great howls of sheer anguish. "Let it go, let it go," Lucy crooned, "it's okay, just let it go."

Images from childhood, long buried, broke open the leaden casket of repressed memory and forced their way to the surface. Episodes of physical abuse when he was small and defenseless bubbled across his inner sight. His arms rose convulsively and his hands flexed open to push the scenes away until they became too many and the long unacknowledged grief and rage became a foam so thick and overwhelming he feared he might drown in it but for the sound of Lucy's soft voice. He clung to her voice and the touch of her hand, which had moved to his chest and seemed gently to be rubbing warmth into his heart. His arms and hands collapsed once more onto the bed, and his rage and grief subsided into soft sobbing.

When he was calm once more, Lucy sat down on the bed beside him and reached for a tissue to blot away the tears.

"I think I need the box," he said. "I have tears in my ears. I feel like I've been underwater."

"You were," Lucy grinned.

"What did you do to me, lady?"

"I just balanced your energy bodies," she answered, "then I channeled a little energy into your head, throat, and heart chakras."

"I don't know what that means," he said, "but it sounds like weirdness from the crystal-granola people."

"Never mind," she countered. "Let's just say I know some places in the body where people sometimes hold pain and grief. And lots of times they don't even know they're holding it. Can you tell if the numbness has subsided any yet?"

He ran his right hand down his left arm and felt the sensation. "It's not quite back to normal, but I can feel it."

"Probably within the next 48 hours you'll be back to normal. But in the meantime, you may experience headaches, or other aches and pains, or I don't know what all. Or you may have images of painful past experiences. If that happens, just start breathing the way I showed you, relax, and let everything flow through you, then up, out, and away. And drink plenty of water. I don't know what you were carrying, but it was pretty heavy, I could tell. Whatever it was, it was affecting your body."

"So," he said, "can I expect to be able to go back to work within a couple of days, doc?"

She looked at him thoughtfully, then shrugged. "I shouldn't advise you one way or the other," she said. "But if I were you, I'd think about the connection between whatever it was you just released that could cause you all that anguish, and the kind of lifestyle you are living right now. There usually is a connection between our *dis*eases, our past experiences, and our present path."

She looked thoughtfully around the room, then continued. "You have a very classy place here, good taste, very expensive. You probably have a fancy car, too, and I know you wear expensive suits when you go out. So you're working at a big, important company and earning lots of nice money, no?"

He nodded.

"Then maybe you should consider that this problem was a warning," she said. "Nature's way of telling you to get out of the passing lane and over to the right, where you can pull off at a rest area if you need to."

"You're telling me you don't like my lifestyle," he said.

"I don't feel one way or the other about your lifestyle," she replied, "but I realized long ago that I don't need too many possessions to be able to do what I enjoy doing most."

"And what is that?" he asked.

"Two things," she said. "Painting. And helping people heal themselves."

"And that's what you're doing," he asked, "helping me heal myself?"

"Well, as the proverb says, you can lead a horse to water, etc. *I* can't heal you. Accepting healing is your choice, not mine. But I can show you what I know to be true. I can show you how I live my own life, and why. If you want to know more about why I make the choices I do, then maybe we have some grounds for conversation."

Lucy got up, straightened her blouse, and looked at her watch. "I have to get down to the gallery. I'll call you in a couple of days to see how you're doing. Or you can call me and report if you like. Or if you want to talk about any of the stuff you let go of just now, I have an ear."

He moved to get up, and she extended her hand. "Careful now, you may find you're a little wobbly."

"I've been wobbly since I went numb, so it's nothing new," he said.

They walked hand in hand to the door of his apartment, and he was elated that he could really feel the pressure under his feet.

"How do you feel?" she asked as she put her hand on the knob.

He shifted from foot to foot a couple of times. "A little spacey," he said, "and I seem to be balancing a little differently." He shook his head. "How long will the symptoms last?"

"You'll settle back into your body within the next couple of days. And I hope all sensation will return for you and you won't experience any recurrences of the numbness. But my intuition tells me you are going to have to make some changes—in your thinking, at least, and probably in your lifestyle."

To his surprise, she opened her arms and hugged him. It was warm, close, loving, and totally asexual—not the kind of embrace he was at all used to, but he had no desire to end it.

Finally, she sighed, pulled away, and opened the door.

"Just remember," she said as she stepped out into the hall, "we're not here to collect; we're here to connect." And she was gone.

*****

"This will be your bedroom, honey," said Sophie to a solemn Cassie.

36

The child had barely smiled since Georgia had dropped her, her suitcases, and the few boxes of her personal possessions at Sophie's McLean home.

"I just finished putting away the pictures and knick-knacks that were in here, so when you feel like it, you can unpack and decorate it any way you like. Do you have posters or pictures you want to put up?"

Cassie shook her head but didn't say anything.

"If you'd like some other color for the curtains and bedspread, just say so. These have been here quite a while, and I wouldn't mind letting you pick out something new."

"The room is very nice," said Cassie. "It's just fine the way it is."

"Well, I'm sure you'll find some creative way to make it your own," said Sophie.

Cassie nodded, sat down tentatively on the bed, looked appraisingly around the room, then let her eyes meet Sophie's.

"*Things* don't matter to me very much," she said softly.

Sophie mentally weighed Cassie's statement for a moment, then asked, "Do you want to talk about what you're feeling?"

Cassie nodded.

"Do you want to talk about it over cookies and milk?"

Cassie nodded again, this time with a tiny upturn to the corners of her mouth.

"Let's go to the kitchen. You'll find I'm not a wonderful cook in many ways, but I do make pretty good cookies," said Sophie. "About 30 years ago, I started asking the volunteer mothers who brought goodies to my classes to send in recipes to be shared with other students. I've collected lots of cookie recipes over the years."

While Sophie poured milk and arranged cookies on a plate, Cassie pulled out a chair at the kitchen table, then perched sideways on the seat, her arm over the chairback. Around the corner from the laundry area came a gray and black striped kitty heading straight for her. It rubbed itself against her legs, then hopped unceremoniously onto her lap, put its paws on her chest, and licked her face.

"That's Emerson," said Sophie. "Usually he's a bit standoffish, but he seems to like you. If you want him on your lap, you'll have to sit back and make a bigger lap. If you don't want him on you, just put him on the floor."

Cassie settled further back on the chair seat, and Emerson curled up on her lap and looked adoringly up at her, purring like a locomotive.

"I acquired three cats during the year after my Saul died—Emerson, Thoreau, and Whitman, named for the three American Transcendentalists," explained Sophie.

Cassie looked a little quizzical, so Sophie continued.

"Ralph Waldo Emerson, Henry David Thoreau, and Walt Whitman were 19th century writers who believed all men are brothers, that men should learn to be self-reliant and independent, that we should learn to do without as many *things*, like you were talking about earlier, and that war was always a great mistake. They lived during the time of the Civil War. Whitman went to the war and worked as a battlefield nurse, but Thoreau protested the war by refusing to pay his taxes, and at one point he was thrown in jail, like some of the people today who protest things they think are wrong."

Cassie was munching a cookie she held in her left hand and stroking Emerson with her right, but Sophie could tell she was listening attentively, so she continued with her lecture.

"The Transcendentalists also believed that we're all a part of God, or as Emerson called it, the Oversoul. They believed that the true part of ourselves is like a little drop of light from the great, abundant light that is the Oversoul. They thought when we're born, that little drop of divine light breaks away from the Godhead and comes to this plane and animates our body. And when we die, they thought that little light returns to the great light that is the Oversoul."

Cassie looked at Sophie with wide eyes and put down her cookie.

"You mean," she said, "they knew over a hundred years ago that when you die you go to the light?"

Sophie nodded. "Some people did."

"Then how come Aunt Georgie doesn't know about it? No matter what I said, she didn't believe me."

"Well, sweetie, not everybody believed the Transcendentalists, either. And we've become very 'scientific' in the 20th century, to the extent that people are reluctant to believe anything scientists can't prove in the laboratory. Not taking a stand on anything science hasn't proved is a new-fangled way of avoiding taking responsibility for—whatever." Sophie shrugged. "So they'd call what you experienced 'anecdotal' evidence. Never mind that millions of people in all ages have attested to experiencing similar things. Never mind that millions of people in this country right now would attest to having had an experience like yours. There'll still be people who won't believe you if it hasn't been proved in 'replicable' laboratory tests—or if they haven't experienced the same thing themselves."

Cassie seemed to be mulling over what Sophie had been saying. She took a little sip of milk, and Emerson, seeing the glass in her hand, said questioningly, "Purrp?" She stuck her finger in the glass and let the cat lick it off, after which the feline stood up and put its paws on the table to try to nose into the glass. Sophie scooped Emerson off Cassie's lap and went to the fridge, got the milk carton, and poured a thimbleful into a saucer, depositing Emerson in front of it.

"Where are the other two kitties?" Cassie asked.

"Thoreau likes to sleep out on the back porch during the day, where he'll be ready to pounce in case an unsuspecting bird wanders by. And Whitman is a rugged individualist. He comes by for a meal about twice a week, but he's also been adopted by the rest of the neighborhood, so he gets fed regularly by lots of people around here. Every once in a while, I hear him doing what his namesake suggested people should do, sounding his barbaric yawp—but usually it's from somebody else's rooftop!"

Emerson finished his treat and returned to settle on Cassie's lap again for further petting. Sophie was glad to see Cassie was finally beginning to relax.

"You know," Cassie said softly, "it was so beautiful, being in the light. I just can't describe what it was like."

Sophie nodded encouragingly.

"And I didn't want to leave my family there and come back here," she continued. "And I miss them. But it's funny, it's not like it would be if I didn't know where they were and what had happened to them. It's like they're off at a new home without me, and I got to visit there but I can't move there yet."

Cassie paused for a moment as if thinking about what she wanted to say next, then continued, "But ever since I woke up back in my body, with that paramedic pounding on my chest, I've known I had to come back for some reason. Like there's something important I'm supposed to do here, before I can go back there. I'd like to go back, more than just about anything. But I can't until I find out what I need to do and actually go do it." She looked at Sophie searchingly. "Do you know how I can find out what I need to do?"

Sophie shook her head and said, "No, honey, but ever since my Saul died I've had the same feeling. I feel like he left me behind because he was finished with what he had to do here. But I can't go to where he is until I find out what I have to do and go do it, just like you." She smiled, then continued, "But even if we don't know what we're supposed to do yet, at least we have an edge on a lot of people. Neither one of us is afraid to die."

Cassie nodded. "Maybe if we look for the answers together," she said, "we won't have to be afraid to live, either."

*****

Ray Gonzales was impatient to get moving. He had a sixth sense that told him when there was trouble brewing, and he was anxious to be on the spot when it happened.

"Who're we waiting for?" he asked Barry Levin, the patrol leader for the month. Levin would captain the control center, a backroom in a sub and sandwich shop that fronted on 14th St., and direct the activities of the two patrols during tonight's excursion.

Levin put down the portable phone he held, and opening his briefcase, laid two sets of walkie-talkies out on the card table that served as a desk. Then he drew a steno notebook out of the inner pocket of the case.

"Jesus Rivera, Chad Morgan, and Donna Gilson," replied Levin, checking his master list of the month's volunteers for this evening's crew, then glancing at his watch. "What're you so antsy about? And where's your whistle?"

Ray pulled the police whistle from his pocket, held it up, and dangled it a few times before dropping the chain from which it hung over his head.

"Good," said Levin. "Anyway, there's still 20 minutes before we need to disperse. They'll be here."

Levin turned his attention back to the table, dumping a bag of 9-volt battery packages onto its surface. "Okay, everybody," he said to the six other people sitting in folding chairs around the walls of the room, "cough up a picture of GW apiece for the energizers."

Ray dug into his jeans, tossed a dollar bill onto the table, and watched as the others in the room rose and sauntered up with their contributions. He'd greeted them all earlier when he'd arrived. Fred Templar, Brice Gardner, Alan Cohn, Grace Allison, and Martin Garfunkle were all familiar to him. A new girl, maybe in her late 20s, was Susan Reiner. She was a speech therapist with a clinic in northeast D.C. This was her first time to actually come on a patrol, though she said she'd worked at the control center a couple of times last month. She'd been inspired to do it, she said, because she and her lover had been verbally hassled on their way home from a play about a month before.

She seemed a little nervous, but that was okay. Nervousness usually made people more observant, and it would wear off as they walked their rounds.

Susan was sitting by herself, not talking to anybody. She watched as Ray began to limber up, slowly moving into a crouch, then reaching behind his body to gather energy. "You a dancer?" she asked.

"Tai chi," said Ray, pulling the ball of energy he collected with his hand in a sweeping curve past his body and pushing it out beyond himself to the left with a graceful thrust.

Levin looked up and watched Ray thoughtfully for a few moments. "Real pretty," he said finally. "I've heard it's pretty effective, too, though it looks harmless enough."

Ray slowly drew back, then just as slowly pressed forward with his fist curled and elbow extended in front of his body, and finally completed his movement by gracefully drawing his hand, fingers extended, through the space in front of his body.

Then he drew himself up from his squatting position, gave Levin a little smile, and responded with the understatement, "Yeah, I guess it can be effective. That last flowing gesture I made, for example," and he repeated the movement of drawing his extended fingers through space, "provided it has the appropriate amount of *chi* behind it, can take out your opponent's eyes."

"You're real good at it, huh?" asked Levin, who was aware of Ray's reputation but had never worked with him before.

"I sometimes teach classes in it for the parks departments in my spare time," Ray answered.

"And wha'd'ya do in real life?"

"Right now I'm between jobs," Ray said, and left it at that.

He didn't really want to talk or even think about real life at the moment. Indeed, he had signed up for patrol every weekend this month in order to focus on something else besides his day-to-day reality with Colin, his lover.

"Go," Colin had insisted. "The Panthers can use someone with your special talents, and I can use some quiet time."

In fact, Ray had been one of the staunchest supporters of the Pink Panther patrols since their inception in the D.C. area. Modeled on the prototype founded back in 1990 in Greenwich Village, the Pink Panther movement had spread to other big cities with large gay populations, and the high incidence of gay bashings that often occurred in them. The original group had trademarked its logo—an inverted triangle with a pink paw print in its center—and affiliate groups around the country which ordered two dozen black tee-shirts bearing the logo automatically received a guidebook for setting up a local patrol association, with info on everything from how to establish a good working rapport with the police to simple techniques for self defense.

Mostly, the guidebook encouraged Panthers *not* to engage in physical exchanges with menacing groups or individuals, but to use their police whistles, send one of their number to the nearest pay phone to dial 911, or call control central for assistance from the other patrol, the police, or emergency medical crews.

The D.C. constabulary had responded more favorably than Ray had expected they would to the gay activist group, and the incidence of attacks on gays was down somewhat since the Panthers had begun patrolling. But there was still trouble enough, and incidents of verbal and physical harassment would doubtless continue as long as homophobia existed. And, of course, the AIDS epidemic had only fueled the fires of fear, especially among very young, straight males who considered it incredibly macho to "burn faggots."

The alley door swung open and Jesus Rivera, a high-energy Black-Hispanic sporting a Bart Simpson hairstyle and one diamond eardrop, bopped through it.

"Hey, Miz Ray," he exclaimed jovially, slapping Ray's outstretched palm, "haven't seen you in a coon's age. . .no pun intended," he said loudly, circling as if showing off to the others in the room, and laughing at himself. Turning back to Ray, he asked more quietly, "How's your close encounter doin', man?"

"He's hangin' in," Ray replied with a half smile. "Some days are a little better than others. But we're takin' it one day at a time."

"The only way," said Jesus softly. "How your own tests runnin', man?"

"You know I don't get tested, Jesus. It's against my principles to give in to the system. If you do, they'll have you believin' you need to write your will and select your slice of real estate in the stone garden."

Jesus grinned. "Just checkin'," he said, and punched Ray's arm. "You somethin' else, man," he finished admiringly.

Through the door just then came the last two volunteers. Levin looked up and said, "Hey, Chad, glad you made it." To the woman, a short stocky brunette with close-cropped kinky permed hair and glasses, he said, "Hi, you must be Donna Gilson. Glad to have you."

The woman didn't smile, and Ray realized she was another new recruit, like Susan.

"The name's Dinah," she snapped.

Jesus shot Ray a look that said, "This chick's got an attitude," but Ray sensed she was just scared and didn't want to show it.

"Okay," said Levin, in a voice that just missed being a campy, top sergeant imitation, "now that we're all here, let's get moving. Ray, you're in charge of Patrol 1." He handed Ray a walkie-talkie. "Grace, Brice, Chad, you'll go with Ray. Fred," he continued, handing over the other walkie-talkie, "you lead Patrol 2. Jesus, Martin, Susan, and Alan, you go with Fred. Donna. . .uh, Dinah," he corrected as she bristled again, "you can either go with Ray's group, or you can stay here in command central and help me out—your choice."

"I'll go with the patrol," Dinah replied with what was either a myopic stare or a glare.

"Oh, I almost forgot," said Levin, "those of you who just came in, I need a buck apiece from you for the batteries."

He waited while they each dug out the money and tossed it on the table. Then he reached in his briefcase and drew out two little spiral memo pads and two stubby pencils and handed them to the patrol leaders. Ray turned to Dinah and handed her the pad and pencil.

"I hope you don't mind keeping track of the license numbers of suspicious vehicles," he said, knowing that giving her a job to do would take her mind off her fear.

She took the pad and pencil and stuffed them into the waistband of her jeans.

Ray turned to Grace then, and drawing a roll of silver-backed cloth tape and a pocket knife out of his jacket pocket, handed them to her. She lifted an eyebrow, but put them in her own jacket pockets.

"Okay, Patrol 1," he said, "we're set. Let's go," and headed out the door into the alley with the four volunteers following.

As soon as they hit 14th Street, Ray turned east.

"Not our usual route," muttered Grace, an angular black woman, at his left elbow.

"No," he admitted, "but I've been smelling trouble for the last 20 minutes. Intuition tells me something's comin' down hard in just a little while, and I want to be there. If it hasn't already happened," he added.

They picked up their pace a bit at his words.

"Okay," he said as they moved along, "don't forget to make note of the nearest telephones as we go along. Dinah, mark down make, model, and license of any suspicious vehicles. Chad, you take the walkie-talkie and the whistle," he said, handing them off to the tall blonde, "I think I may need my hands free very shortly."

Chad obediently took the squawk box and dropped the whistle's chain around his own neck. He immediately pressed the button to report to central.

"We're heading east on 14th, just coming up on H," he said, then added before Levin could squawk back, "Ray's got a notion."

Brice, a student from Georgetown with a face like a Botticelli angel, sang softly, "I'm nervous."

"Ain't we all, honey," shot back Grace.

They walked another block or so before turning north. Chad was reporting their turn when Ray suddenly stopped.

"I hear it," he said, and began to run toward a sound only he could discern.

The patrol jogged quickly behind him, saw him turn ahead of them and run into an alley. Then they all understood what he was heading toward. Halfway down the alley a group of four young men had been methodically beating a prostitute. Two held her while two others pummeled her with their fists and booted feet.

Chad blew the whistle with a deafening shriek and began shouting, "May Day! May Day!" into the squawk box. Dinah ran for a phone across the street outside a closed drugstore. And Brice and Grace watched in awe as Ray leapt forward, gracefully allowing his right heel to connect with the general kidney area of one of the assailants, knocking him to the ground.

It became clear to those watching that the prostitute was a queen in drag. His skirt was torn up to the waist, exposing his genitals, and blood ran down his legs, as well as from his nose and mouth.

The two who had been holding the victim dropped him and ran out the other end of the alley, routed by the sound of the whistle and Ray's dazzling footwork, but the fourth assailant, instead of running, revealed a knife in his left hand. He slashed at Ray, whose left leg swung up and caught the young man just below his rib cage, knocking him sideways. The knife wielder stumbled but caught himself, then dropped to a crouch, ready to take an upward jab at Ray's midriff. Ray, crouching in front of him, encouraged him with his hands to come on, hurry up. The young man lunged.

But Ray wasn't there in front of him anymore.

Ray had moved out of the path of the slashing knife and pivoted to a tight position behind the young man, whose right wrist he now locked up behind his back and whose left he twisted, disengaging the knife and kicking it out of the way of the other dropped assailant, who was just beginning to pull himself up.

"Dance with me," Ray whispered, as he waltzed the man he held over to the first one he had dropped and pushed him down on top. "Tell your buddy to stay down," he added very softly, "because I'd truly regret having to damage you."

Turning to Grace, he said, "Tape." She handed him the roll he had given her earlier and opened the pocket knife so he could cut it once he had the first young man's hands bound up. Next he taped his feet together, then taped the first assailant's feet before carefully rolling the young man on top off onto the ground so he could get to the first assailant's hands.

Once the encounter, which had taken approximately 30 seconds, was concluded, Grace, Chad, and Brice hurried to the side of the victim to see if first aid was in order. The body lay like a puppet whose strings had been cut, broken limbs twisted askew.

"My god, this guy looks like roadkill," said Chad.

"Ambulance is on the way," shouted Dinah as she entered the alley.

The police and the medics arrived simultaneously. Within minutes, the victim had been covered with a blanket, placed on a stretcher, deposited in the emergency van, and hurried off into the night. The police, who knew Ray from a couple of previous encounters, took over the two men he held, got the particulars of the episode very quickly, and radioed for other cars to be on the lookout for the two toughs who had gotten away. In less that 20 minutes of their having entered the alley, the Panther patrol was ready to continue prowling the neighborhood.

It was generally conceded the patrols were not to become physically involved with perpetrators of violent acts. All volunteers had a one-day session in self-defense techniques before signing up for a patrol, but it was emphasized that they were not to think of themselves as vigilantes or professional fighters. They were roundly cautioned against going to the rescue themselves.

Ray had occasionally been the exception.

He had never seriously injured anyone. He had never been hurt himself. And he had a sixth sense that usually got him to the scene of an attack before it happened.

But tonight he had unfortunately been too late, and as the Panthers continued their walk, he was inwardly flagellating himself. Perhaps he should have gone out by himself, to be on the spot to prevent the attack. Or perhaps he could have sent his *chi* out ahead of the patrol, to weaken and defuse the attackers before they found the queen. He wondered if a part of his subconscious had been spoiling for a fight. Could he honestly say he had felt no satisfaction in the blows he had landed on the gay-bashing men? How much culpability does a spiritual master actually have for the negativity he encounters? How much of it can he dissipate—if he is *truly* a master?

When Patrol 1 returned to the sub and sandwich shop at 3 a.m., he insisted on using the portable phone to check on the injured man. The victim, he learned, had been DOA; cause of death was blood loss both from multiple knife wounds and internal hemorrhaging as a result of the beating he'd endured.

Ray gently laid the phone on the table. Then he went out into the alley and howled with grief.

*****

Montague Nelson woke to the dissonant sounds of a small plane strafing his head and the wet snuffling of a water buffalo.

As he came up to full consciousness, he realized the buffalo noises were actually snores from his boss, John Logan, and the small plane was really an extraordinarily loud flying insect of some sort.

He wearily paddled his hand at the little pest, but his efforts were ineffectual. Eventually, he forced his eyes open and looked around for the insect, which had settled momentarily on the plasticized top of the nightstand that separated his bed from Logan's.

He watched quietly, not even breathing while the little creature did a circular dance in the sunlight pouring through a foot-wide fissure in the motel drapes. It was oddly beautiful, with a brown, green, and gold striped body and shimmery rainbow wings. It also had a vicious looking stinger, and he was grateful it hadn't attacked while he was sleeping.

He'd always kind of liked insects. When he was a little kid, he'd caught caterpillers and beetles and bally bugs and kept them under his bed in jars with holes punched in the lids. He's even given them names—Moe, Jerry, and Steve, and Larry, for kids in his old neighborhood—and talked to them every morning and night. Until his foster mother found them and had a screaming fit. She'd squirted the jar lids liberally with Real Kill before tossing them in the trash.

Back when he was in the slammer at Lorton Correctional Facility, he'd caught a Japanese beetle out in the yard, and one of the guards he'd been a little friendly with had brought him a jar to keep it in. It didn't live long, but it had been replaced by a succession of cockroaches, all of whom he's named Willie. Yup, he liked insects.

He cautiously climbed out of bed on the side away from the night table and went to the bathroom for some toilet paper. He didn't want to get stung, but he thought he might be able to catch the insect in a piece of tissue and put it out.

As he turned he saw Logan, now awake, bring a pudgy palm down hard on the table top. The bug crunched.

"What did ya do that for?" yelped Nelson. "I was gonna put it outside!"

"It had a stinger a foot long, fer crissake!" growled Logan. "Nasty little begger! What are you, some kind of bleedin' heart for bugs?"

Logan got up and stomped into the bathroom, slamming the door behind him.

Nelson walked slowly over to the bed and sat down to look at the smashed insect. Its wings, which had been so beautiful in the sunlight, were flattened against the table top with goo from its squashed body.

Nelson didn't like Logan. He had to admit, though, that he'd been living better since they'd teamed up. Instead of the fleabag rooming houses he'd been used to when he was on his own, they stayed at moderate priced motels with weekly rates. And the con games and other jobs they pulled together generally came off smoothly—he hadn't had a brush with the law since he started taking orders from Logan.

Yeah, Logan was real smart. He'd been some kind of demolitions expert with the Aussie Navy in Vietnam, and he knew a lot of stuff Nelson didn't about all kinds of things. But he was mean.

Unfortunately, back when they'd first met, Nelson had gotten drunk one night and bragged to Logan about some of his stunts, like an arson and a couple of thefts nobody'd ever pinned on him. One episode he was particularly proud of involved a double sting, which neither the police nor the local organized crime machine had ever realized he was responsible for. Drunk as he was, he'd told his stories with relish, and Logan had laughed appreciatively. And the next morning Logan had told Nelson he was now working for Logan, until further notice. Or else some of those old stunts would be repeated to other ears.

Nelson heard the toilet flush. He wiped up the remains of the bug with the tissue and put it in the trash.

*****

After her visit to his apartment, Adam had called Lucy four times a day for the next few days and pled with her until she consented to spend the following Sunday with him. By then he was nearly back to normal, and he had wanted to take her to a fancy restaurant for a brunch buffet, but she had declined.

"Come to my place, and see how I live," she said. "And don't dress up; my roommate and I are really casual."

Her place turned out to be a small bungalow on a shady, tree-lined street in one of the older Dallas suburban neighborhoods just north of Southern Methodist University. When Lucy opened the door for him, an Irish setter came loping down the hall, skidded into his knees, and stood up on hind legs with front paws on his chest to give him a welcoming kiss.

"Good," said Lucy, "now you've been properly christened. Down, Smoo. Adam, meet my roommate."

Smoo put up his paw for Adam to shake, after which the dog turned and walked back down the hall, disappearing around the corner.

"He's the best roommate I ever had," said Lucy, looking fondly after him.

"What kind of a name is Smoo?" asked Adam, expecting her to come up with some exotic language he'd never heard of.

"I found him one day when I was over on the SMU campus—SMU spells 'smoo.' He came up and made friends with me, then afterward he followed me from building to building. And he didn't have any I.D. or even a collar. I put notices around on bulletin boards and an ad in the paper, but nobody ever claimed him. So I got him his shots and registered him, and now he's my buddy. Here, come in and see where I live."

The living room was small, but bright, with polished wood floors and lots of windows, plants, pillows, and paintings.

"Are all these paintings ones you've done?" asked Adam.

"Yes," said Lucy, "except for the one at the end. That's a Bill Rabbit print. It's called 'The Elders'."

Adam glanced at the picture she indicated, which seemed to be of some council of Indians seated around a fire in a cave. The rocks had images of faces, and the mouth of the cave, through which a starry night sky shone, was shaped like the heads of an eagle and an Indian brave.

"Once upon a time, before his work was popular, I could have bought the original for $400.00 when I was out in Santa Fe. But I didn't have the money then. His work has been a real influence on my painting, though," she said.

Adam thought he saw the connection with Lucy's work. Her paintings were mostly Southwest landscapes, but the American Indian images were there, too, though often partially hidden, lurking just out of reach of casual perception as part of a tree or a branch or a cloud formation. Sometimes the images were human, but more often they were animal.

"These are medicine paintings," said Lucy. "For an Indian, the animal world is very meaningful, and each animal has a special gift or medicine that imparts power to the human who has an association with it."

"I'd been wondering if you were really Indian, or if the name 'Whitefeather' was a sort of artist's pseudonym," said Adam.

Lucy grinned, "Yes, I am Indian, at least part, and, yes, it is a pseudonym. I had a great-grandmother who was Cherokee, and a great-great-grandfather on the other side who was Choctaw. But my real name—you'll laugh at this!—is Smith."

They both laughed.

"When I graduated from high school," she continued, "I had already been painting professionally for four years. Yup," she said, "I sold my first painting when I was 14. Back then I did watercolors, and I'd sell them at craft fairs for $25 and $30. I think it was probably as much luck as talent back then, but anyhow I *knew* what I wanted to do with my life. So I decided that instead of going to college right away, for which my family didn't have the money anyway, I wanted to spend a year getting in touch with my Southwestern roots. I went out to Santa Fe, where I have a non-Indian aunt, who let me move in with her, provided I paid her $200.00 every month for room and board and took care of her little dogs. She had four." Lucy wrinkled up her nose. "Stinko! She didn't train them and they were very badly behaved and very messy. Unlike Smoo, they were *not* the best roommates I ever had. But anyway, I managed the rent by working three nights a week at a restaurant. The rest of the time I wandered from gallery to gallery, learning everything I could about painting techniques and painting lots of watercolors of deserts and mountains in my room at my aunt's house. I'd been there about four months when I met a painter who offered to let me share his studio. He was in his 40s, a very generous, wonderful man. He was also Native American, and he took me to visit some of the reservations around Santa Fe and Taos. We lived together for the next four years."

Adam opened his mouth to ask the obvious question, then closed it again. He told himself it was none of his business.

"Yes," said Lucy with a laugh, as if she'd read his mind, "we were lovers. But we knew from the beginning that the commitment was temporary."

"Why?" asked Adam, stung by her easy readiness to admit an affair with a much older man. "Was he too old for you?" The words sounded a little more petty than he'd intended.

Lucy continued smiling, but now she did so sadly. "No," she said, "he was perfect. But we knew it was temporary because he was dying. He had amyotrophic lateral sclerosis—you know, ALS—Lou Gehrig's disease. And so we crammed 40 years of loving into four. It was because of him that I know all I do about healing. We went to Phoenix, to the Association for Research and Enlightenment Clinic, and I studied out in California with Dr. Brugh Joy, to learn how to heal with my hands. And we went to the wise men and women of many of the tribes, to learn all we could about herbs and shamanic healing."

Adam had been chastened by her story. "I'm sorry," he said. "I guess you didn't find a way to save him."

"No," said Lucy, "but then he never expected we would find a way to save him. And I learned a very important lesson, which he apparently already knew. It was that there is a distinction to be made between 'curing' and 'healing.' When you cure something, you are treating symptoms, usually with medication. But you never get down to the deeper levels where the real illness comes from, so the potential is still there for it to come back or break out in another area of the body. On the other hand, when you heal something, you have removed the cause of the affliction. You have healed the soul. But this does not necessarily mean you will live forever. You can be healed, you see, and still die."

"And your friend," asked Adam, "was he healed?"

"Yes," said Lucy, "and I'm pretty sure his healing had been effected before he ever met me, and he was getting ready to make his transition. But then I came along, and we fell in love, and he decided to stay on this plane long enough to empower me with all that he already knew. It was a great gift and a great blessing for me. And I am very lucky in that he is still with me."

"What do you mean?" asked Adam.

"Exactly what I said," she answered. "He's with me. He's one of my guides."

"You mean like. . . a ghost?"

"No," she said, "he's not bound to this plane. He's with the Ancestors. And when I channel the Ancestors, sometimes he comes through and gives me advice and helps me decide how I'm doing. And sometimes he's with me in my painting, too. I can tell when he takes the brush because the strokes are bolder and he likes the blues and blacks and purples."

She gestured to the painting right behind her, a four by six-foot canvas with a cubistic Indian brave rising from the forehead of a buffalo skull—Adam thought it a sort of cross between a Picasso and a Georgia O'Keefe—with bold purples, murky gray-blacks, and stark whites. "That's one of our collaborations."

"So," said Adam slowly, "you're telling me you channel the spirits of dead people? Like at some sort of seance?"

For the moment he rejected the notion of making a pun about "artistic mediums."

"I don't exactly think of them as 'dead people'," she replied. "See, when I opened up to begin channeling my healing ability, I also opened up to a group of guides, or entities, who were once healers on this plane. I call them the Ancestors, because that's what they call themselves. They are medical doctors, shamans, masters, medicine men and women. One who comes through very often is an elderly squaw whom I call 'Mellis.' I've painted her several times, though I've sold most of the paintings I've done of her; people seem to like her energy. Oh, wait," Lucy stood up, "just a sec, I think I have one in my studio that I brought back from the gallery."

She hurried out, and Adam heard her moving stacks in another room. She came back moments later and handed him a small painting of two ancient trees and a group of rocks. As he looked at it, a face began to emerge—the rocks became the craggy, weathered cheeks of an old woman, who at the same time didn't seem old at all. The trees were her cloud of hair, the trunks of the trees her braids. She was ancient, wise, beautiful, and innocent all at once, a merging of crone, mother, maiden, and tree goddess.

"That's Mellis," she said.

Adam was awestruck. "How do you paint things like this?" he asked. "This is simply incredible."

He looked up at her face, which had seemed so plain to him when he'd first met her—before he had known anything about her. You're incredible," he said. "You're talented, and you're beautiful, and you're magical."

She shrugged. "I'm no more talented, or beautiful, or magical than anyone else on the planet," she said. "Everyone has wonderful skills, everyone is beautiful, everyone can make magical transformations. They just don't all know it. You, my friend, are a truly magical person, but you haven't discovered it, either. You don't know your purpose for being here. And you don't love yourself enough to try to find out what it might be. See, I've been very lucky; I had somebody who knew how to love show me how to love myself. Everything else began to flow from that."

The vulnerability she had opened up in him during her healing session rose to his throat again and his eyes threatened to fill. "But how?" he asked. "If nobody ever loved you, how can you learn to love yourself?"

Lucy took his right hand and placed it on her chest, between her breasts, over her heart. Then she placed her right hand on his chest, over his heart.

"The Ancestors told me before we ever met that I would have an opportunity to help you heal yourself, if you so choose. And so, if it is your will, then it is mine, that we will love and respect each other, and through that you will have an opportunity to learn to love and respect yourself. If you choose not to take on this learning, then you are free at any time to go, for I can live only with a man who knows his own power. So you will have to find your own way, if we are to be together."

He didn't quite know what she meant, but he kissed her then, long and deeply. And afterward they made love.

*****

Cassie lay in bed with the lights out, letting the golden fizzy bubbles wash over her visual field. Since the accident, she'd often had the experience at bedtime of seeing remnants of the light she had floated through then, except now it seemed more like fairy dust sprinkles. It was comforting for her to feel that the place where she'd left Mom, Daddy, and Timmy wasn't so far away. She could, after all, see the edges of it at times like this, even if she wasn't able to get back there yet.

It had been a big help to know Sophie didn't think she was crazy, and she was glad those writers Sophie'd named her cats for also knew about the light that was heaven.

She felt a soft thump as Emerson jumped up to lie beside her; he nuzzled his head under her hand, then raised it and with a questioning, "Purrp?" began looking around the room, as if he, too, were seeing the bubbly, glistening angel lights. As she started to drift off to sleep, Cassie wondered if the lights were really there all the time and if a person—or cat—just had to be in a certain state of mind to see them.

"I can see them day or night, but only when I'm with you," said a little voice in her head.

She looked down and saw Emerson's eyes aglow, as if his pupils were being backlighted by the angel lights.

"Are you speaking to me?" Cassie asked the cat.

"As best I can," came the little voice. "I am not used to being heard, even by Sophie, though sometimes she seems to understand me."

"How come I can understand you? I never understood any animals before."

"It is perhaps a combining of two other things that are also new to you: you do not have the fear that most people have, so you are open; and you are beginning to love without any strings, because you have learned what that kind of love is like."

"This is neat!" exclaimed Cassie.

"It is nice for me, too," said Emerson. "It is nice to be understood."

Cassie stroked the little furry body for a few moments, looking deeply into the beautiful backlighted eyes. Then she asked, "Can all animals talk to people?"

"If people were only open, they would be amazed at what they could learn—from animals, from plants, from the essences of all things. Even rocks have overlighting spirits. Everything at the place where you and I are has energy that people could attune themselves to, if they only would. Of course, not all animals will want to speak, especially if, like the cockroaches and other unloved insects, they have been labeled 'pests' and sprayed with toxic poisons. Once people knew how to live in harmony with all that is. They knew the reasons for the existence of every species, and they knew how to share space with them. But that was a very long time ago."

"How do you know that?" asked Cassie.

"I know because I am attuned to the overlighting spirit of my species," said Emerson, "which is attuned to the ALL THAT IS."

The cat blinked, as if to indicate there could be no argument with *his* perception of reality.

Then he continued, "You are wondering how *you* can be attuned to the overlighting spirit of *your* species, are you not?"

Cassie nodded, though she knew all she really needed to do was to think an affirmative, and Emerson would know her answer.

"Just continue to have no fear," said the little voice inside her head. "Most people who have the experience of traveling to other planes, as you have had, come back to learn things for themselves alone. But you came back both to learn and to teach. To do that most effectively, however, you must love everyone, and you must continue to have no fear. When the opportunity comes for you to do some good thing, seize it! There are many beings, more than you will ever know, who will benefit if you will just trust, hope, and especially love *all* things."

Emerson engaged Cassie's gaze for a few moments longer, then he nuzzled up into her armpit and closed his beautiful eyes.

"Will I always be able to understand you?"

"Purrp," said the cat softly.

Cassie took the sound as affirmation and drifted off to sleep with a smile, hugging the cat to her side.

*****

Celeste Jacobson lay half awake on her side, her hands clasped under her pillow, feeling the motion of the bed as Joe moved restlessly.

His boss had asked him to lunch that day, a rare occurrence, coming to pass only when one was getting a promotion one had not expected, not getting a promotion one had fully expected, or getting canned—gently. In this case he'd been offered the promotion which, though he had applied for it, he hadn't really expected to get: the editorship of the environmental beat.

So why did he seem so worried and uncomfortable? Here he was, working for one of the most prestigious newspapers in the country. Some of his colleagues had actually been invited to the White House, and this promotion made him an even more prominent member of the local press than he had been before.

It meant more money, too, and she and Joe could certainly use that. They both made decent salaries, though by Washington's standards they weren't exactly rich. But Celeste was pregnant, and she'd already declared she wanted to take some time off from being a legal secretary to be with the baby when it was born. When Joe had asked her how long, she'd wondered if they could make it for six months to a year without her working. He'd immediately applied for the environmental editorship.

She knew he'd done quite a bit of writing on the environment in the past six months and was fully qualified for the position. But he'd seemed so very weary lately, and now that the promotion and change of subject matter were realities, he was even acting ambivalent about the whole situation, as if he didn't know whether the added responsibility was going to make him happy or crazy.

Celeste had been so excited about the promotion when he called her at her office.

"Let's go out and celebrate, sugar," she'd gushed. "Maybe to that French restaurant in Arlington you like so much...what's the name of it, Chez Andre?"

He had demurred. "This is only Wednesday," he'd said, "and I need a whole weekend to work off food that rich. Make a reservation there for Friday night, how 'bout?"

"Okay, hon," she'd answered. "We'll just celebrate with a quiet microwave dinner for two at home. Or should I say two and a half? You don't have anything you have to cover tonight, do you? Maybe I could stop by one of the video places and rent a movie?"

They had spent a pleasant evening alone, in front of the television, where Celeste had dozed off on his shoulder, and he had had to guide her to bed when the video was over. And since then she had lain, half dozing, sensing he was still wide awake.

She was just wondering if she should rouse herself and invite him to talk about what was bothering him when she felt him roll toward her and cuddle spoon fashion against her back. His hand slipped up to cup one of her ample breasts, which seemed to be growing more generous as her pregnancy progressed.

She smiled, turned toward him, and without opening her eyes, slowly began to draw circles with her hand on his naked body, moving from chest to belly to thigh until she finally slipped her hand between his legs and gently squeezed his scrotum.

He had come erect through her ministrations, but protested softly, "It's 3 o'clock in the morning."

She continued her gentle massage, half opened her eyes, and growled with a throaty whisper, "Don't argue with me! I know if you don't do something you'll be up all night."

He chuckled at the *double entendre*, but whispered back, "I'm only thinking of you, darlin'."

"That's very sweet of you, but you don't have to worry about me. After all, you can't get me pregnant these days."

She tugged at him, and he rolled atop her as she opened her legs. She guided him in, welcoming the full weight of him as he filled her completely, then tightening her muscles to let him know without words how much she wanted him to stay. And as they rocked together, sifting and seeking their mutual satisfaction, she sensed his weariness beginning to wash away from him in an ever-diminishing tide. With her body, with her spirit, she blessed him, hoping as she climbed on pulsating currents toward her own electrifying peak that he might feel as cleansed and elated as she when he finally fountained inside her.

After they were both entirely spent, had lingeringly kissed and caressed each other in the afterglow of pleasure, he curled around her spoon fashion again and whispered, "Maybe this is all there is. Maybe this is all there should be. Maybe I can just lose myself in you and forget the future."

Gently she guided his hand to her belly, where he felt the quickening of the life she was growing there.

"Now look what we've done," she said. "This little fella's probably going to kick me for the rest of the night."

She sighed as Joe kissed the back of her head. He left his hand resting against her belly, under which was fluttering what she imagined to be a tiny foot.

"And then again," he said thoughtfully, "maybe I'd better be damn sure there *is* a future. *Something* has to be done to save the world for our kid!"

*****

Adam didn't quite know what to make of Lucy. Was she crazy? Was she an Indian witch? Had she hypnotized him? He didn't know. He had been healed of his affliction, perhaps through the power of suggestion, or perhaps really through the power of her hands. She was his own *belle dame*, but with more mercy, more love than he had ever expected to find from any woman in the world.

To his own astonishment, he'd even asked her to marry him, but she'd said, "Not yet. When it is time, the Ancestors will let me know."

At first he'd worried about her attachment to the so-called "Ancestors." He was sure a psychiatrist would label her delusional, or maybe even schizophrenic. That would have been a scary thought if she hadn't been so grounded in day-to-day reality—her painting, what to fix for dinner, giving the dog a bath once a week.

She even had a saying she'd picked up somewhere about the psychic's need for grounding: "After enlightenment, the laundry!"

Maybe she really was channeling discarnate entities. Or maybe she was only channeling another part of herself. Eventually, he came to realize what she called these forces didn't matter as much as the results. Her artwork was truly splendid, as if she were creating several dimensions of reality with every brush stroke. And she really seemed to know more than other people did about things that were going to happen.

She called him late one night, and she'd been urgent. "The Ancestors say you should not park your car under your office building tomorrow."

"Why not?" he asked.

"I don't know, but they told me to warn you."

The next afternoon as he went to get into his car, he was coldcocked by a mugger, and the car was stolen, along with his wallet, keys, check book, and credit cards. He canceled all his credit cards, put a hold on the bank account, and changed the lock on his apartment. The car turned up two days later; it had been stripped before it was totalled, and he collected almost full value on his insurance.

"Okay, you've made a believer of me," he said to Lucy. "What do I do now?"

"If you are ready to make major life changes, then quit your job, sell off all the trappings of this rich life that hasn't been good to your health, and come with me. I have a friend who has a small ranch outside Valentine, Texas. Nobody is there except on holidays, and he's let me rent it for months at a time when I've wanted to get away and just paint. We'll go there for a while and see if we can learn to live in harmony—with each other and with all that is."

Luckily, they both had been renting in Dallas for several months beyond their original leases, so they each gave notice they'd be leaving a month hence. Together they held the granddaddy of all yard sales at Lucy's, where she turned far more money for her unframed canvasses than Adam did for his personal effects. The only equipment he decided to hang onto was his personal computer and associated paraphernalia, which he put in a rented storage unit. At the end of four weeks, they packed all they'd saved out for light housekeeping, climbed into the truck with Smoo, and headed for the desert.

Two days later they clattered the last leg of the journey in late afternoon, a 20-mile stretch of single-lane backroad consisting principally of gravel and dried mud ruts, guaranteed to knock the alignment out of most vehicles.

"When I called him, Clive said the larder is stocked with plenty of canned goods, corn meal, and dried beans, and we're free to use anything we can find. He brought a load up a couple of months ago when he was here last," said Lucy. "If there's something you can't live without, we can always go get it on the weekends in Van Horn."

The ranch was small, really more a weekend retreat, and not all of it in perfect repair.

"Clive's uncle used to work the place when he was alive," explained Lucy, "and Clive came here summers as a boy. He couldn't bear to give it up, but he couldn't take up ranching fulltime, either, so he sold off most of the land to neighbors and just kept the house and stables. He actually has two horses, and when he comes from El Paso for a couple of weeks he brings them with him to exercise while he's here. The rest of the time he boards them outside of town. Maybe if we stay here long enough, he'll let us have the use of them once in a while."

"Why wouldn't we want to stay here?" asked Adam.

"It gets lonely," Lucy answered, "and as much as you like me and Smoo, you may find you'll miss the fast times at Ridgemont High. I mean, we don't even have a telephone! If you can stand the solitude after the first couple of weeks and think you can really stay here a while, we'll try a little light gardening—some tomatoes and chili peppers and fresh beans. I had a garden last time I was here, and it was fun. I like to help things grow."

Lucy didn't suggest it, but Adam realized he'd need something to occupy his time while Lucy painted each day. He made a tour of the house, stables, and grounds with Smoo and created a list of items in need of repair.

"When we go Van Horn this weekend, call Clive and see if he wants to pay for the lumber and other supplies I'll need to make these repairs," Adam told Lucy. His life as a handyman was beginning.

They had been at the ranch about a month, and Adam was thoroughly involved in refurbishing and renovating the house, when he had a strange dream.

Lucy spent part of each morning, between 3 and 4 a.m., in meditation, speaking to the Ancestors. Adam was usually still asleep while she meditated, but one morning during this period he dreamed he was in a doctor's office waiting to be told the results of a test. He was waiting patiently, but the minutes dragged into hours, and people would come in, be seen by the doctor, and go out, without his name ever being called.

Finally, he became annoyed, approached the receptionist, and said, "I had an appointment for 9 o'clock this morning. Why hasn't my name been called?"

"What is your name?" asked the receptionist, although he was sure he had written it down on her list when he'd arrived hours before.

"Adam Loveless," he replied.

She looked down the list. "No," she replied, "there's no Adam Loveless here. Until you know your own name you can't get the results of your test."

Adam awoke highly annoyed and went to the kitchen to make some coffee. He felt affronted by the receptionist's dismissal, and also a little sheepish at his reaction to what was, after all, just a dream.

When Lucy came to find him a few minutes later, he told her the dream and asked her if she could explain why he found it so annoying.

She poured a cup of coffee while pondering her answer, then said, "I think maybe you are on the verge of becoming that 'new person' you came here to be. Your healing, from all the pain you had to go through in childhood and from all the efforts you made to be 'somebody' in the eyes of the world, is maybe ready to be confirmed for you at a deeper level. But you still have to find out who you are in spirit. I think that is why the Ancestors have suggested this morning you may be ready for a sort of vision quest."

"Explain, please," said Adam. "This sounds to me like I'm being told to make a foray into the Twilight Zone."

He had become quite tolerant of her talk of the Ancestors, and he had to admit she got good advice, but when it reflected on him directly, he tended to prickle.

Lucy grinned. "Maybe one of these days you'll realize this plane *is* the Twilight Zone," she laughed. "Where the ancestors are is the true reality. That's grownup land. This is just school." She jabbed at his arm in a mock punch. "For adolescents."

Adam wrinkled his nose and stuck out his tongue at her, then he pursued his question. "Explain 'vision quest'," he said. "What is it, what's it supposed to accomplish, and what do I have to do?"

Lucy's eyes still sparkled with mirth.

"It's literally what its name implies," she said, "a quest for a vision. Its purpose is to help a person find out or confirm who he or she is. It gives one 'medicine,' or power, to more readily accomplish one's purpose on the earth."

"I'm happy doing what I'm doing now, thank you very much," said Adam. "Especially if you like me this way." He opened his arms for a hug, and she came into them readily.

"I do indeed like you the way you are," she smiled, and gave him a light little kiss. "In fact, I love you very deeply."

"Well, I certainly try to love *you* both deeply and regularly," he said, wiggling his groin against her.

She shook her head. "Down, Rover," she laughed.

"I'm not a rover anymore," he objected.

"No, you're not. You get an A+ this reporting period for fidelity," she said. "Of course, my major competition out here is dagger cactus!"

"You can be a little spiky yourself at times," he responded, and fondled one of her breasts until the nipple hardened under his fingers.

She laughed again. "You have to be the horniest man I've ever been with."

"Ever *had the pleasure* to be with," he corrected.

"Yes, ever had the pleasure," she assented. "I think I'll refer to you from now on as my Texas Longhorn lover."

"Not a bad choice of names. You want to give me a medal, I'll brag about it in the UT alumni news!"

"No medals," she said, and changing the subject back to the original topic, added, "and no more sex until you do the vision quest."

"No more sex?" he yelped, and Smoo, who had been soundly asleep by the stove, got up in alarm and came over to nuzzle his leg.

"Hey, Smoo, are you my buddy? This lady is rejecting me," said Adam. "Bite her on the leg, Smoo. Go ahead. She deserves it!"

"Pay no attention to this sex maniac, Smoo," said Lucy. "He doesn't know what's good for him."

Smoo wandered back toward the stove.

"I do so know what's good for me," growled Adam seductively, looking in her eyes and drawing her as close as possible, his hand cupping her neat little bottom. "You're the best thing that ever happened to me, and I don't want to do anything but make love to you for the rest of my life."

Lucy's eyes glowed with pleasure at the compliment and she hugged him tight. After a moment she said in his ear, "But just suppose sex could be even better?"

"It doesn't get better than what we have," Adam protested. "I've been with lots more women than you've had lovers. Believe me, we're having a peak experience!"

She grinned again and said, "But just suppose. Humor me!"

Adam drew back and looked at her pixie face.

"Okay," he said, "let's pretend it could get better. Just tell me how."

"Well," she said, "there are two things I can think of that would make it better."

"And they are . . . ?"

"They are that you are a very fine handyman. I think you are a genius—you can probably make anything out of nothing, and fix anything so it works. But you have a mission that goes beyond just repairing Clive's house and stables."

"How do you know that isn't my life's true mission?" Adam argued.

She looked at him as if she were expecting him to protest her next words, but she shrugged and said them anyway. "Because the Ancestors say you haven't found your life's true work. And they say that when you do, it will be to serve lots and lots of people. And that it will fulfill you totally to serve others. And that until you can find that thing you can do with your whole heart, soul, and mind, you won't be fully happy. You won't have completed that purpose for which you came to this plane."

"Okay, if you're so smart, what *is* my purpose?" he demanded.

"*I* don't know," she answered. "Each one of us has to determine that ourself. I know I am an artist and a healer. But I don't know what your purpose is. I don't know *your* name," she said pointedly, referring to his dream. "The Ancestors say you must go on the quest in order to know just what it is you must do."

"Suppose I come back *knowing* I'm supposed to be a handyman," said Adam.

Lucy grinned at his stubbornness. "Then I guess," she said, "you'll just have to be the best darned handyman west of the Pecos."

"All right," nodded Adam. "If the first thing that could make sex better is my knowing my purpose in life—and I'm not sure I quite see the connection—then what's the second thing?"

Lucy waited a moment before answering as if weighing her words, then she said, "Well, I know you don't much like to talk about spiritual matters . . ."

He grimaced in response.

". . . because of the heavy emphasis you had as a kid on religion. But if you can get in touch with your own high self, you will have really unlimited power. The power literally to move mountains. And that power and energy and—excuse the word—*spirit* will be reflected in everything you undertake to do." She gave him a sly little smile. "Even in sex."

"*Even in sex?*"

"Yes."

"Will you marry me then?" Adam asked.

"Yes," she grinned.

"Okay, coach," Adam nodded. "When do we start spring training?'

*****

"We're doing a unit on South America at school," Cassie reported to Sophie one afternoon, "and our teacher told us a lot of horrible stuff about the rain forests. Did you know the rain forests are what produce a lot of the oxygen we breathe on this planet, and yet the landowners in South American countries are cutting down the trees to raise cattle? But the land they cut and burn up to raise cattle on isn't very good for grazing land, so the cattle are real scrawny, like maybe grade F meat, so they don't get top prices for it anyway. And after a couple of years, the land is just desert and not good for anything, so I don't understand why they're doing it. Boy, am I glad we're vegetarians!" she said breathlessly.

"Anyway," she continued, "our teacher says this problem has been going on for a long time, and the South American landowners are real closed-minded about stopping what they're doing. They say the land is theirs, to do with as they like. Do you think that's right, Sophie?"

They were at the table in the kitchen, where they always went when Cassie came home from school, to have a couple of cookies, review the events of the day, share insights, and get any homework started. Today the cookies were macadamia and chocolate chip.

"No, I don't think it's ever right for either a person or a group or even a country to squander resources needlessly, especially when doing so can negatively affect a lot of other people. And in this case, their actions may affect not just the people who live in the area, but all life on the planet.

"But, honey," Sophie continued, "there may be a lot more to the problem. As I understand the situation, there are developers and farmers who are also involved in rain forest destruction. Some of them want to develop the area so it will be more like industrialized countries. And some of them are the poor people of the area who need to raise crops to survive.

"So it's not just the people who want to sell cheap beef who are creating the problem—farmers who don't know about rotating crops deplete the land and think they have to cut more forests for farming, and developers who want to construct highways and industrial complexes do the same. And then there's the wood industry, that uses rain forest hardwoods for furniture, so they go 'chop, chop.' And maybe even scariest of all are the factions that are trying to use the rain forests to dump nuclear wastes! I mean there's a lot of craziness going on!"

Cassie was so shocked by this last bit of information she stopped munching and gasped.

"But," Sophie continued, "there are people in all the Central and South American countries—some of them indigenous Indian peoples and some of them scientists and anthropologists—who really want to preserve the forests and who are working hard to do so. But it's hard to find a solution that will solve everybody's problems."

"Well, isn't there anything else the people there can do to earn money?" asked Cassie. "Our teacher said there are some plants and animals in the rain forests that don't exist anywhere else in the world. Some of them are used for medicines that can't be made if they all die off. I mean, can't the people who have control of the forests grow and sell those plants and animals and stuff and make money?"

"Yes," answered Sophie, "they could, if the economic markets were set up for them to do so. In fact, I read an article in the newspaper a while back which said if the South Americans were to harvest the rain forests instead of cutting and burning them, they could make three times as much money each year as they do now. This means they'd be working only with the things that are renewable. The real advantage would be that the plants and animals would continue to flourish and could be regularly harvested. So the trees could remain where they are, the landowners and the people could all be much wealthier, and the rest of the world could literally begin to breathe a little easier."

"Then why aren't they harvesting all that good stuff in the rain forests?" asked Cassie around a cookie. "Hey, these are the best cookies you've made yet! I mean, if somebody knows a way to solve the problem, why aren't people doing something about it?"

"Well," answered Sophie, "there have been a few efforts by independent companies in the States to sell products made with things from the rain forests, like a company that sells a candy made with South American nuts, and another one that sells soaps and beauty products made with ingredients from the rain forests. But I guess the main reason they haven't stopped the destruction is that so far, the markets for all the good things the rain forests could provide on a regular basis just haven't been established yet. The cattle market, as poor quality as it seems to be, is already well established world wide. To make the switchover to another kind of market, other countries would not only have to offer to buy rain forest products on a regular basis, but some provision would have to be made to maintain the South American economy until the changeover could be completed. I'm not an economist, mind you, but it seems to me that's what would have to be provided for, at a minimum."

"Okay, then," said Cassie, "who do we talk to about opening up markets for some of these products?"

Sophie thought for a minute, then said, "I guess if the U.S. government were to become interested in the idea of harvesting as a viable solution to the rain forest problem, maybe each congressman and senator could appeal to his or her respective constituencies to open up markets in every state for rain forest products. And I personally think people all over the world would feel good about buying rain forest products, especially if they knew they were contributing to maintaining rather than depleting the forests. So maybe our government could show other countries how it would help the whole world community to support the rain forest economy. If everybody were interested in buying South American products from rain forest harvesting, they could stop slashing and burning, and we'd all benefit—because nobody will live if all the oxygen disappears."

"So how do we get the congressmen and senators interested?" asked Cassie after a few moments of thought and another cookie.

"The usual way is to write letters to them," said Sophie. "Of course, I'm not sure they really look at their mail themselves. And they may not pay a whole lot of attention to letters that aren't from people in their home states."

Cassie suddenly sat up very straight, as if she'd been pushed from behind. "Hey, we live right next to Washington, D.C. Why can't we go see some of these people? I bet if we talked to them in person, they'd listen to the idea."

Sophie grinned at Cassie's wonderful enthusiasm, and though a little cynicism tried to creep into her reply, she said, "I don't know how easy it would be to get an appointment to see a congressman or senator, honey. They're very busy people. But I guess we can try."

Cassie raised an eyebrow. "Have you ever tried to get an appointment to see one?"

"Well, no, not really," answered Sophie. "I never had a reason to do so. I'm just guessing it wouldn't be easy."

"Okay, then," said Cassie, "now we have a reason. We want to talk about saving the rain forests. So let's call and at least see if we can get an appointment. Maybe with one of the ones from Virginia first. How many are there?"

"There are two senators from every state," Sophie answered. Her schoolteacher persona cut in to convey information whenever the opportunity arose. "And I frankly don't know how many representatives there are from Virginia, because that number varies from state to state, depending on population. But I can find out by calling the public library. I know they have a list of everybody in public office. There are 435 congressmen in all," she finished.

Cassie looked at Sophie for a long moment, then jumped up to get the phone book and phone. "Let's call the library right now," she urged.

Ten minutes later, they had a list of Virginia congressmen and senators, complete with office addresses and telephone numbers.

"If you can get an appointment, let's try to make it on a Monday afternoon," said Cassie, "'cause I want to go, too, and I get home early from school on Mondays." She bit into a macadamia nut in her cookie. "Say, are these Brazil nuts?" she asked.

*****

Ray sat in the frayed rattan rocker his mother had left him when he was just a child and listened to the gentle *shush. . . shush* of Colin's breathing through the oxygen tubes that were always taped to his nostrils when he was sleeping. He thought about how things always seemed to come full circle. What goes around invariably comes back around.

Ray's father had been a macho Chicano. He had considered his son a wimp from the time, when Ray was about 7, that Ray had seen Barishnykov on television and had asked to take ballet lessons. Ray's father had threatened to disown him ten years later when he'd found out about his sexual predilections.

Ray's mother had been a beautiful Oriental woman whom he had adored, but who had died when he was barely 10 years old, leaving him to his father's bad disposition until he was old enough to leave home.

He remembered the day his mother had died, how afraid he had been, how abandoned he had felt even before she had stopped breathing. He had sat in this same rocker then, knowing his childhood was over, realizing he had come to the end of a phase in his life, with no idea what would lie ahead. Maybe it would be best, that little boy had thought, if he could just die, too.

The circle had come round, and there were similarities to that other day's dying with what he felt now. Colin would die, as Ray's mother had died, leaving him behind. But Ray was a different person now than the child he had been. And though he felt a phase of his life was over, and he had no idea what lay ahead, he didn't feel abandoned this time. He was peaceful about the letting go.

Ray had garnered the adulation of most of his acquaintances by being something of a local phenomenon in the AIDS support community. He had tested HIV positive back in '84, when standard treatment for AIDS was a prescription to write a will and get one's affairs in order.

Ray had briefly considered giving in, just lying down for the count like so many others were doing, but by accident, or as he had come to think of it, by felicitous synchronicity, he had seen a piece on Dr. Katerina Brenner-Beusch—the famous initiator of hospice care for cancer patients—in a Sunday magazine, about how she was trying to set up a communal farm in West Virginia for people with AIDS. He had decided if he was a dead man anyway, he might as well do something useful with the rest of his life. So he had called Katerina to see if he could volunteer to work on the farm.

As it had happened, the Sunday magazine article had caused such a furor among the populace of the county where Katerina owned her farm that there was an immediate backlash. The good people of the county didn't want the spectre of AIDS being brought into their midst and began a campaign to block the doctor's plan. She was harassed both openly and covertly, called "Satanic," had rocks thrown at her windows and threats made to her person and her property.

When Ray called her to offer his services, she told him it might be some time before she could realize the dream of having anyone there and discouraged him from coming to visit just then because of the conflict with all the locals. But in their conversation, she'd recommended books to him that might help him heal some of the issues in his life while he still had time to deal with them. She wished him well and said she hoped to see him at one of her healing workshops in the spring. Later, she had sent him a schedule of where she'd be holding her weekend intensives for the seriously ill.

Some of the books she had recommended dealt with creative visualization, some with the effects of attitudes and emotions on the physical body. Others dealt with the death and dying process. And still others offered diet and exercise regimens for better health.

Ray was fascinated with the variety of ideas in the books; he became a New Age psycho-pop junky, reading everything from the Seth and Michael materials, to the Edgar Cayce books, to *The Course in Miracles*, to diet and exercise manuals.

To support the physical body, he got regular massages and changed his diet to include only clean, fresh, pure foods. And for exercise, he began doing Tai Chi. He realized later he had chosen it because its grace and fluidity reminded him of his mother; in fact, when he practiced in front of the mirror, he sometimes caught a glimpse of her in himself.

To heal his mind, he did visualization exercises, picturing every cell of his body as perfect and unblemished. To heal his emotions, he began doing forgiveness exercises. He meditated twice daily. He consciously made a list of all the hurts and rejections he had both endured and inflicted throughout his lifetime—from childhood to the present, and he consistently began working to heal those incidents.

Sometimes he telephoned people he had had conflict with in the past and reopened lines of communication. One of those people had been his father. He still treasured the phone call.

"Dad," he'd said, "this is Ray. I don't know if you want to hear from me, but I have ARC—AIDS related complex. Guess you figured me for it, huh? Anyway, I'm sort of tidying things up. So I just thought I'd call and tell you I really do love you, and I understand where you were coming from all those years."

When the old man didn't answer, Ray had just continued rambling.

"So, anyway, I'm not sorry for my lifestyle or anything, I mean, we all are what we are. But I do understand you better now than I did then, and I just wish we could see each other again sometime."

There was a long silence, and Ray was afraid his father wasn't ever going to respond, until he recognized the sound of soft weeping over the phone and realized with gratitude that he'd been incredibly lucky. Too many gay men who tried to heal their relationships with their fathers tended to meet with rejection, even in the face of death. Colin had. But that one phone call had healed all the past for Ray and his father. They'd seen each other a couple of times since, and his father had expressed a certain pride in Ray's obvious expertise at Tai Chi.

When telephoning an old adversary wasn't possible, Ray would sit and visualize the person being immersed in the rays of healing pink light that issued from his heart center. He did a lot of such visualizations, and he kept doing them over and over with each individual until he felt his burden lift for that person.

And then one day, a miracle happened. As he sat cross-legged on his bed in meditation, trying to let flow into his mind whether there was anyone else in his life he had forgotten to send love to, it seemed as if a skylight opened above his head, and a brilliant light streamed into it, flooding him with wave after wave of love. It was physical, emotional, and spiritual. It was asexual, and yet almost orgasmic, intensified to the tenth power. It was joy, ecstasy, bliss, rapture. It was fulfillment. It was beyond words.

And as he was washed in the deluge of brilliant energy, he heard a voice, melodious and somehow androgynous, as if it were for him both father and mother, speak inside his head the words of balm and benison, "You are my beloved son, in whom I am well pleased."

And, incredible as it seemed, he knew it was true.

From that day forward, Ray stopped being tested by his doctors. He effectively dropped out of the system, and out of its statistical frame of reference. So far as the compilers of AIDS statistics knew, he was already pushing up Jimson weeds.

It amused him to note that the Center for Disease Control in Atlanta had undertaken a study with 135 longterm AIDS survivors, those anomalous individuals who had tested HIV positive but who had survived more than five years, and who continued living long and well in spite of the odds. Center officials admitted they would only be able to examine physical influences on these survivors, the effect of attitudes and emotions being beyond the scope of their capabilities.

Ray had laughed when he read that. He knew without doubt that attitudes and emotions were the crucial key to any real healing.

But he also knew he would someday die. Perhaps he'd get hit by a truck while crossing K Street. Maybe he'd misjudge an adversary on one of the Panthers' patrols and catch a knife or even a bullet in a vital organ. But he wouldn't die from AIDS. That was no longer part of his belief system.

Ray was also aware of many more people who, like himself, had chosen not to accept the standard death warrant of the United States medical monolith. There were groups all over the country where those with AIDS were encouraged to take responsibility for their illness and their healing. The disease had made gay communities in New York, Chicago, San Francisco, Los Angeles, and other major cities create real networks of love and support. And they had opened their hearts when others besides themselves began needing advice.

For it had become increasingly clear AIDS was not just a gay disease, not just a disease of illicit drug users. It affected men, women, and children; it affected 96 percent of the hemophiliacs in the country. And as other populations had begun to evidence cases, the network of gays had rallied with all the energy they could muster to offer hope. Ray had been so proud of their continuing positive response to the crisis.

There were hopes of an actual cure—he'd read that doctors in Europe and Mexico were experimenting with such things as ozone treatments, superoxygenating the blood, and medications not available in this country. He'd also heard of a physician in Georgia who was treating her patients with radionics; many of them were doing extremely well. But as long as the FDA and the AMA continued their vise-grip control of the testing and dispensing of unorthodox treatments in this country, AIDS victims would continue to die in large numbers unless they somehow found the hope, will, and discipline to heal themselves.

Ray only wished there could be a magic bullet for Colin, the lover from his past with whom he had reconnected when he was in the midst of healing his old relationships. Shortly after his experience with the light in meditation, he and Colin had gotten back together, but it was clear their reunion was only temporary. Because Colin couldn't believe in miracles.

Ray had to respect Colin's right to die. But in the months they had been together again, he had experienced the joy of mutual giving in a way he'd never known it before. Perhaps because he truly loved himself now, he could give without reservation. He had no neediness, so he could love without fear of rejection.

Ray had tried to offer his spiritual approach to Colin, but while Colin was admiring of Ray's conviction, he'd insisted from early on, "The spiritual trip won't work for me."

He had, nevertheless, taken good care of himself, had meticulously followed his doctor's orders, and he'd had three more years of life after he and Ray had joined forces. But Ray knew Colin's sojourn was just about over.

It was okay, though. A year or so before he'd managed to get Colin to one of Katerina's workshops, and Colin had finally been able to express the pain and anger he had been carrying, not just about his disease, but about how he felt he'd been used by other people all his life, had experienced so much rejection, had never really been happy, because his family, friends, religion, and culture wouldn't let him be okay just being himself.

He'd even expressed to Ray how hurt and angry he had been when the two of them had broken up, how he had *known* Ray was about to leave him, so he'd left first instead, and how when they'd come together again, he really didn't trust that this time the commitment could be real. But he admitted he'd needed it so badly he'd decided to take the risk.

Then he'd wept openly, saying, "I think I've been using you to put a bandaid on my pain and anger."

Ray had held him and said, "No, love, you can't *use* anybody else unless they let themselves be used. I *love* you, man, I always did, I always will. And nothing you can do or say will stop me from loving you. So, no guilt, okay? What went before doesn't matter. It doesn't even exist. Stop turning your pain on yourself."

It had been a very healing experience for Colin, and in finally expressing his sense of never having been loved, but of needing love so badly, he opened himself to the possibility of receiving. At the end of the workshop, the other people participating came to him and selected him for a special "love ceremony," hugging and kissing him, lifting him on their shoulders and singing, "I Love You Just the Way You Are."

After that weekend, a sort of calm settled in for Colin. It wasn't so much that he'd given in to his disease, but it seemed to Ray as if he'd agreed to let it become a teacher. He had arranged to visit his parents in Florida for a week, and had come back looking relaxed, tanned, and peaceful. His mother, he said, had been totally supportive when he'd told them about his illness, and though his father had become quiet and had distanced himself during the visit, Colin hadn't felt hurt or rejected, just sad that his father couldn't make peace, too.

Later, when the lesions of Kaposi's sarcoma had worsened and begun to appear on his extremities, he had told Ray he would understand if Ray didn't want to touch him anymore.

"Touching you," Ray responded, "has been one of the great pleasures of my life. You'll always be beautiful to me, no matter what."

And he'd really meant it. He'd even begun giving Colin regular massages during the last couple months to help make him more comfortable.

Ray sometimes thought the very best part of being together with Colin again was the music. Colin had been trained as a classical musician, played both flute and piano, and he'd actually earned his living performing with music and theater companies in the D.C. metropolitan area.

Ray sat enraptured when Colin played for him alone. Sometimes he would play Mozart or Chopin, sometimes pieces of his own composition, and though Ray himself had never been able to carry a tune except when holding a Walkman, he was aware that since Colin had made peace with himself, his music had become more brilliant, more splendid.

Colin had continued to play professionally until just a few months before, when he'd become too ill. Now most evenings he and Ray would just sit and read together, Colin in his bed and Ray in the rattan rocker, listening to recordings of James Galway or Jean Pierre Rampal, or tapes Ray had made of Colin playing. But either way, it was a peaceful pleasure.

Ray had quit his own job, as an administrator for the Virginia Recreation and Parks Service, when he calculated Colin had only about two months left to live. Except for his weekend forays with the Panthers, he and Colin spent virtually all their time together.

Ray sensed that as soon as Colin made his transition, Ray himself would be called to some other kind of service. He just didn't know what yet. But in the meantime, there was only a little time left for them to be together, too little for them to waste any. They both had money set aside, so there was plenty for rent, groceries, and the few medical needs not covered by Colin's insurance. Colin had chosen to die at home, with Ray in attendance, so when Colin had become very weak, they'd rented a hospital bed so he could be as comfortable as possible. And they'd made arrangements with a local funeral parlor to come when their sharing of the dying was past.

Once again Ray remembered his mother's dying at home. While his father hadn't rented a hospital bed for her, his memory of watching with her was eerily similar to what he was experiencing now, though her emaciation had been from the cancer that was strangling her and the deadly drugs the doctors had given her to kill it. The drugs had ultimately killed her instead. She'd had an oxygen tank, too, much like the one beside Colin's bed.

Ray, who would have liked to deny his sixth sense this time, thought today might be the last day for Colin.

About 2 p.m., with the afternoon sun streaming through the windows and just beginning to touch the foot of the hospital bed, Colin opened his eyes and turned to Ray, extending his hand a little. Ray reached for it and stroked his fingers. Colin tried to lift his hand to remove the oxygen tubes in his nostrils, but the small effort seemed almost too much for him, so Ray rose and helped him take them out.

"I had a wonderful dream," Colin said smiling, his face bright with the memory of it.

His voice was ragged and raspy as he spoke, but Ray didn't try to stop him, for he sensed what Colin would say was perhaps the most important sharing they'd ever had.

"I was walking through a door," said Colin, "and I was all dressed up in a white tuxedo. And this beautiful man, also dressed in a white tuxedo, came to meet me; I think he must have been an orchestra conductor. First he embraced me, and then he took my hand and led me down the aisle of this magnificent amphitheater, where all sorts of gorgeous people dressed in white were waiting to hear me play. And the spotlight came on, and it was just a brilliant, brilliant light, and I sat down at a stunning white grand piano and played for this audience. It was the concert of my life, because I played all my own compositions, and they were glorious!"

He stopped speaking for a moment, transported with the memory of his dream vision, then he added with tears in his eyes, "Ray, that's where I'm going! I'm going to get to play. . . for the angels." He spoke the last words more softly, awed by the reality of what he had just said. "You were right, Ray, there's something after this life. You really were right!"

Ray couldn't think of anything to say, but his own eyes welled with tears, and he brought the hand he held to his lips and kissed the fingers as he nodded.

"You'll have to help me get ready," Colin said, with excitement, and he grasped Ray's hand more firmly. "Ready for the concert! Will you?" He could barely move, so his intensity was astonishing.

"Of course," Ray said. "We'll get you bathed, and then you can put on that white silk robe I gave you for Christmas, and you'll be ready."

Ray fetched the plastic tub they'd been using for bath water, tenderly undressed Colin, and gently began the bathing process, washing him with soap and warm water, being careful of the lesions. He removed the disposable diaper, which they'd also been using for the last couple of weeks when Colin's bowel and bladder function had become unpredictable.

Colin, who had been calm and patient up to that point, frowned a little and turned his head to the wall. "I do so wish," he said, ". . . that's the thing I wish I could still do for myself. It's like being a helpless baby again."

"It's okay, love," said Ray. "'Homo sum; humani nihil a me alienum.' That's Terrence, as I recall. It means, 'I am a man; nothing human is alien to me.'"

Colin looked at Ray in amazement, but Ray just shrugged in return. "Four years of Catholic school Latin."

When he'd finished bathing and drying Colin, Ray just looked at him for a moment. He realized this was probably the last time he'd ever see his lover naked. Even wasted from the disease, even splotched with the purplish lesions, in Ray's eyes Colin still had a beautiful body, though Ray's feelings were more of tenderness than of desire.

"I have become like his mother," Ray thought, and knew with the thought he was somehow closing the circle of their relationship, a relationship that had once both come and gone with erotic passion, and had come back again—and would go again—with generosity and what St. Paul had called *agape*. He smiled at the wonder of it and went to fetch the white silk robe from the closet.

When he'd diapered Colin, dressed him in the robe, and refolded the sheet and blanket over his body with his arms resting on top, he kissed his forehead.

"You were right all along, weren't you?" said Colin.

Ray raised his eyebrows questioningly.

"About there being more to life than just the body. The 'spiritual trip' I didn't want to take. You were right about it."

"Yeah," said Ray with a smile, "the nice thing is you don't have to believe in it for it to be true, or for it to work for you, for that matter."

Colin nodded.

"And see," Ray added, "you did what you needed to do. You finished your unfinished business. Now you can get on with whatever's next."

Colin nodded again, then wiggled a finger toward the oxygen tank. "I won't need it again," he said.

"I know," said Ray.

"Will you kiss me one last time?" asked Colin.

For answer, Ray leaned over and touched his warm lips to Colin's cool ones.

"Thank you for loving me," whispered Colin. "Please promise not to grieve."

Ray nodded.

"Now just hold me," Colin whispered.

Ray slid a hip onto the bed and encircled his lover from behind, leaning Colin's head against his chest. They sat that way for a few minutes in silence, and Ray listened to Colin's breathing. Colin's eyes were shut, and for a moment Ray thought he had drifted off to sleep, but he suddenly opened his eyes and looked at something in the near distance.

"Here he is!" said Colin, and his eyes were luminous. "He's come to take me to the concert!"

Then his body shuddered violently, as if something inside, perhaps his vital energy, were being released. Ray didn't see it, but moments later, he felt the spirit leave Colin's body.

Ray sat there, holding the body for a while longer, rocking it and whispering, "Goodbye, love, goodbye." Then he gently closed the eyes of his departed friend, laid him back against the pillows, and straightened the covers.

He went to fetch two white candles, two silver candlesticks, a carrying case of tapes, and a portable player. With reverence, he placed the candles in the holders and lit them. Then he sat down in the rocker, placed one of the tapes he'd made of Colin playing his own compositions in the portable machine, and turned it on.

Taking Colin's hand in his, he sat back and listened to the concert until nightfall.

*****

Lucy explained to Adam that a vision quest was generally a tribal rite of passage for young people entering adulthood, but that lots of non-Indian adults in recent years had chosen to go on such a quest as a means of breaking through the barriers in their lives and finding more meaning.

"It is," she said, "a means to growth, both for the self and for the whole community. The warrior is a person who is willing to go outside the comfort of the group to find a new truth, then brings it back to share so that everyone may be more fulfilled. In finding *your* truth, you will enhance the understanding and body of truth of the whole group."

"You mean you and Smoo will be better off if I find my truth?" said Adam.

"Smoo and I will be *immeasurably* enhanced if you find your truth," she answered laughing, "but so will everyone else on the planet."

"But I don't know everyone else on the planet," he argued.

"Trust me," she said. "You don't have to know them for them to be improved by your growth. Just be willing to go with the experience with your whole self—heart, mind, body, and soul—and don't try to rationalize whatever happens. Just let it be, and at the same time let yourself be."

She told him the Ancestors had given her a simple set of instructions for his quest. He was to cleanse himself for a week with a vegetarian diet. Then he was to go to some wilderness place and find a spot in which he felt he could communicate with his natural surroundings. He must then fast for three days and nights and keep silence, to await the advent of his vision. He would, as part of the experience, receive or choose a new name, which he could use when he felt it was appropriate after he returned.

Lucy encouraged him to take a notebook with him, to keep track of his thoughts and feelings during the three days while he fasted and kept the silence. He had never kept a journal before, so it was a novelty for him.

They thought of nearby places that might offer Adam both the close contact with the earth and the solitude he would require.

"I'll bet," said Lucy, "you could find the kind of place you need in Big Bend. It's just a couple of hours from here and encompasses the Chisos Mountains. Why, Smoo and I could go with you and camp out at one of the campgrounds while you are off questing! That way, I won't be so far away when you are finished."

She'd said the last sentence almost shyly, as if she didn't want him to think she was horning in on his experience, but was really eager to share what he was to learn.

"I'd be honored if you'd join me," he'd said gallantly.

Even though he'd been thinking of his idyll here in Valentine with Lucy as a sort of vacation from "real life," the idea of taking a break from Clive's ranch made his handyman activities, which were actually a pleasure to him, seem more like authentic work. Well, as Mark Twain had once said, "The secret of success is in making your vocation your vacation," and he had to admit he enjoyed building things a lot more than he had ever enjoyed creating flow charts or business plans. But perhaps, he thought, that was because he was working for himself now and not for someone else.

A part of Adam—perhaps it was his left-brained rationalistic side—didn't really think this quest was going to amount to much. That part of him wasn't expecting anything to happen, but it said at worst he'd have to make up some sort of vision to please Lucy.

Another part of him, though, was really eager to undertake the quest. It seemed a little like a game, like the Dungeons and Dragons roleplaying he'd sometimes done as a teenager. He was an Arthurian knight, setting out in search of the Grail, or perhaps in search of a dragon to slay. The kid in him got a little flutter of excitement when he thought about spending three days alone in silence, challenging whatever gods there might be to make a miracle for him.

They decided they would camp together for seven days and scope out the park for likely sites where Adam could spend some time alone and in silence. A friendly park ranger with whom they chatted at the visitor center told them the desert had been blooming all the last year, so if they were wildflower fanciers, they were in for a treat. Lucy's eyes lit up; she'd brought plenty of painting supplies to keep her occupied for the days Adam would be by himself.

"The downside," said the ranger, "is that the desert only blooms like this when the rains have been excessive, and when the rains have been excessive the river swells. So some of the campgrounds along the Rio Grande aren't accessible at present, and Santa Elena Canyon is periodically closed. Also, Burro Mesa Pouroff is a good place to stay away from in a heavy rain."

"We'll be careful," said Adam, taking a copy of the park map.

They chose the primitive campground at Government Spring near the center of the park for their base of operations during their week together, where they slept in the back of the camper truck while Smoo took the seat in the cab each night.

"Saves getting dog hair all over our blankets," said Lucy, "if he has his own binky and his own space."

They kept their diet simple and spare for the week, eating only fresh apples for breakfast and lunch and fresh vegetable salads for dinner. By the fifth morning, Adam was ready to swear off apples, and he complained to Lucy after his third trip to a park portajohn, "Why do I have to fast for the last three days? I'm already clean as a whistle!"

She'd just laughed at him and handed him a Golden Delicious.

To get him into the discipline of writing his thoughts during his quest, he spent a few minutes each night before bedtime commenting on his observations of the day. He surprised himself with some of them; when he just blanked his mind and then wrote down whatever came into it, he discovered he was capable of some pretty profound things.

One morning they'd gone to Grapevine Hills very early. The path to the mountainside was in shadow on their way in, so all he noticed were the rocky pebbles. But an hour later, on their way back, the sun was higher, and he could see that strewn among the pebbles were many little pieces of quartz crystal, glittering like diamonds. He couldn't resist picking them up; by the time they emerged from the brush and climbed into the truck once more, he had about 30 of the little crystals in his pocket.

That night he wrote: "The path that lies in darkness seems to be strewn with rocks. But the path that lies in the light seems strewn with diamonds. You can choose to walk in darkness, or you can choose to walk on diamonds. But your perspective will be a result of your choice."

Another day they decided to go to the little town of Boquillas, a tiny Mexican village across the Rio Grande from the easternmost campsite in the park. Unlike most border crossings, this one was totally unpoliced, and navigating it turned out to be a popular tourist adventure.

Leaving Smoo for a couple of hours with a friendly camper they'd met, they picked their way carefully on foot through the muddy brush to the edge of the rushing water, where they were met by a unique and enterprising ferry. The only way to get to the little town was in a rowboat manned by two Boquillas residents, one of whom would row very rapidly with a short oar, and the other of whom would bail out the leaky boat to keep it from sinking. Round trip fare was a paltry $3.00—a bargain in any market, thought Adam, considering the laugh the trip gave them.

Once on the other side, they were importuned by the local equivalent of taxi drivers to ride mules to the village, but since they could see it in the distance, they decided to walk instead.

"We can't get lost, at any rate," said Adam. "All we have to do is follow the donkey droppings!"

"Hansel and Gretel should have had it so good," Lucy answered.

Once in the village, they decided to have lunch at the town's one restaurant, where they had their choice of eating either tacos or burritos and drinking either Coke or Mexican beer. They chose the tacos but eschewed both the soda and the beer in favor of the water they carried in bottles on their belts.

Then they had their choice of shopping at the town's one store for blankets, ponchos, leather goods, or jewelry carved of onyx, or buying liquor at the town's one bar. Adam, feeling a need to support the village economy, bought a blanket and a cowboy hat. And on their walk back to the river, Lucy succumbed to the pleas of two tiny, brown, barefooted salesgirls who offered them a selection of colored rock crystals at the bargain price of a quarter apiece.

"Don't laugh," she said to Adam as she stuffed about a dozen of her selections into her jacket pocket. "We can always use more rocks!"

"Of course," he responded. "We need them to replace the ones I'm finally getting out of my head!"

They had to wait about 30 minutes for their erstwhile boatman to return for them from the U.S. side of the river with another load of passengers. As they sat quietly waiting on the bank, Adam looked at the flowing water and thought of the friendly people he'd met in the village, eking out a living in a variation of the tourist trade in whatever way they could. The boatmen with their leaky boat, the restaurateur with her tiny but delicious menu, the little girls with their colored rock crystals. He was sorry now he hadn't taken a mule ride after all, just to support the taxi drivers.

That night, he amazed himself by writing in his journal: "On this side of the border, the river runs from right to left. On the other side, it runs from left to right. The division between our country and theirs is totally arbitrary, for the land is the same, and the water that divides us supports the same kinds of vegetation on both banks. But oh, what a difference of economy and lifestyle separates our peoples. Would that we might someday overcome these arbitrary boundaries and become *one* people."

"Where did that come from?" he asked himself, and realized he wasn't, even now, the same person he had been at that fateful New Year's Eve party.

On their fifth day in the park, they visited Cottonwood Campground, which was open to picnickers, but closed for camping because high water had inundated it several times in the preceding year. Its two portajohns were tipped over as a result, and the one permanent outhouse building had silt on the toilet seats, clear testimony to the height the water had reached. In fact, Adam thought he could make out a water line on the wall of the building; it came to about his shoulder.

Here Adam finally found a place where he wanted to spend his three days of solitude. A few hundred yards downriver from the campground, and not on the beaten paths of the park, he found on what amounted to a little hillock a circle of trees that formed a natural shelter. He would be out of the sun's direct rays during the day, and at night he'd be reasonably protected from the worst of any wind. But the best part of all was that from this vantage point, he could climb a tree and look at the river flowing by. He had become addicted to the river.

As it happened, the days Adam would spend by himself were the first three days of April, which he would normally have expected to be pleasant so far south. Ironically, the last days of March were balmy, but a late season norther blew down from the Great Plains just about the time he was to go off by himself.

"Maybe we should go back to Boquillas and buy you a couple more blankets," said Lucy worriedly.

"I'll be fine," he said, though he was glad he'd had the presence of mind to pack long underwear and two sweaters.

"At least take my rain poncho," she insisted. "You'll have the pup tent, but while it's supposed to be water tight, if you get caught out of it, you'll need something else to keep you dry. And you'll need as many layers as you can get to stay warm, so take your sleeping bag. Even if you're not planning to sleep, you can curl up in it for warmth."

"Why are you worried?" asked Adam. "Aren't the Ancestors supposed to be taking care of me?"

She stared at him for a few seconds, then she said, "You ever hear the story about the man who when the hurricane was coming kept thinking God would save him? So a man in a jeep came by and offered to drive him to safety, but he said, 'No thanks, God will save me.' And the rains came, and the waters rose, and he had to climb up to the second floor of his house, and a man in a rowboat came by and offered to row him to safety, but he said, 'No thanks, God will save me.' And the waters rose even higher, and he had to climb out onto his roof, and a man in a helicopter came by and offered to fly him to safety, but he said, 'No thanks, God will save me.' So he drowned. And when he went to heaven, he was very upset, and he said to God, 'Why didn't you save me?' And God said, 'I sent you a jeep, and a rowboat, and a helicopter. What more did you want?' So take your sleeping bag."

Adam laughed and hugged her. She hugged him back fiercely.

"And take care of yourself," she whispered as he held her close, "because I sort of like having you around."

"I'll take it under advisement."

She dropped him the next morning just before dawn at Cottonwood Campground, with his sleeping bag, watertight pup tent, blanket, and two gallon jugs of drinking water. He was dressed for the cold, with thermal underwear under his jeans, a shirt and two sweaters, his jacket, a poncho, a pair of gloves, and his new Boquillas hat. In his sleeping bag he had the park map, a snake bite kit, a knife, a flashlight, and his notebook and two pens.

"That's more paraphernalia than you're supposed to take, but if you get into trouble I want you to be prepared," said Lucy as she kissed him goodbye and Smoo gave him a slobbery lick. "I'll pick you up here just after sunup three days from now."

"Go paint some flowers," he said in response, and picking up his gear, he turned and marched into the campground.

*****

Cassie was bubbling with excitement as Sophie parked the car in a lot near the Cannon Congressional Office Building. She reached behind the seat and extracted Sophie's large canvas Environmental Defense Fund shopping bag from the back, then locked the door on her side of the car.

She really liked the big black bag with its beautiful color picture of the planet Earth, and Sophie had suggested they use it to carry the "tribute" they were bringing to the offices they would visit.

"May as well make a statement in any way we can," she'd said.

Just inside the front door of the Cannon Building they had to go through a metal detection gate and be inspected by a security guard.

"Ooh," whispered Cassie, "it's like at the airport. What do they think we're gonna do, bomb the place?"

"They just want to make sure we don't," said Sophie quietly. She gave the security guard a big smile.

"I'll need to look in your bag, ma'am," he said, and she turned her large canvas Environmental Defense Fund shopping bag over to him.

"No bombs," said Cassie brightly, and the guard stifled a little smile. When he seemed puzzled at the contents of the bag, Cassie decided to make conversation.

"Would you like some cookies?" she piped. "We made them ourselves, and you can have some on one condition."

The guard obviously thought Cassie was cute. "Okay, what's that?"

"Well," she responded, "we're going upstairs to see *our* Virginia congressmen and ask them to do everything they can to help save the South American rain forests. So these are cookies with Brazil nuts in them, to help them get the message. See, if the South Americans would just leave the rain forests alone, they could harvest them each time they replenish themselves—they could get herbs, and nuts, and flowers, and plants, and some of these things have medicinal properties and aren't grown anywhere else. And they could make lots more money than they do cutting down the trees and burning them. And if we don't all do something to get that message to the South Americans, we aren't going to have any air left to breathe, because without trees, there won't be any oxygen. And in addition," she added with studied preciseness, "when trees get burned, the carbon released into the atmosphere accelerates the greenhouse effect. Anyway, you can have some cookies if you'll promise to speak to *your* congressman—or congresslady," she said, glancing at Sophie, who nodded, "and tell him or her that *you* want the rain forests saved, too."

The guard had been nodding at her speech, and he handed her back the shopping bag.

"Promise?" asked Cassie.

"Yeah, okay!" agreed the guard cheerfully. "Sounds like a good idea to me!"

"Thank you very much," said Cassie as she offered him a package of Brazil nut and chocolate chip cookies. "I just know you're going to love these cookies."

"Cute kid," said the guard to Sophie. "She's pretty grown up, isn't she?"

"Yes," said Sophie, smiling. "Uh, what direction do we go to find Congressman Ryder's office?"

The guard consulted a list and told her the office number. "Upstairs, second floor, hall to the left, then at the end of the hall, left again. Numbers in each corridor are posted at the end of the hall."

It took them about five minutes to climb the stairs and find the office they were looking for in the maze of corridors. They hadn't managed to get a real appointment with Congressman Ryder over the phone, but his aide said he'd be glad to meet with them if the Congressman was unavailable, provided they could get there by 4 p.m. According to Sophie's watch, it was 3:55 p.m. when they arrived at the proper office.

"Hi," said Cassie to the receptionist at the desk just inside the door of the office.

"Hi," responded the attractive girl.

"We have an appointment either with Congressman Ryder or with Mr. Tennyson, his assistant," said Sophie.

"Well, I'm afraid the congressman isn't in this afternoon," said the girl. "And Mr. Tennyson is in a meeting right now."

"We'll wait," Sophie said, and gave the girl a smile.

"While we're waiting," said Cassie, "would you like some cookies? We have some wonderful chocolate chip and Brazil nut cookies for the congressman, and you can have some, too, on one condition."

The girl smiled a little, and Sophie could tell she was responding to Cassie the way the guard downstairs had.

"What do I have to do?" asked the girl.

Cassie gave her the same speech she had given the guard, and the girl agreed that she would, indeed, contact her congressman, which in this case was easy because it was Representative Ryder.

"And, just in case you forget," Cassie said, "there's a message in the middle of the package to remind you, sort of like a fortune cookie message."

"And what does the message say?" asked the girl.

Cassie looked around as if she wanted to be sure no one else was listening, then she whispered conspiratorially, "It says, 'Don't forget to speak to your congressman about saving the rain forests—before you run out of breath'." She grinned and asked, "What do you think? I made that up myself."

"Not bad," said the girl. "We should hire you as one of the congressman's speechwriters!"

"Here," said Sophie, while they had the girl's attention, "have some literature about what we're trying to get the congressman to do, and how it will help both South America and the U.S. from an economic standpoint, among other things. We have our suggestions outlined." She handed the girl a sheet, at the top of which was another of Cassie's slogans, "Saving the rain forests makes cents!"

At that point a group emerged from a back office, and shook hands all around. One of them was Mr. Tennyson, who couldn't have been more than about 23. Sophie was pretty sure he wasn't the congressman's top aide—he was probably just the assistant assigned to politely brush people off.

The receptionist called his attention to Sophie and Cassie, and he shook hands with them and ushered them into the office from which he and the earlier group had emerged.

The receptionist, left to herself in the outer office, opened the package of cookies and bit into one as she glanced down the list Sophie had handed her.

"Quite an unusual pair," she thought, "for lobbyists."

*****

The first day of Adam's silence was anything but quiet, with the howling of a cold wind, the shushing of the cottonwoods and other flora as they rocked and groaned in the onslaught, and the rushing of the river's water. He set up his pup tent immediately, to be prepared in case of rain. Stowing most of his gear inside it, so nothing would blow away, he then took a walk back toward the campground. It wasn't likely anyone would be picnicking here in the middle of a blue norther.

As he walked, he noticed the dried mud from the last flooding, which had been baked by the sun and cracked. In some spots, the pieces were large enough to contain his whole foot, like asymmetrical adobe tiles; in others, the cracked pieces were small and curved, like broken potsherds.

He walked a circuit of the entire compound. As he neared the river, he became aware that there had once been a road into the campground. He'd not noticed it the first time he'd been here earlier in the week; now he saw that the last flooding had sheared off a portion of the river bank, and a large section of what was considered unstable ground had been roped off with a string of red flags.

A thought came into his mind: "Change is inevitable. But the more we change within, the more the external world will be able to stay the same."

"What the hell does that mean?" his reason asked him.

"I don't know," he answered, "but I'm going to write it down. I have a feeling it's a useful piece of information."

And he wandered back to his ring of trees to find his notebook.

During the course of the morning and afternoon, he walked the compound again several times. Four times he spied black feathers stuck in the dried mud but fluttering now in the wind. Each time he found one, he extracted it from the baked mud and stuck it in his hatband.

"It would be sort of ironic," he thought, "if Lucy Whitefeather were to marry Adam Blackfeather."

"That is not your name," said a little voice in his mind. "Be patient. This is but the first day."

There had been no real sunrise, just a subtle graying of the black until it was apparent that somewhere above the murk the sun had risen. Sunset occurred in much the same way, with a darkening of the gray until it became black.

The wind hadn't diminished throughout the day, so the sound never let up. Before the light disappeared completely, Adam checked to be sure he knew where all his supplies were, especially the flashlight, then crawled into the sleeping bag inside the tent. He didn't intend to sleep, but in the dark and the wind, he knew he'd have a difficult time if it began to rain.

Funny, when he'd thought about this vision quest, he'd romantically expected to be sleeping under the stars, not worrying about being blown over a precipice into the river. Ah, well, he didn't have to choose this place, did he?

"Yes," came the thought into his mind, "the river is a symbol of the Mother. You had to choose to be near the water for this time."

Dutifully, he reached for the flashlight, turned it on, and wrote the thought in his notebook.

He wondered what the bears and the mountain lions of the park were doing. They were the only predators about which visitors were warned, the only thing to guard against if one was foolhardy enough to stay out alone at night. Which, by the way, all the park literature warned against.

"Though any intelligent bear or mountain lion wouldn't be out in this wind storm. Only stupid humans do things like this," he thought.

If he slept, he wasn't aware of it. The wind was consistent all night, and he lay simply listening. He could remember having been afraid of windstorms when he was a little kid, or at least he was afraid of them until his father beat the fear out of him.

He hadn't really thought about his father much lately. The old man hadn't retired from the service until a couple of years before. At that point, he and Adam's mother had moved to sunny Florida to some community mostly filled with retired military. He'd had lunch with his mother once when she'd been on a long layover between planes at the Dallas airport. He hadn't seen his dad in probably five or six years, since the folks came to his graduation from U of H.

He probed some old wounds, memories of whippings for infraction of rules, memories of being pushed and yelled at when his grades weren't perfect or his shoes weren't shined or his bed wasn't made just right. And he remembered how his father had guilt tripped him for at least two weeks the one time he didn't make a team in sports. He couldn't even remember now which team it was—soccer? basketball? Anyway, his dad had had him in the basement every night that semester doing pushups and chinups for what seemed like hours so he'd be in shape the next term for any tryouts that came up.

No wonder he didn't like rigid exercise programs!

And then there was the religious routine. Dad had been hard enough on him when he was little, but at least he was away a lot, and even when he was stationed in the continental U.S. where Mom and Adam could join him on a tour, he was often out evenings bowling, or taking some class or other, or just at the NCO club drinking with his buddies.

Then came Vietnam. Something happened there. But Dad came back and next thing they knew, he went to OCS, then signed up for another tour in Vietnam as a officer. By the time the war ended, he'd made captain. And he'd become a religious fanatic.

In retrospect, knowing what he knew now about the war, Adam wondered if his father hadn't done some things in that military action he felt he needed to make retribution for. It was just one of those strange quirks that the whole Vietnam action caused for people: some men got cynical; Adam's father got religion.

The particular brand of religion was strict, rigid, hardshell fundamentalism. For Adam, it meant that at the age of 11 he was suddenly thrust into some serious indoctrination, too late for him not to question its validity and logic. But any argument would cause more beatings. Frankly, he didn't relish crossing his father, at least not until the day when, at 16, his father threatened to strap him and Adam stood up to him. At that point they were both 5'10", but Adam, because of all the pushups, chinups, sports, and calisthenics, was stronger. When his father lifted the belt to hit him, Adam just caught his wrist and shook his head.

Funny, he hadn't thought about the old man at all since Lucy had done her magic healing thing on him back in January. What was even more interesting to him was that the anger thoughts of his father used to generate seemed to be missing. The old wounds had finally scabbed over. Being loved by Lucy—and loving her back—was making all the difference.

He thought about her sweet pixie face and her gentle little body. Even putting the sex aside, which in his experience was extraordinary, he missed being able to roll over and reach for her, cuddle around her and go to sleep warm together with her, like squirrels in a nest. They hadn't spent a night away from each other in about three months, and he certainly missed her now. Good god, he felt so married to her, it would break him apart if she ever went away.

Then discomfort started niggling his consciousness. What would happen if nothing happened? Suppose he didn't have any experience worth mentioning? Suppose he had to make something up and she caught him in a lie? Would she give up on him, write him off as a bad job?

"Come on, Ancestors," he thought, "don't let me down. Give me something worth reporting."

He remembered later he was thinking this thought when he heard thunder in the distance. He opened the pup tent to get a look at what was going on in the sky and saw lightning off to the northwest. He slid back into the comfort of his tented sleeping bag, but lay listening to the distant storm. An hour later, he could still hear it raging and looked out again. It didn't seem to have moved, but was still going on at about the same intensity.

About another hour later, dawn—such as it was—broke in the east. There was no sun to speak of, just that pale, bleak lightening of the eastern sky. Off to the northwest, the storm continued to rage.

Adam crawled out of his warm burrow and tidied it up. He took a few gulps of water straight from the jug, then decided to make his way up to the campground. The wind wasn't any stronger, but he did think it was colder today than it had been yesterday. And even though he'd worked up to it gradually, he felt light headed from his fasting for the last 36 hours.

Once outside his ring of trees he relieved himself; then he decided to walk the compound one more time. As he walked, he became profoundly aware of being the only living creature moving in the area. The winds had effectively forced all other birds, beasts, and humans under cover. And as he recognized his aloneness, he began to experience an intense loneliness. Why had he let himself be talked into this ridiculous venture? Here he was, cold, hungry, lonely, and before long he was likely to be very wet.

When he came to the river's edge and looked down at the water, he was abruptly aware of a heightening of all his senses. The rapidly rushing flow, the bits of wood and floating branches in it, the current, the ripples, even the sound it was making—he seemed more acutely aware of these things than he'd ever been before. He was seeing with more clarity; as bleak as the sky was, he was perceiving it with a peculiar acuity. And when he turned his attention to the fireworks still going on in the stormy western sky, it became a hypnotic dance of light. He stood watching it at length, until he realized he'd been standing still so long he'd grown stiff.

He shook out his legs, then made his way back to his circle of trees, where he sat, sleeping bag wrapped partially around him, and began to write his perceptions about his vision in his journal.

At some point, sitting there, back against a tree, he must have dozed off. Looking at his watch, he was surprised to find it was nearly 4 p.m. He'd been without food about 46 hours, but he wasn't particularly hungry. Or thirsty, for that matter, though he dutifully took a drink from the jug while he was thinking about it, just as a matter of course.

The wind hadn't varied much in intensity for the time he'd been here; it was still loud and complaining. And the storm that had wakened him this morning was still sitting off to the northwest, pouring an excessive amount of rain on somebody else's parade a few miles away. A fact for which he was grateful! The only thing different from when he'd dropped off to sleep was that the sky was darker. Old Sol, wherever he was above the clouds, had moved far enough west now that the whole sky was uniformly murky.

When night came again, he didn't bother getting into the pup tent, though he did extricate the flashlight from it so he could write down any extraneous thoughts in his journal. Then he just sat staring at the blackness around him and wondered how this compared to a sensory deprivation tank. That morning his senses had seemed so acute; now it was almost as if, with nothing to sense but the wind, all his senses but his hearing had become depressed.

There really was a voice in the wind. It was indistinct, but he intuited it was trying to tell him something. He sat up most of the night listening to it, trying to make out its nuances, hoping the language it was keening to him would somehow start to make sense. Toward dawn of that second night, he began to understand it.

"Give in," it cried. "Give in." Over and over, just those two words. "Give in. Give in." Had it been singing this to him all along? And what did it mean? Give in to what?

As the sky lightened once more to the east, Adam realized the on-going storm had moved somewhat south; it was now almost directly west of him. It had been raining somewhere within a 50-mile radius for over 24 hours now, but nary a drop had fallen on his head. Was he lucky or what? Maybe the Ancestors were taking care of him after all.

He realized a while later that he hadn't needed to urinate for nearly 24 hours. With nothing coming into his body, his systems had apparently put themselves on hold. At that thought, he reached for the jug and began to chug the water down. He had a gallon and a half left, and barely 24 more hours to go, so he decided he didn't need to be sparing with his supply. Almost immediately he felt a need to relieve both his bladder and his bowels.

He debated just letting go right here near his circle of trees, but something made him change his mind. "Sacred space," were the words that came into his mind; he chose not to pursue the thought. Nevertheless, he sloughed off his sleeping bag and began the walk toward the john at the campground. If nothing else, it was too damn cold to comfortably drop his drawers; in the campground john at least he'd be out of the wind.

He had no more extraneous thoughts until he came out of the john and realized in amazement that he really *wasn't* having any extraneous thoughts. Somehow he'd slipped into a state where the "words" in his head had been turned off! At least for the time he'd been in the john, he'd had no thoughts beyond just "being" in the john. Could this be what was meant by getting in touch with your shit? He laughed out loud, long and raucously.

God, that felt so good, he thought. He began laughing, whooping, howling with delight, shouting yahoos of ecstasy. The noise he made—no, the *rapture* he made—went on and on, exploding in wave upon wave of delight until he flung himself prostrate on the cracked mud tiles of the compound floor.

He lay giggling for long minutes, experiencing something akin to orgasmic relief. Perhaps it was a cleansing of the soul. Perhaps it was just a reaction to his having fasted for so long. It didn't matter; he was in bliss.

When he finally stopped laughing, he lay a long time on the dry ground with a grin on his face. This was joy! This was ecstasy! This was the most positive experience he'd had in. . . he couldn't remember when.

Perhaps he slept again, prostrate on the ground outside the Cottonwood Campground toilet facilities. But lying there in the pleasant lassitude of aftergiggles, he heard a buzzing in his ears, like the approach of a large insect, except it seemed as if it were coming from *inside* his head. And then it felt as though he were rising up out of his body, and floating above it. He could see in a sort of half-lighted way, and he turned and saw his body lying on the ground; but *he* was free to float or fly or do flips. And so he did, joyously swooping up to the tops of the trees, then zooming down to the ground again. And then he buzzed his body like an airplane, but as he did, he realized he had a great tenderness toward it, something he had never felt while he was inside its confines.

And he thought, "What keeps me from feeling this way toward myself all the time?"

And he saw a mass of light floating in front of him, and it became the face of his father, and he felt a surge of anger, as he often did when he had to interact with his father. But he saw himself as a child, and he and his father were playing catch, and his father was forcing him to the limits of excellence as he always did with every sport, something that always made him angry and hurt and exhausted and feeling diminished when he thought he couldn't please his father.

But this time his father was saying to the child, "You are the best. I never told you, but you always were the best. You were better than I ever was, and I was jealous and proud at the same time, and I couldn't tell you and I couldn't bend." And then his father turned and looked at the adult astral Adam that stood watching, and he said again, "You were the best part of me, but I was afraid of you, and afraid for you."

"Afraid of what?" Adam asked.

"Afraid of making you weak like me," said his father.

The thought was so strange that for a moment Adam couldn't comprehend it. And then he said, "I never thought of you as weak."

And his father answered, "What you thought of me didn't matter. It was what *I* thought of me that counted. Just as what I think of you, or ever thought, does not and did not reflect the truth."

And then the image of his father popped, like a bubble.

Adam looked down again at his unmoving body, lying on the ground, and with a start he was back in it and conscious, as cold drops began spattering his face.

He leapt up, and only later did he realize he'd left his Boquillas cowboy hat behind, for when he got back to his ring of trees, he was bareheaded.

He unzipped the pup tent, extracted Lucy's rain poncho, and slipped it over his head. It was long and heavy with a hood and would keep him reasonably dry if the rain didn't turn into a deluge.

He looked at his watch and realized it was mid-afternoon. Where the heck had the time gone? It seemed to be telescoping! He thought he'd just gone off to the campground a few minutes earlier, and here it was hours later. He had to have fallen asleep.

He felt drunk—that was the problem. Did this happen when one fasted for—how long had it been? Had it really been 70 hours since he'd had anything to eat?

The rain was beginning to fall a little faster, and Adam decided he needed to retrieve his hat from the campground, so he hurried back in that direction. But when he got there, he was dismayed to find it wasn't where he had been lying outside the toilet facility. The wind must have picked it up and blown it elsewhere. He looked around to see if he could spot it; even with the hood of the poncho, he felt exposed, and he really wanted the hat to keep the rain off his head. But it was nowhere to be seen through the increasing drizzle.

Finally, he decided to jog around the perimeter of the compound and see if the hat had been blown into some of the uncleared brush surrounding the area. It was about 20 minutes later when he found it, wedged between two bushes very near the path he took to get to his circle of trees. He jammed the hat onto his head. He'd found it none too soon, for the rain was picking up its tempo, increasing to a downpour.

As he started up the path to his campsite, he noticed a sound he'd been impervious to before because he'd been so focused on reclaiming his hat, though as he thought about it now, it had for some time been underlying those other sounds of the everblowing wind and the pattering rain. It was a shushing sound, and he finally realized it was the river itself.

He went near the river's edge and looked down. When he'd arrived at the campsite two days earlier, the river had been at least 40 feet below the bank on which he stood; now the surging water was less than 10 feet from the top of the gorge. The sound he was hearing was the river, flowing higher and swifter than it had been before. The rain which had been falling steadily some miles distant for the last day had caused the river to swell and rise, and he realized the waters which had flooded the area in the recent past were very likely to do so again.

The swollen river seemed to be rising rapidly. He picked a spot on the side of the opposite bank, checked his watch, and timed how long it took for the water to reach the spot. He quickly estimated the water was rising at the rate of about a foot every five minutes. Which meant he had about 45 minutes before the water would reach the bank on which he stood.

Realizing he should get out of the area as soon as possible he hurried back to his ring of trees and packed up his gear. In the interest of saving the weight he had to carry, he decided to leave the water jugs behind, though he took the time to drink his fill from one of them before wedging them against the trunk of his favorite tree.

When he got all his gear together, he slung it on his back and turned to bid farewell to the river. And to his horror he saw it was rising much more rapidly than he'd expected it to—it was now within a foot of the bank!

He needed to get across the compound and to the entrance road. And he needed to get there in a hurry, before the road was overwhelmed by the rapidly rising water. He hurried toward the compound, but just as he reached it, he heard a great retching sound and watched in shock as a huge section of the river bank sheared off and began floating away, red flag markers and all. He no longer had an easy access to the campground and hence to the exit road. And the river kept rising; he knew it would soon become a lake of swirling, churning water. Something, some dam upriver must have broken loose.

At this rate of rise, he acknowledged all in a rush, even if he tried to make a run for it, straight north from the river, he had no idea where to find a road through the brush. There were no paths, either, and he had no compass. Why hadn't he brought a compass?

He couldn't think logically, but instinctively he started back to his ring of trees. It was higher ground than the campground, and the cottonwoods were taller there. He thought about the water level ring he'd seen on the side of the men's toilet at the compound. It hadn't gotten more than five feet up. Maybe if he could climb up a tree which would allow him to go higher than five feet, he could outlast this deluge!

He looked around the circle for a likely candidate to climb. One sturdy fellow caught his eye; it had some branches lower down which would make easy rungs for his feet, and a limb forked with three tines about 15 feet up would give him a platform for sitting. And, if he had to go even higher, he could.

He stepped up into the tree and realized immediately his gear was going to hamper him. Reluctantly he looked for someplace to stow it and spotted another tree with some broken off limbs about five feet above the ground. He hooked his equipment to the short limbs and went back to the tree which would hold him. The water was creeping into the circle, and he needed to get up fast.

And to top everything else off, or more precisely to untop it, as he struggled upward toward the place he had selected as his seat in the tree, he knocked his hat off. It was immediately picked up by a gust of wet wind and floated off down the river.

From his vantage he watched for the next couple of hours as the water covered the ground of his campsite and then crept up and up the trunks of the trees. Helpless, he saw the churning waters reach his gear and float it off the limb on which it hung and away down the river. Well, at least he had nothing left to worry about except his own person.

Too late for God to send a jeep, but he wouldn't turn down a leaky Boquillas rowboat if one were to show up!

Then it got too dark for him to see what the water was doing. Finally, hanging there on the tree in the dark listening to the unabating wind and rain and realizing he was probably going to drown, he began to howl in frustration and fear.

"What was this all for?" he thought. "Why did I have to come on this fool's mission?"

Lucy's face came into his mind, and he remembered that morning two weeks ago when he had dreamed he didn't know his name and Lucy had said the Ancestors wanted him to go on a quest for it.

Weeping, he broke the silence and shouted into the wind, "Okay, God. Or Gods. Or Guides. Or Ancestors. Or whatever You are. If You save me, I'll assume You have a plan for me I don't yet recognize. And I'll go wherever You want me to go." Then he added defiantly, "But if I drown, I just want You to know I do it without understanding a thing that's happened, and I'll die thinking I've been a very foolish person!"

Are you asking for a sign? came a questioning voice in his head. Or perhaps it was a voice in the wind.

In any case, he shouted, "Yes! I'm asking for a sign! What the hell do you think I'm asking?"

Perhaps it was coincidence, but at that precise moment, the rain stopped, though the wind continued. He could still hear the water rushing below him, but he was no longer being pelted with the violent deluge.

Well, he thought, if Lucy were to find out about the flood—and she certainly would when she came in the morning to pick him up, if not before—she could notify the park rangers, and maybe they could arrange to have a helicopter come in and rescue him from his tree. She knew precisely where he had planned to camp. All he needed to do was hang on. And perhaps he wouldn't drown after all.

He didn't know what he believed about the Ancestors, and whether he had been saved by forces outside himself. But he did experience immense relief, and hope, and gratitude. And he began murmuring over and over, into the wind, "Thank you, thank you, thank you, thank you."

And while he murmured his thanks, as if it were the real key to his understanding, to his knowing, he looked out into the blackness of the night and found he could see with a kind of inner sight.

It began with the tree to which he clung. He could see what he could only describe as its "essence," as if the truth of the tree was not its trunk or its branches, but the lifeforce that permeated it. He could see this even in the darkness, and he was amazed. And then he found he could see the other trees in the grove in the same transcendent way, and inexplicably he realized they were all connected to each other.

And the water swirling below him had a light essence, too, and he was able to perceive it in all its kaleidoscopic beauty as it flowed toward and away from him. And the mountains and the sky, which he shouldn't have been able to see in the darkness, took on a glow, as if they had become enchanted. But what impressed him most was the unity of the light force—it connected mountains and sky and water and trees and Adam himself as if all things were one with him, and he not just a part of the whole but a reflection, a holographic fragment of the whole, with the all in himself.

How long this perception went on he couldn't say. It might have been moments or hours. But he continued murmuring his thanks into the wind, even after the light of his vision faded.

Just before dawn, the wind finally abated. Adam sat contentedly in the tree, waiting for the light, a grin on his face. The flood waters were about six feet deep, so far as he could estimate. He wasn't going to drown after all. And for the first time in three days the sky was free of gray clouds, though the moisture in the air cast a rosy haze to the east.

But as the sun rose, something almost miraculous caught his attention. He found he was looking at sunrise through a gleaming spider web, about five feet away from him, made golden by the sun's rays. Without the backlighting, he would never have seen it.

Had it been there throughout the storm, clinging like Adam to the tree branches? If so, how had such a fragile thing lasted through the wind and rain?

And then the little voice in his head said, "This is the source of your name and your mission. You have seen the light that connects each and all. You will be a weaver of the sunlight."

Adam sat in awe at the voice. He didn't know quite what it meant, but he trusted he would learn. He had had his vision, he had received his name, and soon Lucy would send help to rescue him from the flood waters.

He was captivated by the glorious spider web, but as the sun rose higher, it was no longer backlighted and try as he would to shift his position, he couldn't find a place where he could see it glowing anymore. The experience—the vision—was over.

Then he heard at a far distance the sound of a car horn. He looked down, and for a moment he was in shock at what he saw, or rather what he didn't see—there were no flood waters at all! What's more, on the ground, in a neat pile, was his camping gear. And on top of it sat his Boquillas hat, jaunty black feathers intact.

Had it all been illusion? Adam thought of Lucy's comment about the reality of the plane of the Ancestors, and he smiled. No, he thought, it had just been a day at school.

He climbed down from the tree, took off the rain poncho, packed it away, and put on his hat. Then he hoisted his gear and started off for the Cottonwood Campground compound.

And as he walked toward the sound of the honking car horn, he also began to hear a dog barking, and he grinned as he went to meet his beloved future wife.

*****

When Sophie and Cassie had finished visiting the offices of all the Virginia representatives and senators and still hadn't met anyone but staffers, they were feeling a little disappointed. But Cassie decided she wanted to try the representatives from Ohio, because that's where she'd lived all her life until now, and Sophie went along with her wishes. So they just kept visiting offices, though with the same mediocre results.

And then one afternoon in early April, they were walking down a corridor in the Cannon Building when a lady stepped out of an office and said, "Hi! I'm Representative Billings from California, and I understand you're doing a little lobbying for the environment. I've been hearing about your visits to some of the other offices here, and I'd like to hear what you have to say since I'm on the committees that handle both environmental concerns and foreign affairs."

It was their first real boost, and they decided after their talk with Representative Billings they just might be going in the right direction after all. They even started visiting the congressional offices every afternoon when Cassie got out of school.

They had been doing their canvassing for nearly a month when Sophie got a call from Representative Ryder's secretary that the congressman wanted them to come back and actually talk to him. In person.

It was Ryder's secretary who decided to call the newspapers about their unusual lobbying practices. And it was Joe to whom her call was forwarded when she dialed up his particular paper. As environmental editor, he would have to decide whether to assign anyone to cover their activities.

Joe initially envisioned the story of their campaign as a little filler piece, possibly being run, provided it was really a viable story, in the middle of the news section.

He found Sophie's home number in the Northern Virginia book and dialed it from his desk at the newspaper one evening just before he left work for the weekend. Cassie answered, and after he had identified himself, he asked her if she was indeed the little girl who was passing out cookies to congressmen to ask help in saving the rain forests.

"Well, yes, but I'm not doing it by myself," answered Cassie. "My friend Sophie and I are doing it together. And next week, all the kids in my class are going to write letters to congressmen, too. Our teacher heard what Sophie and I are doing, and she's going to have our whole class write letters. And the principal of our school is thinking of having an assembly for the whole school, where Sophie and I can talk about our project, and maybe get all the kids in the school to write letters, too. But, frankly," she finished, "I'd rather go talk to people than write them letters. My penmanship isn't so hot."

"I see," said Joe. "So tell me, this woman who is going around with you to the congressional offices, is she your grandmother?"

He'd been told by Ryder's secretary that Sophie was an older woman, and not the child's mother.

"No," said Cassie, "I guess she's my guardian. But I just think of her as my friend. I mean, we live together, but she's more like a friend than a parent or anything. Anyway, we're doing this project together. See, she had all these magazines from environmental groups, and so we started gathering facts about the rain forests, and then she typed up some stuff—like information, you know?—and I thought of making cookies to take with the information packets, sort of what my dad used to call a gimmick to get people's attention."

"And where are your parents?" asked Joe, his curiosity piqued by her mention of her dad.

"Oh, they died in a car accident last Christmas vacation," she said. "My little brother Timmy did, too."

Joe wondered about her matter-of-factness when she stated this information; almost as if she'd said they were all off on a cruise.

Then she added, "My Aunt Georgia, who is my father's sister, was too busy to have me live with her. That's why I live with Sophie. She was Georgia's friend. And now she's my friend."

"Is your friend Sophie there right now?" asked Joe.

"Sure," said Cassie. "You want to speak to her?"

"Yes, if I may."

"Okay," said Cassie. "Just a minute."

Joe doodled a picture while he waited for Sophie to answer, a tree with bulky branches that looked a lot like a bunch of broccoli when he got through with it. In a couple of minutes he heard Sophie's voice say, "Hello? This is Mrs. Nussbaum."

Joe identified himself and his position on the paper. "I understand you and the little girl I just talked to are conducting a sort of unusual lobbying effort with Congress right now."

"I guess you could call it that," said Sophie. "We just feel more attention needs to be given to the way the whole earth and the global family of man are connected. So we thought we'd draw some congressmen's attention to the problems and some of the possible solutions by making a point about how the rain forests are in large measure responsible for the very air we breathe, and how if we want to save them we have to provide means for the people who have them in their stewardship to find other ways of supporting themselves than by destroying the forests."

"And the little girl Cassie," said Joe, "what's been her role in this effort?"

"Goodness!" said Sophie. "It was her idea to call congressmen in the first place. She had a school project on South America, you see, and she was really concerned about calling attention to the rain forests there."

"Mrs. Nussbaum," said Joe, "just what is your relationship to the child? She called you a 'friend,' and she indicated you are not a relative. Her parents are deceased, is that correct?"

"Yes, although I've always thought that terminology was awfully final. I'm the child's legal guardian. I'm a long time friend of her aunt, to whom custody went upon her family's transition. Her aunt travels quite a bit, so I have guardianship of her at present."

Joe, who was beginning to smell a story in the relationship of these unusual lobbyists, continued carefully, "Would it be a problem for you to tell me about her background and what happened to her parents?" He was still puzzled that Cassie didn't sound particularly perturbed by their demise.

"It's no problem," Sophie began. "She and her family—mother, father, and little brother—were in a car accident last December.

She survived. They didn't. Well, actually, she had what is known as a near death experience. Are you familiar with the literature on near death experiences?"

"Not particularly."

"You see," said Sophie, "the people who have such an experience usually become very interested in learning all they can about how things work. And they usually become highly aware of the interconnections of human beings, and show a sort of open lovingness to all people everywhere. But most of all," she continued, "the near death experience, especially in children, makes them aware they have a purpose for being on the planet—that indeed we all have such a purpose. But experiencers want to fulfill their purpose. So as her guardian, I feel I have a responsibility to help facilitate whatever it is she believes she needs to do. She's a bright, loving child who wants to see if she can help make a difference in the world to which she has returned.

"I see," said Joe. "So this is a sort of one-person campaign to save the planet?"

"I suppose you could look at it that way."

"And you're telling me the child thinks she has a special mission because her life was spared, is that correct?"

"In a sense, yes," said Sophie, "although I believe that's really oversimplifying the motives behind the project. She doesn't think she's the only one who has a special mission. She believes we all do. Maybe she's just more awake to what needs to be done than many of us.

"And she has no delusion that the two of us can save the planet by ourselves, as your question implies. Indeed, that's why she hit upon petitioning Congress to assist. In this country, Congress has the power to get things done—fund research, support particular business enterprises, send information to the United Nations, and so forth. Never mind that the power isn't always used wisely—it's there, and it's one of the ways things work and wheels get turned in our country. So that's why the 'campaign,' as you call it. And did she tell you her whole school may get involved in a letter campaign to Congress? We think that's very exciting!"

"Yes, she told me," said Joe, who had sensed the slightest bit of defensiveness in Sophie's explanation. He decided he should try to charm her.

"Please don't be offended by my questions, Mrs. Nussbaum," he said. "I'm just a crusty old newspaperman, and I try to get to the heart of a story as quickly as possible."

"Yes," said Sophie, "I understand. Unfortunately, as a former teacher of literature and of writing, I'm fully aware that the objectivity newspaper people prize is often lacking. I mean, it really isn't possible, is it," she asked rhetorically, "to keep ourselves and our opinions totally out of what we write? By the very selection and organization of certain facts instead of others, writers shape their presentation and so influence what others perceive as 'reality' or 'truth.' Writers and editors, no matter what they may say to the contrary, shape the news by what they choose to write or print and by how they choose to present it.

"And I actually do read your paper every day, Mr. Jacobson, so I'm fully aware of the cynical undertones of many of the stories, even those which are supposed to be 'straight' news. Be honest with me—don't you agree a story is shaped as much by what you don't write as by what you *do*?"

Joe hadn't expected to be interrogated, but he answered, "Yes, ma'am. What you say is true to a certain extent. But as newspeople, those of us in journalism are charged with presenting the facts in as unbiased a way as possible. So what seems like cynicism is often really our effort *not* to put personal feeling into a story."

He was beginning to register a little defensiveness himself.

"I only asked in order to establish ground rules for what I assume will be your request for an interview. You *are* calling about wanting to interview Cassandra, aren't you?"

Joe wondered briefly if Sophie really was a sort of stage mother-manager for what she considered a hot little property in this child she was currently fostering.

"Yes," he replied, "I thought I'd try to send someone out to talk to you, provided I think there's really a viable story here."

"That's what I expected. But you see, I don't know if it would be wonderful for Cassie if the paper published a cynical, negative story about the project. So I guess what I'm asking is, how do you plan to slant your interview? I mean, I'm very sensitive to the power of the press to make or break a project by the coverage they give it, and I think we're beginning to get people in Congress to listen to us, so I don't want any coverage at all if it's going to be negative."

"Well, Mrs. Nussbaum, suppose I give you my word as an editor I'll try to keep the story, if one gets written, from being slanted in a negative way, or in a way possibly detrimental to your project. But that presupposes you've been totally open with me about your and the child's motives and that I don't find anything negative to write about. I mean, you don't know me, but then I don't know you either, do I?"

"It's true you don't know me," said Sophie. "Well, I guess the best we can do is find out about each other."

"Good!" Joe said. "Then I'll see who on the staff or among our stringers would like to take on the story. You'll probably be getting a call from someone who will come do an interview with you."

"I see," said Sophie. "You wouldn't be coming yourself, then?"

"Not likely," said Joe.

"A pity," said Sophie, and after a moment she added, "I really do know who you are, Mr. Jacobson; I've read your articles for years. And I was particularly touched by the appreciation piece you did last summer on Dave Shumacher."

"Oh," said Joe, flattered at the unexpected recognition. After a pause, he continued, "So, someone will be in touch with you in the next few days about the interview."

"All right, Mr. Jacobson, I'll be expecting a call."

After they'd hung up, Joe sat drumming his desk with the eraser of his pencil. Something about this lady and the kid and their project intrigued him. Maybe it was the frank way the little girl had talked about the gimmick of the cookies; maybe it was the unemotional way she'd mentioned the death of her family; maybe it was Sophie's insistence on a positive story. Most people were just flattered by the attention of a big newspaper; she'd been cautious.

Who to assign to the story was a problem. And where to print it was another. In the editorial hierarchy, Joe was nearer the nadir than the zenith. He could see this story having only marginal news interest and being relegated to eight column inches in the back of the news section. But, presupposing the child really had had a mystical experience of some sort, and that it was part of her motivation for her project. . . he could also see the story as a nice solid feature in the Style section.

He'd talk to Martha Halifax, the Style editor, in the morning.

Then, looking at the blipping space marker on his computer screen, Joe thought of Dave Shumacher. How uncanny for this Nussbaum woman to have brought up his story of last summer about Dave. And her comments about shaping the news. . . . Maybe, just maybe, he should cover this story himself.

*****

When Joe rang the doorbell of Sophie's McLean home, Cassie answered, with Emerson draped round her shoulders.

"Hi!" she said. "You the newspaperman?"

"Yes," he answered, "I'm Joe Jacobson. I'm the one who's going to interview you."

"Come into the kitchen," she said. "We're making cookies for our Monday visit to the Rayburn Building."

Joe thought how mundane and homey were the aspects of this interview compared to many he'd been on. Usually people put on their best clothes and put out their best china to offer him tea in the living room. But Sophie and Cassie were both in jeans, and Sophie had to wash her hands in order to shake the one he extended.

"We spend a lot of time making cookies these days," she laughed. "The security guards indicated we're becoming something of a *cause celebre* these days, and that all the representatives and senators, no matter what state they're from, are now interested in receiving a batch of cookies. I guess if we leave somebody out, he or she will feel slighted, so it'll probably take us 'til the end of the summer to canvass the whole Congress!"

Joe took a small tape recorder out of his pocket and set it on the table. "Well, maybe while you're involved with cookie baking I could start with some questions for Cassandra."

"Sounds okay to me," said Cassie. She clumped down on a chair, and Emerson carefully picked his way down from shoulder to tummy to curl in her lap.

Joe clicked on his tape recorder. "Looks like you have a friend there," he said, indicating the cat.

"Yes," said Cassie. "Sophie has three cats, but Emerson is the one who likes me the most."

She proceeded to explain to Joe about the three cats being named for the three American Transcendentalists. Then she explained, with what Joe considered very adult philosophical implications, Ralph Waldo Emerson's concept of the Oversoul.

"Did your friend Sophie teach you all of that?" asked Joe when she paused for breath.

"Of course!" said Cassie, in a tone of voice indicating he'd asked a too obvious and relatively dumb question. "I mean, she's an English teacher, so she knows all this stuff about writers. But it was a big help, you know, for her to tell me about the idea of the Light of the Oversoul, and how all of us here are little sparks of that big Light. Because nobody would let me talk about what it was like to me to die and come back. But Sophie did. And she didn't tell me that what I saw was just a dream or anything. And she taught me lots of other stuff, you know, like that lots of people in all countries and throughout history have had this experience. And lots of people have had the experience of seeing the Light without having to die to do it."

"And what," asked Joe, "does your experience have to do with your lobbying Congress about the rain forests?"

"Well." Cassie looked pensive. "I guess it's just I feel I'm still here because I have something to do. And maybe what I have to do is to help bring people's attention to some of the things that need to be done to save the planet. I know saving the rain forests is part of the job I have to do. And part of *that* means I have to learn how things work, you know, where the power is to get projects and people moving. I mean, Sophie says if we could get lots and lots of people just thinking it's possible to make a difference, then we *can* make a difference.

"She says getting people *thinking* about and actually *visualizing* world peace was part of what caused us and the Soviets to come to terms and begin working together, and it's part of what caused the *people* to take down the Berlin Wall. So it seems to me if lots and lots of people could visualize a healthy, safe world, a world with healthy rain forests and a pollution-free environment, then we could have it. So we're just trying to get people to *think* about ways to make all this good stuff possible."

She looked as if she were listening to something far away, and then she nodded and looked Joe in the eyes. "And I'm supposed to tell you also that once I've contributed to changing thinking about the environment, I have one other thing I'm supposed to do."

"And what's that?" asked Joe.

"I'm supposed to teach other people that no matter what happens to them, there's nothing to be afraid of. And that, no matter what you do. . . the Light still loves you." She finished the last part of her sentence very softly.

Though he wasn't sure he understood her, Joe sat there nodding for a moment. Then he asked gently, "Cassie, what religion were you brought up in?" He wanted to know if what she had just said was indoctrination by some sectarian group.

"Well," she answered, "my mom called herself a Judeo-Christian. She said that meant she was a product of her culture. But my dad said he believed in God, but he didn't much believe in organized institutions. So we didn't go to any church as a family.

"And once, about two years ago, a school friend of mine invited me to go to church with her. It turned out it was a really strict church. And the preacher said if we didn't come up and get 'saved,' all kinds of terrible things would happen to us, and eventually we'd end up going to hell. And it really scared me, so when I got home I talked to my dad about it. And he got pretty mad and said he wouldn't let me go back there, because any church that scared little kids didn't deserve to have converts!"

Joe laughed.

"But anyway," she continued, "the important thing was, he said there wasn't anything about God to be afraid of. And he was right, because the Light really loves you, no matter what. Except that when you know that," she said, and her voice became soft again, "you really want to show everybody else the kind of love you've experienced from the Light. You want to love everybody that same way, you know, without judging them. And you want to love the whole earth—the whole planet—that same way, and make it the very best place you can. Do you know what I mean?"

"I think I do, honey," said Joe. Then he added candidly, "Even though I haven't been in the Light, I guess I'd like to see the planet become the best place it can be because I love my wife, and she and I are going to have a baby pretty soon."

"Congratulations!" said Cassie and Sophie simultaneously.

Joe looked up to discover Sophie had taken off her apron.

"All finished with the cookies for now, " she said. "Would you like to try one while it's warm, perhaps with a cup of coffee or tea?"

"Certainly," said Joe, and he clicked off the tape recorder while she and Cassie set the table.

When they were all seated and he'd tasted and commented positively on the cookies he was given, he clicked the machine on again and asked Sophie for her perspective on their project and what she expected it to accomplish.

"A problem," she began, "exists in that much of the rain forest land is owned by private individuals who don't have any incentive to change their business approach. The key, we think, is to make it more profitable for them to employ the local people in doing the harvesting than to keep doing what they are doing now.

"If they can be convinced to develop profit sharing enterprises with their own people, they can actually increase their personal profits, improve the economy of their whole culture, salvage the rain forests for future generations, and become a model for other countries to follow. But Mr. Jacobson, you know all this as well as I do. I mean, you're the environmental editor!"

Joe smiled. "Yes," he said, "but I'm here to get quotes from you. And maybe you'll say some of these things in a way that will penetrate to those readers who haven't thought about them."

Sophie smiled. "Okay, then, you asked for it; I'm about to climb onto my soapbox! What we need in the United States is a consciousness that will make us not the world's watchdogs but the world's motivators. If we can just show other countries how to improve their economies on their own, then everybody wins."

"But what about the greed factor?" asked Joe. "Won't the landowners want *all* the profits for themselves? Why should they share with the local people if they haven't shared before?"

"From what we've read on the subject," said Sophie, "it would be more advantageous, and more profitable, for them to use local people as employees—to train them in forms of skilled labor, to raise them up, to offer them incentives and education that will help them improve themselves. The landowners can't harvest the forests all by themselves, but if they make the people of their country their loyal employees, they'll make more money because then they can diversify into lots of businesses, with a variety of new products. And this is especially true if they'll train their women as well as their men. Women's cooperatives in various places around the world have shown that if given a chance, women can become wonderful skilled workers, foremen, small enterprise entrepreneurs, farmers, bank owners—you name it.

"And the greed motive you mentioned—that's just one of the many faces of fear. It comes from a consciousness of lack, a consciousness which says there's only so much of anything to go around—money, food, or whatever. But a creative thinker can show this simply isn't so. I mean, with respect to money, did you realize there's enough in circulation right now for every man, woman, and child in the world to be a millionaire if it were all distributed equally—it's true, check it out!

"Anyway, any good, *honest* American businessman could show a South American landowner how to harvest, diversify, increase profits, establish a loyal employee base, and eliminate the consciousness that breeds greed. It's just a matter of creative thinking."

"So you really believe people could be convinced to do what's in the best interests of the whole of humanity?" asked Joe.

"I believe that people who do not act in ways beneficial to the whole of humanity are unconscious as to their connection to that whole. But, at the risk of oversimplifying the situation, I also think most people who haven't learned to do good for its own sake, just because it feels good, or because they know that what they do for others they are doing for themselves—these people can nevertheless be encouraged to do good for other reasons. Those who don't do good for its own sake are like some of the children I used to teach who hadn't been taught to love learning for its own sake. But they could be encouraged to do well in their school work for other reasons—for example, because it got them good grades, which in turn got them the approbation of their parents and the school faculty, or won them awards, or permitted them to participate in sports, or whatever. And I found most every child could also learn to be creative in some fashion, and when their creativity was rewarded, they actually began to love creativity—and by extension *learning*—for their own sakes.

"So what we need to do as world leaders, and hence in effect as the 'good teacher' figures for the rest of the world, is come up with ways to help those in other countries discover creative ways to solve their own problems.

"My late husband and I were both in the teaching profession for 35 years. Together that constituted 70 years worth of teaching and motivating experience. And what we learned was that the best teacher, and parent, and *leader* was the one who said to his or her students, or children, or followers, 'Here's what I know to do about a given subject. Now you see if you can improve on my approach or come up with a better approach of your own.' Believe me, if all leaders were motivators, there wouldn't be any need for discipline. My Saul always said he never had to discipline a student who felt good about himself.

"So if we can become the world's motivators, we just may find we no longer have to be the world's militaristic disciplinarians!"

"So," said Joe, "are you saying that if we act the role of military disciplinarians, we're not being particularly creative about solving world problems?"

"I guess that *is* what I'm saying," Sophie smiled. "But if you'd permit me to oversimplify again, let me suggest that one reason we're in the pickle we're in as a world power is we really haven't ever been into empowering other countries."

Joe raised his eyebrows and looked as if he might protest; Sophie quickly responded to his facial expression with, "Oh, I don't mean empowerment as military powers—we've done too darn much selling of arms to other countries in the past, if you ask me. And it seems to me by giving or selling arms to other countries, we've been like parents who tell their kids not to fight with other kids in the neighborhood, but then encourage the fighting by giving the kids brass knuckles or brickbats or even rifles! We wouldn't encourage our kids to fight by giving them weapons, would we? Then why do we encourage other countries to fight with each other, when we say we really want peace?"

"Because arms sales are a lucrative business, perhaps?" Joe interjected.

"Oh, dear," said Sophie, "I guess I've ignored the greed factor again, haven't I?"

"Well," said Joe, "I do feel it's a very powerful motivator, and probably a stronger force for action than idealism. But then, I'm a bit of a cynic, and it's clear you're an idealist, so go on with what you were saying about empowerment," he smiled, and nodded toward the tape recorder, "at least until the tape runs out."

Sophie continued, "Well, I guess what I mean is that this country has always acted as if it had to caretake third world nations. Maybe it's a carryover from that ridiculous concept of the 19th century of the 'white man's burden.' Or perhaps it's another aspect of that 'face of fear.' We seem to think if we teach everyone else what we know, we'll end up being bettered by everybody else. But in reality, when we all try to be the best we can be, and we share what we know, everybody just gets better and better, provided we're all actually motivated to be the very best we can be, and to really share."

"What about all we hear about Oriental kids besting our kids in school?" asked Joe.

"As a former teacher, I believe we in the U.S. *don't* motivate our own youth to excel—certainly not the way the Oriental cultures currently do. But it's our lack of motivation and not our sharing of knowledge that is allowing the Pacific Rim countries to become greater economic powers than we are.

"See," she continued, "what we've had in the way of leadership in this country has been exactly the opposite of the kind of motivation we should have had. Too often we've viewed the third worlders as people to be taken care of in a somewhat paternalistic fashion.

"But it's terribly chauvinistic to think that because we have had a rich economy for a long time we should naturally have all the answers to everybody's problems. We don't need to play daddy to other nations, and besides, they resent it when we try to do so, especially when it includes a lack of respect for their cultures and traditions and values. Better we should play teacher, and help other nations to come into their own, as equal members in the world family.

"It's the difference, I think, between the masculine and the feminine styles of leadership. Men most often lead through a kind of leadership ladder, with the boss at the top, and other figures of power under him in descending order. We speak of the 'corporate ladder,' with the CEO at the top and his vice presidents of this and that under him, and the junior executives under them, and then all the support staff under them. And it's the structure of the military, with generals at the top, and the colonels under them, and the majors, captains, lieutenants, and warrant officers under them, and then the non-coms, and so on, down to the privates at the bottom. Very paternalistic, those leadership ladders.

"But the feminine model of leadership isn't a ladder. It's a network, sort of like a spider's web. The feminine leader is not the 'boss' of the ladder model. She's a teacher or motivator, who sends her power and influence out along the rays of the web or network, and she encourages those who work *for* her to think of themselves as working *with* her—all on the same plane, all empowered to do their best and in their own fields of expertise to create their own webs or networks.

"Now, you may think I've come a long way from the original idea we had of saving the rain forests, but actually what we really want to do is show that in the networking model, it's not just the presidents of nations or the heads of corporations who have the power to save the world—it's everybody on the planet. Because in the webwork model, everybody is both at the end of a strand of the web of being influenced *and* at the center of a web of influencing.

"In other words," Sophie finished, "even a little old lady and a 10-year-old kid—if they have the will and the energy—can make a political statement just by doing what they do best, which in this case is baking and passing out cookies. We're beginning to get the attention of the Congress members who hold this country's power; we're beginning at the same time to get the attention of others of our peers, especially in Cassie's school, to write letters themselves. And each one of those people at the ends of our strands of the web has a web of his or her own that she or he can influence. So our Cookie Lobby is really a model for world transformation!"

She grinned at Joe. "Was that enough of a harangue?" she asked.

"Just about," said Joe, "although I do have one more question."

"Which is?"

"Do you think a woman should be president?"

"Darn right," said Sophie. "I think it's just about time. But it needs to be a woman who has as her leadership model the web rather than the ladder."

Joe switched off his tape recorder, then as an afterthought he jokingly asked, "Have *you* ever thought of running for public office?"

*****

Joe had found himself charmed by Cassie and Sophie, and he put his best effort into the feature he did on them. It came out on the front page of the Style section a couple of weeks later, under the alliterative headline, "Cookie Lobby Canvasses Congress."

He'd taken the trouble to call some of the offices they had visited and interviewed the staffers they had talked to. Uniformly, everyone who'd had contact with the child and her guardian were positively impressed with both their personable manners and the research they had done on rain forest ecology and economics. For lay people, they had plenty of facts and figures to quote, and—to Sophie's credit—plenty of authorities who agreed with their contention that a way could exist to support the third world societies which had stewardship of the forests better than they'd been supported in the past, provided the rain forests were harvested, not destroyed.

Joe then took it upon himself to do one other thing he'd never done before. He called some contacts he had at the major television networks and talked to them the day before his story was going to appear.

"This lady and kid," he said to each of the network news editors, "they make an unlikely but interesting human interest pair. And they're both amazingly articulate."

The afternoon of the day his story appeared, Sophie and Cassie were accosted by reporters on the steps of the Rayburn House Office Building. They appeared that evening on the national news of all the major networks. And by the next Monday, Sophie had received phone calls for appearances on several talk shows around the country.

When Sophie called Joe at the paper to tell him about the upcoming appearances on talk shows, Joe laughed and asked, "So how'm I doin', teach? Is this what you'd call exercising my influence? Hey, is this fancy webwork, or what?"

After they hung up, he glanced at the blipping space marker on his computer screen. "How'm I doin', Dave?" he thought. "Sorry I never managed to do as well by you, though I guess you got your share of airtime."

That evening when he left the elevator on the ground floor of the newspaper building and waved goodnight to the security guard on duty, he was surprised to realize he was whistling a happy tune.

*****

Since Colin's death, Ray had allowed his days and nights to turn upside down. He'd decided the best way to deal with the grief he had promised Colin he wouldn't experience but which had come unbidden anyway was to spend as much time as he could patrolling. On nights when the Panthers had no patrols, he cruised the streets alone, hoping to provide a buffer not just for gays but for runaway kids, prostitutes, and homeless street people who might be in trouble.

He would come home around dawn, have soup or a salad, climb into bed, then get up mid-afternoon, go through his Tai Chi form for an hour or so, shave, shower, and eat breakfast. And usually, just to keep up with the day's events, he'd then sit down and watch the evening news before getting dressed to go out on the streets.

He knew this routine wouldn't last forever. Eventually he would come to terms with the sense of aloneness he felt now that Colin was gone. Eventually he would probably look for some kind of work, perhaps as a Tai Chi teacher with his own studio. But Colin had left him well supported in his will, and Ray could afford not to participate in the work world for a few months while he allowed the grief to play itself out.

And so it was that he happened to be at home in front of his television set on the evening Sophie and Cassie were featured. The woman he thought he recognized; he felt sure she had been a student in one of his Tai Chi classes with the Northern Virginia Parks Department a couple of years back.

But when the camera panned to the child and she began to talk, he sat up abruptly and stared at her. Watching her, he started having that uneasy feeling he got in his abdomen when something bad was going to happen. It wasn't as strong as when danger was imminent, but it was definitely there. He could almost smell the taintedness of whatever was out there that the little girl was attracting. It was like milk just on the edge of going sour.

The kid, he thought. Something bad is tracking the kid. She's in need of protection. If she's to be out in public, she needs a bodyguard.

He got out his Northern Virginia phone book, found Sophie's number, and dialed.

*****

Under the electric blue of the El Paso sky, Adam Sun Weaver paused in his stone masonry and wiped the back of his hand across his forehead. In the old days, when the El Paso chamber of commerce had touted the city's "360 sunshine days a year," it would have been too dry to sweat this much and really feel it, but these days the humidity was up from unprecedented rains of the last several months. He pulled a bandanna from his pocket and tied it around his head as a sweat band.

He looked up at the Franklin Mountains and then at the sky beyond, so close it made his eyes and throat ache with pleasure. No rain today, that was certain, so he'd be finished with this repair job by evening.

It was the third bracing repair job he'd done in a week. Lots of people in the Kern area had had similar problems because of the rains, and he was Juan-on-the-spot to do all the little jobs he could because he and Lucy needed the nestegg.

They'd known for sometime they'd soon be moving to the East. Just after his vision quest, an invitation had come for Lucy to participate in a special show of Southwest artists at a gallery in Washington, D.C. So they had packed up and moved temporarily to El Paso, where Adam could push his handyman business with a little more ease, and earn the necessary money for the trip. In just a couple of days they'd be hitting the road.

The Kern area was El Paso's older, better neighborhood, and folks there generally had the money to pay cash at the time of service. Adam knew it well; he'd grown up here. So when the rains had hit, he'd printed up his flyers for "MAÑANA HOME REPAIR SERVICE—We'll Give You an Estimate No Later Than Tomorrow!" and begun casing the neighborhood, leaving the flyers where he saw damage and suspected repairs might be needed. Then he'd had some magnetic "Mañana Home Repair and Contracting" signs made for the truck and, ¡Ole!, he was in business as a handyman.

The name of his business was a kind of personal joke. Back when his dad had been stationed at Ft. Bliss and his family had owned a house in a suburb way out on Dyer St., his mom would often call up businesses in the area for repairs or services and get the response, "Maybe we can send someone out *tomorrow*." Ah, tomorrow, and tomorrow, and tomorrow—the time usually ran from two to four weeks before they could even get a bid. Good old El Paso and its laid back *mañana* attitude—truly life in the slow lane.

When he'd finished the bracing job, he knocked on the door. He could hear the chatter of a television talk show in the background as the lady of the house padded toward the door in a pair of soft houseshoes. She opened the door just a crack, and he said, "All finished!"

"Oh, good," she replied. "Let me get my checkbook."

She invited him into the cool living room as she went to the kitchen to write him out a check. And he noticed what was on the screen was the Oprah show, with a middleaged woman and a little girl as the guests. He just stared absently at the screen for a few moments, drifting into the alpha state so often triggered for him by watching television, when he suddenly recognized the woman Oprah was interviewing.

"Hey," he said aloud as the lady of the house returned from the kitchen, a check for the bracing job extended toward him, "that's an old teacher of mine from high school, Mrs. Nussbaum. I was in her class one year when my dad was stationed in Washington, D.C. and we lived in McLean. She was the best darn English teacher I ever had."

"Here," said the lady of the house, grabbing a wooden chair from the dining alcove for him to sit on so he wouldn't get sweat on her good Queen Anne wingback chairs, "have a seat and watch if you like."

He accepted the offer and sat listening as Sophie discussed the transformational tools of motivational leadership, incentive economics, individual responsibility for change, and the power of networking.

Then, to the millions of viewers in Oprah's audience nationwide, she said, "There are 17,000 peace organizations in this country. And there are thousands and thousands of local groups nationwide that are interested in environmental issues. What a powerhouse we would have if we could get all the people in all those groups to network together for the common goal of a safe, healthy, peaceful, pollution-free planet! I don't know how to create such a network of networks, but if we could, I believe we'd be unstoppable."

Oprah broke for some ads at that point, and when she came back, she shifted her attention to the child Cassie and began to ask questions guaranteed to titillate the audience about her near-death experience. Was it her brush with death that had caused her to want to do something to make the world a better place?

Adam barely listened. His mind was churning with the idea of networking networks.

When the show was over, Adam thanked the lady for allowing him to watch, went out to his truck, and drove home to Lucy, grinning as he sang out loud a new variation on a silly old tongue twister: "How many networks could a Sun Weaver weave, if a Sun Weaver could weave networks?"

He was pretty sure he had found the focus of his mission.

PART II
Weaving the Web

The first few times Ray tried to call Sophie and Cassie, he got no answer, and no answering machine. In fact, it wasn't until after their appearance on the Oprah show that he finally connected with Sophie by phone. To his gratification, she recognized his name immediately.

"Goodness," she said, "your Tai Chi class was one of the best workshop series I ever took through the Parks Department, and I think I've about done them all! So, Mr. Gonzales, what can I do for you?"

"Well," said Ray, "I know this is going to sound a little, um, odd, but when I saw Cassandra on television the other night, I started getting some. . . uncomfortable. . .vibrations concerning her safety."

He told Sophie about his patrols with the Panthers and his uncanny ability to sense trouble *before* it happened.

"I don't generally talk much about this ability I seem to have," said Ray, "but I thought maybe since you'd had a class with me, you'd take the warning with an open mind."

There was a short pause before Sophie said, "Are you free to come over for dinner this evening, Mr. Gonzales?"

And of course, he was always free these days, if he chose to be, so two hours later he was at Sophie's house in McLean.

Ray was as charmed by Cassie as everyone else was, and he, Cassie, and Sophie got on a first name basis immediately. During dinner, Cassie prattled about what fun it had been to see herself on television the first time, and about how she and Sophie were going to make an appearance at her school at assembly the next day. After dinner, Cassie and Ray sat in the living room together while Sophie fixed coffee and dessert in the kitchen, and when Emerson chose to put in an appearance, she talked about the Transcendentalists, about her NDE, and finally, in a more conspiratorial tone, she mentioned that she and Emerson sometimes had chats before they went to sleep at night.

"Ah," he punned, "if only you were French, you could have a nightly chat with your *chat!*"

"Oh, but if I were French," she said immediately, "what we do wouldn't be called a chat, would it?"

"Perhaps a *tete a tete* with your tabby?" he suggested.

She grinned, but when she spoke again it was in that more conspiratorial tone. "Actually, the only person I've told about this is Sophie, and though she believes me, she said maybe I shouldn't mention it to anybody else. But Emerson really does seem to talk to me, only it's in my head and not with his lips."

"So you hear him answer you in your head?" asked Ray.

Cassie nodded.

"In English?"

"Well, certainly not in French," she laughed.

"I just thought maybe it wasn't really in words, you know, but just impressions about ideas," said Ray. "But anyway, if Sophie told you not to talk about it, why are you telling me?"

"Because Sophie told me you had a psychic impression of something about me when you saw me on television the other night. So I figured you'd understand about Emerson talking to me, and not think I'm crazy."

"No," said Ray, "I certainly don't think you're crazy."

"So, what sort of thing did you pick up about me?" she asked.

Ray was uncomfortable telling the child his impressions without Sophie in the room, but just at that moment she arrived with a tray of cups and slices of rhubarb pie.

"Gosh," said Ray, "I think I've had rhubarb only about two other times in my life. This is a real treat!"

"I have 14 rhubarb plants out back, which is enough to supply an army. Most people don't realize just how easy rhubarb pie is to make, and after the first season how easy rhubarb is to grow. And rhubarb season goes on and on all summer. So I have a whole freezer shelf full of rhubarb. Take some home with you if you like. I'll even throw in a pie recipe if you'll just get some of it off my hands!"

Ray smiled and began heartily working at his slice of pie until Cassie, still full of curiosity, brought up the subject of his psychic impression again.

Ray set his plate down and looked first at Sophie and then at Cassie. Finally, he said, "As you know, I'm a Tai Chi teacher. Some would even call me a master. One of the things that happened when I began learning Tai Chi was I started to have impressions of what other people were feeling."

Sophie and Cassie nodded their understanding.

"The more centered I became within myself," he continued, "the better became my perception of what other people were experiencing. In fact, I found when I was around someone who was feeling ill or bereaved, I had to put up a shield in order to block their discomfort or pain, or else I'd begin to feel it, too, even though it wasn't mine. I believe what I experience would put me in the category of 'empathic.'

"Eventually, I got so I could receive an impression, determine whether there was anything I could do to assuage it for the person, and then, for my own protection, screen it out. But when I started patrolling for the Panthers, I realized there was one negative impression I didn't always want to screen out, so instead of blocking it, I started trying to enhance it, to make it even sharper. I honed it. I fine tuned it, so that when I picked up on it, I could judge where it was coming from and maybe be in the right place to do something about it.

"And that was. . . ?" said Sophie.

"It was what I think of as the vibration of animosity, of anger, of hatred, of violence. . . which are bred by fear. Fear of difference, fear of otherness, something like that."

He glanced at Cassie, wondering if it would be all right to refer, even obliquely, to his sexual bias. His logic told him not to say anything, but his intuition said she was sophisticated enough to accept him for whatever he was, and that she and Sophie would be neither offended nor judgmental. Still, he decided to get Sophie's permission before being too frank.

Looking at Sophie, he asked, "Does Cassie understand about AIDS and the community I'm a part of? Is it okay for me to talk about my work with the Panthers?"

Sophie nodded with a sad little smile, for she thought she knew what was coming.

"If there's anything she doesn't understand," she responded, "she'll either ask you directly, or she'll talk about it with me later."

Cassie nodded vigorously, and said, "I always do!"

"As you probably realize then, I am a part of a community that the rest of society views with both fear and animosity, simply because we do not conform to what is considered the norm in our choice of sexual relationships. On top of that, as the AIDS epidemic has grown, the anger at the gay community has grown increasingly as well, at least from some quarters. So at first, when I began picking up these negative vibrations, I thought they were specifically directed toward gays and bred by homophobia and fear of this dreadful disease.

"But then," he continued, "I was on the Mall near the Lincoln Memorial one Sunday, and there was this group of pro choice supporters having a rally, and I began to get those ugly feelings. So I started to track where they were coming from, and it turned out they were being generated by a group of guys near the Vietnam Memorial who were with the antiabortion side of the issue. They had some boxes with them, and I knew they were going to do something negative, because of all the anger that was coming off them."

"What did you do?" asked Cassie.

"I called the cops on them. Because of my work with the Panthers, I know a few folks in the D.C. police department, so I just went up to the nearest cop, did a little name dropping, and got them to go investigate. Sure enough, what this crew had in the boxes were some heavy duty fireworks, some of them illegal, like rockets and so forth. These clowns were getting ready to shoot some of their fireworks *into* the crowd, and a lot of people could have gotten hurt."

"Then it's a good thing you were there and followed your instincts!" said Cassie.

"You bet!" he exclaimed. "But anyway, that's when I realized I wasn't just tuning in to the homophobic vibration, but could pick up anger and violent tendencies from all quarters. And see," he said, pausing to be sure they were clearly understanding him, "it goes one step further yet. I don't just pick up on general animosity. Like for instance, the vibrations of domestic squabbles would be at such a low level I'd normally screen them out without even thinking. And I would automatically screen out the anger and frustration of rush hour drivers on the Beltway."

Sophie and Cassie both laughed, since they spent a lot of time in traffic each evening coming back from the congressional office buildings.

"But," Ray continued, "what seems to draw me is animosity connected to *premeditated* violence. Those guys on the mall were plotting to hurt people. And if one of the partners in a domestic quarrel were to have in the back of his mind to take a gun and shoot the other party, that's something I'd likely tune to. That's why, when I go out on a patrol, either with the Panthers or by myself, I have such a good record of sensing where violence is going to erupt. And I can either be there on the spot myself or call the cops. Fortunately, after the first couple of times I managed to head off some really bad stuff on a patrol, the cops started paying attention when I called something in."

Ray looked down at a spot on the floor, as if he were rehearsing what he was going to say next.

"So, you're wondering. . . what does all this have to do with Cassie, right?" he said, looking from one to the other of them.

They nodded, and Sophie said, "I guess that's the punch line, isn't it?"

"When I saw Cassie on the news the other night, I began to get some really uncomfortable feelings. Now, it's never happened before that I'd pick up these negative vibes just watching television. But this time I did. There's somebody—or perhaps some faction—that's highly agitated in a violent way by her appearing in public. Somebody is very much afraid of you, honey, though I don't know why anybody would be afraid of a sweet little girl like you."

"I guess that makes us even," Cassie countered, "because I sure don't understand why people would ever be afraid of a nice man like you, either."

Ray nodded in acknowledgement. What a friendly little kid, he thought. Then he continued, "But what bothers me most is I began to get the uncomfortable feelings just seconds after you came on the screen, as if your appearing in public was acting as a sort of lightning rod for somebody's fear and hostility. And it was like the energy force, whatever it was, was all ready to do you harm, if only it could.

"Now, I just can't imagine it was being generated by somebody you've never met before, who saw you for the first time at the same time I did, on the news that night. So my logical mind says it has to be someone, or some group, that already knows you, and that's had time to work up a good mad about something!"

"There's one other possibility," said Sophie. "Joe Jacobson's article about the two of us came out in the paper that same morning. Potentially, a million and a half people could have seen the article and found something to be hostile about before we appeared on television."

They sat quietly thinking about what Sophie had said for a few moments. The situation was sobering at best, and could be really frightening if they let themselves succumb to it.

Then Sophie spoke again. "Well, I know there are a lot of crazies running around loose, so you may be picking up on a sociopathic personality. But I'm also thinking the source may be one of the strict religious types. Some of them are very fearful of anything that doesn't conform to the exact letter of their interpretation of the Bible. And I understand that people who claim to have had NDEs are condemned by some of these more fanatical types as being either hallucinatory or deluded by devils."

"Gosh, that's so silly!" said Cassie.

"You and I think it's silly, honey, because we believe there's more to reality than just three dimensions. But if you'd been warned all your life by your mom and dad and maybe scared by the preacher like you were at that revival that any out of the ordinary experience had to be the work of devils, then it wouldn't seem silly at all. What I mean is, a lot of people have been told that psychic experiences, precognitive dreams, out of body experiences, and everything of the sort are all the work of the devil. So even if they were to have some sort of experience like your NDE or the perceptions Ray has just been telling us about, they'd immediately invalidate it. Because they believe recognizing it might put them right into Satan's clutches."

They all sat silent a while longer, until Sophie was struck by another thought.

"Ray, what are you picking up on Cassie right now, while you're here with us? Are you getting anything negative now?"

He shook his head. "Nothing at all. Whatever it was that was aimed toward her, it's not focused on her right now."

"Then it would seem she is only in danger when we make public appearances?"

"That would be my guess," he responded, "but I'd need to be around her frequently during public appearances, or on the set at TV appearances, to really know what the source of the vibes is."

"Could you do that?" asked Sophie.

"Do what?"

"Could you be with us when we go into public? Maybe come with us a couple of times to the congressional office buildings and sort of snoop out any bad vibrations we may be drawing to us there? I mean, all we've ever picked up is that the staffers like us, and that it's become a real coup for whoever we pick to visit—sort of an ego boost, though I can't imagine why congressmen need such a thing! One receptionist told us they hate to see most lobbyists coming, but the Cookie Lobby is welcome everywhere! We really don't have any idea who might be finding us a threat. So, could you come with us? I mean, the only alternative for us is to stop what we're doing. We can't afford to endanger Cassandra."

"Well. . . ," Ray began.

"No, I guess you're probably too busy, with your classes and patrols and all. It was just a thought."

"It's not that," said Ray.

They both waited expectantly for him to continue.

After a long moment, he said, "Okay, sure. I can meet you in D.C. the next time you go, and walk the halls with you."

Cassie went to bed shortly thereafter. Sophie walked Ray to the door, asking as an afterthought, "So what are your plans?"

"I don't have any classes with the Parks Department just now," he said. "I've come into a little money and I've been thinking about opening my own studio. But I just don't seem to have the drive for it at the moment."

He told her about his relationship with Colin, and about how he was really searching for something he hadn't done before, trying to find a meaningful focus to put his energy into.

She said she understood both his grief and his search for meaning. She'd been through the same feelings, the same search after Saul died.

"Really," said Ray, "I want you to know I'm quite grateful for your invitation to join you in your visits to Congress. But maybe you ought to think twice about my coming with you."

Sophie raised her eyebrows. "Ray, you seem a bit at loose ends right now. We have some television appearances coming up during the next couple of weeks. Would you consider traveling with us? Sort of as a companion, or bodyguard? I'd be happy to pay you, and to take care of your expenses on the trips."

"I'm flattered you should ask me," he replied. "But like I was trying to indicate before, you have to realize, consorting with a known homosexual may not do your lobbying effort any good. And I have to warn you about another thing, as well. Some years ago, I was diagnosed as having ARC. And while the disease seems to have backed off, and I haven't had any tests for months—actually for years!—I probably am still a carrier. I mean, I know of only one person who has overcome the virus—Niro Asistent—and she carries little scars on all her blood cells. But anyway, I may very well be a carrier of AIDS, and I just think you ought to know that."

"Well, then," said Sophie facetiously, a little smile playing at her lips, "I guess Cassie and I just won't have sex with you."

Ray snorted a laugh. "You're a very funny lady, Sophie," he said. "And a very wise one."

"My name isn't Sophia for nothing," she replied, and gave him a kiss on the cheek as she wished him a pleasant goodnight.

*****

Lucy had been right, Adam decided. Their sex life really had become better. But not because the physical nature of it was more intense than it had been before.

They hadn't camped out on their way up to D.C. because the camper plus a trailer they'd had to rent had been full of Lucy's paintings. They'd decided since they were going East themselves anyway, they'd take her artworks with them rather than having them shipped. Which meant unless they wanted to share the pup tent—and risk having Smoo insist on joining them as their resident pup—they had to stop at motels every evening.

On the trip, Adam discovered a fondness for motels. Maybe it was the energy they contained from those previous occupants who had used the space for illicit encounters. Maybe it was just that the rooms were clean and empty of the clutter and chores one had to take care of in daily life, and so one was left with nothing to do but sleep, read sleazy novels, or make love. In any case, he found staying in a motel an erotic adventure.

126

But the subtle heightening of his libido due to circumstance wasn't what made the difference in his sexual interchanges with Lucy either.

It was simply the light.

Since his experience up a tree at Big Bend, when he had seen the inner life force connections of all that is, he had begun seeing an inner light in lots of other people and things. He'd seen it in Smoo, when the lumbering ox came up to give him a slurpy kiss and be petted.

And once, when he and Lucy were having a beer and some nachos at an outdoor cafe in El Paso, he'd watched a little boy go past them on the sidewalk, bouncing a younger sibling on his hip. The kid was singing a sort of tuneless little chant to the delighted, giggly baby that went, "Boop-de, boop-de, boop-de-do . . . you're my baby, and I love you." And both of the kids were radiating the light as they bounced along.

And he saw it constantly in Lucy—when she was painting, when she was cooking, and most of all when she turned her whole attention on him in their lovemaking. She glowed. She shimmered. If one could make love to an angel, this must be what it would be like.

When he'd told Lucy about it, she'd said, "You are beginning to see with your inner eyes. You are seeing the auric field that surrounds all created things."

He didn't know if that was quite true. It seemed to him maybe what he was seeing was the radiance of unconditional love, emanating from those—like Smoo and those little kids and Lucy—who gave themselves without reservation to others. And he saw it sometimes in nature—in the mountains, and the sky, and plants and animals.

And then again, maybe he was just hallucinating.

But if he was, he didn't want to stop.

*****

Senator Snailer was in a cold rage.

He'd experienced such a state several times in the last couple of months, every time he'd seen the old lady and the brat with the cookies in his building again. He'd experienced just this intensity of rage with this pair the first time he'd seen them on television, back when they were visiting congressional representatives in the Cannon Building, before they'd even appeared once in the senatorial offices. Now they'd been on television several times, and they seemed to be in this building at least twice a week. And each time he saw them, he'd get a rush of the rage, starting in the pit of his stomach and flushing through his whole body.

This afternoon, just a few minutes before, he'd seen them in the hall; as usual, they'd passed his office right by, and he'd stood and watched as they passed. They acted as if they didn't even recognize him.

Except for the man they had with them—he'd looked Snailer right in the eye; a glint of recognition had crossed his face, and he'd given a little sneering half smile.

Snailer was quite sure they'd gotten smart and checked the voting records for environmental issues, and then they'd decided he wasn't worth bothering with because of his consistent record of voting against environmental controls on big business! Well, what did they know anyway?

Oh, he'd seen their literature—with all the publicity they'd been getting on the news and on major talk shows, he'd made it a point to get copies of everything they were passing out from one of his colleagues who'd already been a recipient. And he'd noticed something missing in the literature that most of the other members of Congress hadn't and very likely wouldn't.

Snailer smiled to himself at this knowledge that the Cookie Lobby seemed unaware of one very important economic factor in the determination of U.S. policy toward South American rain forest management. They'd got all the stuff about the cattle market and farming and industrialization and wood in there, and all of those factors had been important in the past, and to some extent they still were.

But the most important factor at the moment was so significant for the global economy that no amount of talk about harvesting the rain forests was going to shift policy. No amount of wailing and gnashing of teeth by the bleeding hearts was going to cause American financial interests to get gracefully out of the area. And the vast majority of the public and the media weren't even aware of it as a factor in rain forest management.

The factor was gold.

Snailer knew, because he had some personal interests and investments in the mining of gold, that the rain forests of Venezuela, Guyana, Suriname, French Guiana, and upper Brazil had recently been designated as the newest and richest source of gold in the world. Currently, the demand for South American gold was very high world wide, especially in Pacific Rim markets. U.S. business interests in the area anticipated a growth in "gold futures" that would effectively assist in solving the economic problems the U.S. had long been experiencing. So there was no way the U.S. was suddenly going to give up its mining interests in the area. No way.

And Snailer knew, because he'd been an investor in gold for decades, that gold mining was not a clean business. He knew there'd been complaints from some of the native tribes in Guyana and Venezuela about the poisoning of their water and food supplies from the mercury that was used in the gold separation process. And he knew that to even set up equipment for drilling, processing, and refining the ore, it was necessary to burn a lot of the forest.

But there was no point in trying to save the environment—the end of the world was coming at the end of the decade, and he couldn't imagine that God gave a holy damn about the environnment this close to the end!

Nevertheless, he'd had his aide check up on these so-called "Cookie Lobbyists," and he'd found out some pretty interesting things. Like, for instance, the old lady was a New Age freak, associated with all the fringe groups in the whole metropolitan area, like the Aquarian Spiritual Science Center, and the Network of Humanistic Development, and the Modern Metaphysical Institute. Everybody with any sense knew organizations like that had Satanic leanings! How the hell had these freaks made such a splash in the news?

And now, for the last week, here they were wandering the congressional halls with a bodyguard, and Snailer's aide had found out the guy was a certified homosexual. So he'd had his aide call up Joe Jacobson, that guy at the newspaper who'd written the story about them in the first place, and spill the beans about their occult leanings and their consorting with this faggot. And what had Jacobson done? He'd laughed! That's what his aide had said, the sonuvabitch had actually laughed. And then

he'd said, "Thank Senator Snailer for doing my research for me."
And he'd hung up. Damned black bastard!

When Snailer had seen the Cookie Lobbyists pass him by, he'd
told his secretary he was not to be disturbed, and he'd gone into
his office and locked the door and gotten down on his knees and
he'd prayed. Fervently!

"Oh, thank You, God, for instilling in me, Your faithful servant
Marvin Snailer, the devotion to right thinking that will lead me to
salvation. Thank You for not making me weak like other men,
but strong to obey Your commandments, a general in Your army
of faithful soldiers, who will fight Your enemies on every front.
Thank You for showing me from my very youth the shining path
that has kept me from damnation, and that has made me so very
able to seek out wickedness in all its disguises and smite it hip
and thigh for Your glory. I promise You, oh Lord, that I will
continue to fight the evil elements threatening to corrupt this
country, and I will do my best to help it reclaim its economic
dominance.

"And I thank You, God, for having shown me I am one of Your
chosen, and that I will be among those You select to experience
the Rapture when the final battle of Armageddon comes, when I
will see your face in Glory. Hallelujah! Amen."

When Senator Snailer got up from his knees and unlocked his
office door, his secretary took it as a sign he was once again
available for business, and his intercom lit up.

"Yes?" he said, as he pressed the button.

"Senator, the Cookie Lobby people were here a few minutes
ago. I know you've been looking for a visit from them, so I told
them you were unavailable at the moment, and that they should
phone to make an appointment, perhaps for next week. Was that
all right?"

"Thank you, Miss Pender," said Snailer, almost preening
himself. "When they call back, allot them about 15 minutes next
Wednesday afternoon. And, uh, tell them their appointment is
about a half hour before it's actually scheduled—do you get my
drift?"

"Yes, sir," said Miss Pender. She smiled, for she admired the
senator greatly. He was a true soldier of righteousness, totally
tuned in to the instructions of God, and a bulwark against all the
evil elements in society. He was strong on all the traditional

values that had made this Christian country great—and when a vote was called in the Senate, he could be counted on to know the *right* way to vote, to keep America from the evils of socialism. And one of the little tricks he sometimes played on people he knew to be unrighteous was to make 'em wait!

She also felt privileged, for now she knew what virtually nobody else in the congressional halls knew—the Cookie Lobbyists were corrupt! She was so lucky to be the senator's secretary, to be privy to so much inside information, and thus to know who to trust and who not to.

Yes, it was of great value to know your enemies!

*****

When they stepped out of the Russell Building into the sunlight, Ray said softly to Sophie, "I've just pegged one of your enemies."

She lifted her eyebrows questioningly.

"Snailer." He said the name as if it did indeed belong to a slimy slug. "He won't commit a violent act himself, but he has it in him to spearhead a lot of dangerous actions by other people."

"Well," she said, "it's good to know your enemies."

*****

"Your lady has a beautiful soul," said Sophie to Adam. "It shines through in all her work."

Sophie, Cassie, and Ray were attending the opening of the Southwestern artists' show at the Dupont Circle gallery where Lucy had been invited to participate.

"Yes," answered Adam, "I'm very lucky she found me and salvaged me."

"Oh," said Sophie, "I imagine you're still a prize catch. As I recall, you were at least *one* of the answers to every high school girl's prayers about 10 or so years ago."

"Let's just say I've had some of my own prayers answered in being with Lucy. I really want you to meet her. She's talking to the gallery administrator right now, but she'll be down here soon," said Adam. "In the meantime, would you like some wine and cheese?"

They strolled to the refreshment tables in the central gallery to which Ray and Cassie had already found their way. Since he'd signed on as chaperon for Cassie, Ray rarely let her out of his sight in public, and together they were analyzing the merits of what looked like a curry dip with crudites.

Adam poured a glass of Zinfandel for Sophie and one for Ray, but Ray demurred with a shake of his head and a softly spoken, "Thanks, but no," so Adam kept the glass for himself and proposed a toast.

"To your network of networks—may it soon be a reality!"

"Ah," said Sophie, eyes gleaming, "you caught the Oprah show!"

"Yes, indeed!" said Adam. "And since there are no accidents in the universe—or so my beloved wife tells me—then I must surmise it was not by chance that we came to Washington, D.C. just at a time when you're in need of a super business administrator. Dear lady, I've been an admirer of yours since I was just a sprout. Indeed, I had a considerable crush on you when I was in your American literature class in the 11th grade, and I hope you'll accept my services in helping make your vision a reality.

"And," he added, "I also happen to be an expert fixit man, so if the roof should start leaking or the plumbing should go or your car should break down while we're creating this network of enlightened beings, I'm your man!"

At that moment, a lovely woman with high cheekbones and a flare for dramatic, gauzy costuming came walking toward them.

"Ah, it's my bride, arrived at last!"

After the introductions, Adam poured yet another glass of wine for Lucy and said, "I've just been prostrating myself before Mrs. Nussbaum and begging her to accept my services as a weaver of her network of networks. Support me, love, and tell her I'm wonderful."

"He's wonderful," laughed Lucy. "A little nuts, but wonderful! You really should take him up on his offer, Mrs. Nussbaum, since he works cheap. Free, even!" She gave a classic shrug. "What more can you ask than that?"

Sophie grinned. "Not much, except to find out what the bottom line is. And please, call me Sophie."

"Oh, do you know what we used to call you in the 11th grade?" asked Adam. "Saint Sophia!"

"Yes, I did know," laughed Sophie. "I assumed it was because I had a direct line to the principal, rather than to God."

"Actually, it was because every word out of your mouth seemed both illuminating and elevating to our callow spirits. Except, of course, when you said, 'Your research papers are due tomorrow'."

Sophie smiled again and sipped her wine, then asked once more, "Now tell me, just why do you want to help make my network of networks a reality? I mean, I was just speaking off the top of my head on the show, and I have no idea how to go about creating a coalition of groups around the country. And what makes you want to be a part of the scheme, anyway? That is, assuming there's a viable scheme here somewhere."

"Because," said Adam, "the planet is in need of saving at the moment, and unless a whole lot of people get together and realize such saving has to become a top priority in their personal lives, the pinball game we've been playing is going to tilt, and all the lights and sirens are going to go off, and then the game will be over."

"I like your allusion, but I didn't think anybody played pinball these days. I thought it was all Mario Brothers in the arcades," said Sophie.

"It is!" piped Cassie, who had been an old hand at video games in her other life. "And Teenage Mutant Ninja Turtles! My dad and I used to play arcade games together."

She said the last just a little wistfully, then she added as a soft aside to Ray, "Sometimes I really miss my dad and mom and Timmy."

Taking her hand, Ray led Cassie to some chairs along one wall of the gallery, where he allowed her to continue her remembering with more privacy. Sophie silently blessed Ray and thanked heaven for his sensitivity and his many talents. Then she turned back to Adam and Lucy.

"So," she said, "back to the pinball game of life. Yes, I do believe the planet needs saving, and I'm pretty sure a lot of other people across the country and around the world are concerned about it, too, if they aren't overwhelmed by a need just to supply the bare necessities of survival. And I'm confident one of these days, if we can just hold everything together long enough, we're going to reach a critical mass of consciousness."

"The hundredth monkey," said Lucy.

"Right! Or the hundredth sheep!"

"I haven't heard of that—what are you talking about?" asked Adam.

"Which?"

"Both! Or either."

"Well," said Sophie, warming up to her old schoolteacher role, "it's a common New Age concept that when enough people begin to *think* a certain thing, that thing suddenly becomes a part of common or collective consciousness. The New Agers cite a phenomenon discovered by a group of Japanese scientists, who found that on a certain Pacific island, where monkeys had always dug their sweet potatoes up and eaten them straight from the ground, dirt and all, one little monkey decided one day to *wash* her sweet potato before eating it. And, watching her, other monkeys also began to wash their sweet potatoes, until one fine day, the practice became a part of monkey collective consciousness, so that all the monkeys—not just on that island, but *on the whole chain of islands*—began to wash sweet potatoes before eating them.

"And more recently Rupert Sheldrake cited a similar phenomenon among sheep in Great Britain. You know those cattle guards that have the rolling cylinders? Well, one little sheep discovered that he wouldn't have to walk on them if he'd just lie down and roll across! And pretty soon, all the sheep, not just in his pen, but all over Great Britain, were lying down and rolling across the cattle guards!"

"So what you're saying," said Adam, "is that if enough people begin to think *responsibly* about the planet, we'll eventually reach a critical mass, and it will then be important for all people to be responsible."

"Yes," said Sophie, "And maybe I'm saying that in the process of working together to save the planet, we'll learn we really are a global family, and that every single one of us is important and necessary to the whole, and that we're not just sisters and brothers, we're actually connected by a webwork of light and energy. And that *nobody is excluded from that webwork!*

"Now if it's true, as the positive thinkers and psychocyberneticists and creative visualizers and maybe even the quantum physicists suggest, that what we *think* is what we *manifest*, then how much more might we be able to manifest if we could *all think the same thing at the same time!* But that," she finished, "was too esoteric and far out for me to say on the Oprah show!"

"That's right," said Adam. "Save it for Geraldo!"

*****

Sophie and Adam had met Joe for a late breakfast at a hotel coffee shop in D.C. near the newspaper office building. It was a tiny space, with booths along one wall, and a lunch counter arrangement along the other. Joe liked the place for its relaxed atmosphere—friendly, easy-going waitresses, unlimited coffee refills, and a TV on the wall behind the lunch counter going constantly, which Joe glanced at as they all slid into a booth.

He registered with a smile that what was playing was the regular morning episode of "I Love Lucy." He'd always felt there was something soothing about old reruns of "I Love Lucy"—a continuity with a simpler past, and in the person of Lucille Ball, with a consciousness that could take itself lightly.

"So, how can I help you out?" Joe asked Sophie as he stirred Equal and non-dairy creamer into his coffee.

"Frankly," she began, "I'm not sure. Adam has convinced me that before the 15 minutes of fame Cassie and I are experiencing are over, we need to do what we can to launch our collective project."

"Which is?" Joe asked.

"Which is to start some kind of clearing house or association for networking networks around the country. There are hundreds and hundreds of groups around the country presently focusing on positive action in some area. Groups of peace activists, groups of citizen diplomats, groups to feed and shelter the hungry and homeless, groups of environmentalists, groups of animal conservationists, groups to protect children from abuse, groups for women's rights, minority rights, gay and lesbian rights, *human* rights—and groups just dedicated to developing human potential, through firewalking, vision quests, meditation, and so forth.

"Now, as I see it, all of these groups are doing good work, but they're all like scattered energy—you know how you feel when you have too darned much to do and so you spread yourself around trying to do it all? And then you're spread too thin, so even though you may manage to get everything done, you find you haven't done anything very effectively. Well, that's the effect these groups often manifest; sometimes the return on their effort is so small they get really frustrated and feel like Sisyphus, pushing that boulder up the hill only to have it roll back down again immediately.

"An example comes to mind from the peace activists. There we were working so hard to solve our problems with the Soviets, and there was that breakthrough in '89 when there were all those summits, and the sense of elation was wonderful, especially when it was all topped off by the tearing down of the Berlin Wall. But then we surely all felt a certain frustration when before you know it we were embroiled with Iraq. I mean, you think you've got a problem licked, when up pops another threat to peace that's maybe even scarier."

When Sophie paused for breath, Joe stopped stirring his coffee and said, "I'm not unfamiliar with that sense of frustration. But how do you propose to overcome it?"

Sophie looked at Adam, and he answered, "To build bridges between networks that will help focus energy collectively, and thereby maybe make all of the positive actions a part of collective consciousness.

"Now it's true all of these different groups of activists have their own agendas. But Sophie has pointed out to me how people who are interested in saving whales and dolphins are likely also interested in saving African elephants and Siberian tigers and rain forests. Maybe they're even interested in saving people! However, they probably don't have the time or the energy or the money to support more than one project at a time.

"On the other hand—and this is where we hope to come in—all these people of good will *might* have the *psychic* energy to focus once a day for five minutes on somebody else's project besides their own. And they might have the *physical* energy once a week to write a letter to a congressman or to the president or to the United Nations or to a political leader of another country urging positive action on a specific issue other than their own. Now at five minutes a day for six days, plus 30 minutes on Sunday to write a short letter or even a post card and mail it, that's an outlay of only one hour a week, plus the cost of a first class stamp.

"And what do you think would happen if every person of good will in this country actually focused together on a single cause—like maybe saving the whales—at the same time every day for a week, and at the end of that week wrote a letter to someone in power urging positive action? I'm talking thousands and thousands of people focusing all at the same time every day, just for five minutes—why, the energy would be tremendous! And then, at the end of the week, every one of those people would write a letter to someone in power. If it didn't do anything else, the focusing every day for a week would help the people get clear on what they could say in their weekly letter.

"Let's say for the sake of argument that there were only 100,000 people interested in doing this. But let's say also if each of them wrote an assigned congressman, that's nearly 200 letters to each congressman! And if half of them wrote their congressmen and half wrote the president, that's 100 letters per congressman and 50,000 to the president! Or let's suppose 25,000 people were committed to writing the president and 25,000 wrote the United Nations. Or maybe just 10,000 each wrote the president, the U. N., and the heads of those countries which have refused to stop their whale hunting. That's a terrific batch of letters!"

Joe held up his hand to put a rein on Adam's enthusiasm and said, "I have a couple of questions before you continue. The first is, do you really think there are as many as 100,000 people who are interested in this kind of positive activism?"

Sophie fielded the question by replying, "According to one recent estimate, there are 50 million Americans who lean toward New Age sympathies in one form or another. So I think 100,000 is really quite conservative. I honestly believe we could harness a million or more. I mean, that's only two percent of those with futurist leanings."

Joe looked impressed with the figure. "Okay, then," he said, "my other question is, why would people want to do this kind of focusing and letter writing on a regular basis? I mean, what's the real incentive?"

"Ah!" said Adam, "We think the incentive would be mutual back scratching. We think save-the-whale activists would be willing to meditate and write letters for builders of shelters for the homeless if they knew the shelter builders were going to meditate and write letters for them the next week. And remember, we think most people who want to take action are interested in more than one kind of activism, but they just don't know how to be effective in more than one area at a time. Not to mention that many activist organizations dun their members for contributions just about every month, so you get so you have to be selective as to which good causes you feel you can afford to support."

"Also," said Sophie, "the RESULTS lobbyists—they're the ones who write monthly letters to congressmen and heads of state about legislation and positive actions that can be taken to alleviate world hunger—they've shown that people are more likely to sit down and actually write letters if they know other people are doing the same thing at the same time. You just feel you'll have more effect with a letter if you think lots of other people are writing, too.

"And another example of how people will do something together they ordinarily wouldn't think of doing by themselves is the World Healing Meditation that John Randolph Price inspired some years ago to take place at the same time round the world on New Year's Eve. And thousands of people participate every year. So I think the idea of having people do something like this collectively and focus on a different specific problem area every week is really good, and certainly not without precedent. It's just that nobody has suggested doing it with quite this scope before."

"Okay," said Joe, "I've been thinking about what Adam said about some of these organizations dunning their members with great regularity, and that brings up the matter of money. How are you planning to pay for this networking collective? I mean, what service are you going to provide, and how will you get paid for it?"

"If we do it by computer," said Adam, "which I think is an effective way to start it, it should cost subscribers no more than $5.00 a year to link up with us. And," he glanced at Sophie for support, "if you can provide us with some ideas about free publicity, Joe, it may not even cost people that much to participate. But we'll get to that in a minute."

The waitress came at that point and refilled their cups, thus interrupting Adam long enough for Joe to say, "It sounds to me as if you're talking about a system which could possibly be incorporated as a non-profit organization, and which could eventually support you. But while you're getting it going, how are you all going to support yourselves? And what happens if it *doesn't* work out? Where's your security?"

Sophie answered, "Cassie, Ray, and I are in the somewhat enviable position of having a small but steady income which makes us financially independent. I have my and Saul's retirement income, Cassie has a monthly stipend from her parents' estate, and Ray seems to have invested wisely in the past, in addition to having recently come into an inheritance. On top of which, we are all currently living together in my little, crooked house—which is totally paid off."

"And I," shrugged Adam, "am not opposed to leaching off my lovely wife, who has been selling more paintings for more money than she ever thought possible since coming to Washington."

"We can turn my basement into an office," continued Sophie, "until such time as we find we can afford—or need to afford—to expand into office real estate. I mean, after all, we don't need much room to house a computer or copying equipment. We aren't going to interview clients or anything, so working out of my basement ought to suit us just fine."

Then Adam added, "The thing that's kind of a unique experience for me is that none of us is particularly interested in getting rich, or 'making it' in the usual sense. I've been there, and I can tell you the rewards are pretty empty. To paraphrase something my bride once said to me, I'm now more interested in connecting than in collecting."

"I'll admit," said Joe, "it's kind of unusual to meet up with folks who are more interested in making changes than in making money." He thought of his late heroes Martin Luther King and

Dave Shumacher. "So, okay, I've got the picture—I think!—of what it is you're going to try to do, namely, catalyze all the scattered energy of all the hundreds of groups already out there doing good things so that they're focused effectively on helping each other."

"You've got it!" exclaimed Adam.

"And the beauty of the project," said Sophie, her eyes beaming, "is it's not a solution to the world's problems that's being imposed from the outside, but is one that empowers everybody, wherever they are, to link up with other people of like mind across the country—and maybe eventually around the globe!—to be real world changers. If we can visualize change, and focus all our collective energy on it, we can bring it about. Remember the 'Hands Across America' project back in the summer of 1986? I was part of that, and the energy of that line of people was overwhelming. I felt then if we could only maintain such a connection, we really could move mountains together. And this venture I believe will be like that—it has the potential for making everybody on the planet a magician!"

Joe smiled at her enthusiasm and said, "So, now, what's your plan of action, and just what is it you want me to do to help?"

Adam answered, "As we've discussed the possibilities up to this point, several schemes might work to create the link. One is to establish a computer connection among all the groups with visionary agendas. In fact, there's something called Peace Net/Eco Net that offers to connect all organizations of peace or ecology activism. And quite frankly, with all the computer equipment I have in storage in Texas, and with an outlay of around another $5,000—which Sophie and Ray and I think we can easily pool from some savings we have—I believe I could probably set up a system and a program that could handle the kind of connection we're talking about.

"The *modus operandi* of the system would be that individuals or organizations would contact us by sending in their one-time only link-up fee. We would send them back a password to use to modem into our system. What we would provide on an on-going basis would be the focus project of the week, including a description of the issues involved, plus a suggested letter format they could follow in writing their own letters, plus a list of those to whom they should send their letters. I see no reason why we can't have a listing by state of people's elected representatives with mailing addresses—lots of people don't really know who their congressmen are, or how to get in touch with them.

"In addition, I don't think it would be too difficult to create a running cross-directory of associated individuals and organizations, filed both by zip code and by area of interest—for example, groups that save whales and dolphins, groups that oppose pollution, groups that work for specific human rights, etc. That way, if a particular interest group wants to contact other groups with their same agenda, we'll be providing them with a service to let them know about each other. And, if a group wants information on other activist groups in their local area, they can get that, too, from our zip code listings."

"Also, as a simple alternative for individuals or groups without access to a computer with a modem," said Sophie, "we'll have a telephone hotline number people can call from which they can get a three-minute recorded message updated weekly on the focus of the week's meditation and letter, the key issues of the focus, and who to write to request action. We'll also have our mailing address on the hotline so people can write to us if they have specific questions—for example, if they want a list of congressmen or what not. And there'll be a number they can call if they want to talk to a real, live person."

"So our principal concern with launching this venture," said Adam, "isn't money to support it. It's publicizing the project and piquing people's interest in it. We truly believe people will want to participate. It doesn't require a lot of time. It doesn't require much at all in the way of money. It's going to encourage people toward responsible thinking and responsible action. And the more people who participate, the more effective it will be. But people have to know about it before they can participate. And that's your area of expertise."

"Cassie and I have two more upcoming appearances on talk shows before summer vacation. We can hype this networking project on them. But that's only two shots, and there are lots and lots of people who won't be watching who would like to be part of our mobilization plan. So how do we go about getting the kind of publicity we need?"

Somebody turned up the television behind the lunchcounter, and Joe turned to look. And there—not really to Joe's surprise because if the guy could show up on a computer monitor, why not on a television screen behind a hotel coffee shop lunch counter?—was Dave Shumacher.

"Hey, Joe," he said, "this is it, man! This is your chance to step out and show your mettle! You've got the contacts. You know who to call in New York, Chicago, San Francisco, L.A. so these people can get some column inches! You know who the TV bigwigs are, and how they can maybe get some free service announcement spots. And you can help 'em write their press releases, can't you? And maybe you can even write some stories for magazines and stuff, right, or maybe even the script for some TV spots?"

"Yes," said Joe to the face on the television. "And I didn't really need to be told to get involved."

"Just thought you might need the moral support, buddy!" said Dave as he gently faded into the face of Vivian Vance.

"What did you say?" asked Sophie, following the direction of his gaze toward the screen behind the lunch counter.

"Umm," said Joe, "I guess I'm not too old to get involved."

"Certainly not!" retorted Sophie. "You're still just a young whipper-snapper! Do you two realize I turn 60 tomorrow? And believe me, references to age are not welcome."

"Hey," said Adam, "I didn't realize! We'll have to have a party!"

"You're both invited to a soirée tomorrow night at 7:00 at La Mirabelle in McLean," said Sophie. "It was my Saul's favorite French restaurant. Bring spouses please, and I promise to break a long standing rule and let everyone talk shop at dinner, since I would welcome everyone's opinions on our prospective venture."

"I'll check with my wife and see if we can make it—I'd like to have you meet her," said Joe. "But one thing does occur to me right now which you might consider. If you acquire non-profit status, you might be able to get some of the television stations to run public service announcements for you for free. Of course, it could be very expensive to have the spots filmed."

"Not necessarily," interjected Sophie. "I have some friends in AARP who've been learning television studio production over at Channel 10. It's the Fairfax Community Access Cable station, and

142

as long as the shows they produce run there first, my friends say they're then free to bicycle them anywhere they like. So maybe it wouldn't be so expensive to create public service announcements as you might think."

"Definitely worth looking into," Joe agreed, and waved the waitress a scribbling sign to ask for the check. "Well," he said, "I need to get back to the office. But you can expect me and my wife tomorrow night, unless you hear otherwise between now and then. Our baby's due in about two weeks, so you never can tell. In the meantime," he added, "I'm happy to say I think your venture may be just the thing we need in this country to wake a few people up!"

*****

The venture turned out to be bigger than any of them had expected, though the auspices should have been perfectly clear when the Jacobson's baby arrived halfway through the entrée of Sophie's birthday party dinner.

Sophie, Cassie, and Ray had chosen the vegetarian option; everyone else had decided on the fish. But just as the waiter was placing her plate in front of her, Celeste said, "Ooops!" and clutched her belly as a look of consternation crossed her face.

"Oh, my," she said, "I do believe the baby has dropped!"

"What do we do?" asked Joe nervously.

"Oh, nothing yet," she said nonchalantly. "The doctor indicated I'd have some time to wait before the baby would actually come after it drops into position. Maybe even a couple of weeks yet."

She took two bites of her fish, then registered a look of intense pain.

"Are you okay, sweetheart?" asked Joe.

"Oh, yeah," she said. "The doctor indicated I might have some false labor pains. Not to worry."

A couple of minutes later, however, the pain occurred again. And yet again a couple of minutes after that.

"Celeste," said Lucy, "those pains are coming pretty fast. I attended some deliveries on the reservation, and you might want to call your doctor and tell him what's going on."

Celeste said, "Do you really think so?" but before the words were out of her mouth, Joe was on his feet and heading for the telephone.

When he came hurrying back, he said, "The doc is gonna meet us at the hospital. He says it wouldn't do any harm to get there pronto and see what's going on."

But when Celeste stood up, her water broke, flooding the chair and floor.

"Maybe we'd better get you to the ladies' lounge before you head off," said Lucy, and all the ladies including Cassie moved en masse to assist.

Cassie was back in about three minutes, first to inform the headwaiter that a baby was about to arrive in the ladies' room and would he please provide some fresh tablecloths for the event, and then to inform Joe his wife expected his presence at the impending arrival of their offspring. She also calmly told Adam to call for an ambulance and Ray to guard the door of the restroom.

When Adam got off the phone, she was standing behind him again.

"Sophie says she read a long time ago that if a baby was being born and you needed something sterile to wrap it in, you should use an unread newspaper, because that's germ free. So she says you should go get a newspaper, please."

Before the time it would have taken to have dessert, the Jacobsons were the proud parents of a 6 pound, 7 ounce female child, duly named Adonna Mirabelle Jacobson. She was handed to her father wrapped in the Style section of a copy of the paper he worked for.

"A newspaperman's daughter, born in style," said Joe to Adam later. "It's a good thing you didn't bring a product of our competition!"

Though they didn't fully realize it then, the seven people who had been participants and witnesses to Adonna Mirabelle's rather dramatic arrival had been bonded for life.

"It was," thought Sophie in retrospect, "a very clear sign we were giving birth to something astonishing."

*****

Cassie had expected the beginning of summer vacation to be a relief. No more school assignments, no more trying to cram homework in while she, Ray, and Sophie crept through late rush hour traffic on George Washington Parkway or I-66. Now, she thought, they could get comfortable with their cookie deliveries to Congress and do them earlier in the day. And then maybe in the afternoons, she and Ray could do something fun.

What happened instead was Sophie decided Cassie needed to be in on all the plans for the Consortium of Light, as their networking of networks was to be called. So when they weren't in the congressional office buildings handing out cookies and literature, they were making public appearances at luncheons, or they were talking to representatives of businesses and philanthropic foundations to get grant funding for their project, or they were talking to media administrators to try to get free publicity, or they were videotaping public service spots—which they had to do three times because of production glitches before they finally had a product Joe said was professional enough for them to air on the major networks.

It really wasn't a summer vacation for a kid, thought Cassie, and she begged Ray to take her to a movie or find an arcade where they could play video games.

"When I get the computer all hooked up," said Adam, "you can play video games on it. That is, when it's not directly in use for the project."

"I think there won't be any time for you to use the computer for games," said Sophie, and invested in a Nintendo system for Cassie that she could use with the television set in the living room.

The unspoken message was that they were all afraid for her to be out in public in case she became a focus of some of that still unidentified hostility. Ray had gone with Sophie and Cassie to the taping of their final two talk shows, and though he picked up nothing negative during the tape sessions, when the shows aired his belly began to churn from the hostile vibrations that poured in.

"This time," he told Sophie, "it's not just Cassie who's the focus. It's both of you. Whatever the faction is that's afraid of you, it's still out there."

"Well, then," said Sophie, "I think Cassie had better not go anywhere unattended. We don't want to take any chances, do we?"

Still, Cassie yearned to get out, so one afternoon, Ray and she went to the Tyson's Corner mall to see a new cartoon feature that was making its summer debut. Everything was fine until about mid-way through the show, when Ray began to have one of his negative sensations in the pit of his stomach. It grew stronger and stronger until after the show, when Cassie, who had had a giant economy size lemonade during the film, told him she needed to go to the bathroom before they started home.

Out in the lobby he looked around, trying to pinpoint who might be generating the negative vibes, and spotted a woman who seemed to be perusing the offerings of the candy counter. She was half-turned away from them so he couldn't see her face, but he was absolutely sure she was the source of the vibration.

He sent Cassie to the restroom and stood nonchalantly examining his fingernails. Sure enough, the woman turned and went in the same direction, but before she reached the door, Ray was standing in front of it blocking her entrance.

"Sorry," he said, "you can't go in. It's being cleaned."

"No, it's not!" protested the woman. "A little girl just went in."

"Ah, yes," he said, "but you can't go in. No one over 10 allowed."

Just then two giggly teenage girls came out.

"If you don't let me in, I'm going to miss my movie!" said the woman angrily.

"I'm sorry," said Ray calmly, "but you'll just have to wait until everybody else comes out, after which it's going to be cleaned."

The woman narrowed her eyes and glared at him. "I'm going to call the manager!" she said in a loud voice.

"Go ahead," said Ray, but before she could move, he raised his hand almost in an attitude of blessing, and he added, "but perhaps what you really want instead is just to become very calm, isn't it?"

The woman didn't move. Her chest was heaving with angry breaths, but as Ray began sending out his *chi* toward her, her eyes became very wide, her breathing slowed, and a look of shock spread over her face. Ray, who was consciously attempting to calm her by lowering her blood pressure and sending her peace and love, smiled ever so slightly.

They were both aware of the sound of a flush from inside, of the water faucet being turned on as the child washed her hands, of Cassie's voice humming a little tune, and throughout, they stood unmoving, eyes locked. Then Cassie opened the door and came out, and Ray felt the woman struggling to reenergize the negative vibration. But she wasn't able to do so.

"Oops!" said Ray cheerfully as the restroom door swung shut. "My mistake. I guess it's not being cleaned after all."

He gestured toward the door as if the woman should be his guest and enter its inner sanctum. She lifted her hand to her throat, backed toward the restroom door, and mumbled some unintelligible sounds. Ray hurried Cassie up the stairs.

"What was that all about?" asked Cassie.

"Just one of those people who doesn't like you for some reason," said Ray, who didn't want to frighten Cassie but felt it would be wrong to lie to her. "I sent her some good vibes and lowered her blood pressure so she wouldn't have a chance to hurt you."

"Goody!" said Cassie, and slipped an arm around his waist as they walked out of the mall and made their way to the parking garage.

Ray didn't discuss the incident any further with her then, but on the way home he had time to really think. The negative vibes hadn't started until the middle of the film. But the woman was waiting for them to come out of that particular screening theater. The obvious conclusion was that they had been followed by someone else, someone who had no real animosity toward Cassie, or at least had no intention of harming her. *That* someone had called the woman who Ray's instincts said *was* capable of doing the child harm.

As soon as he could get her alone, Ray told Sophie about the incident.

"She's a wonderful little ambassador," said Sophie, "and people love to have her speak, but until we find out just who or what is generating your negative vibes, we'll need to keep her out of the limelight as much as possible."

She had no idea how difficult that was going to be.

By the first week of August, just a little over six months after they had conceived of it, the Cookie Lobby had concluded their regular visits to the congressional office buildings. By Sophie's count they had delivered cookies, literature on the rain forests, and some sort of verbal speech to 1,842 people. That included 63 senators, 312 representatives, 1,428 staffers (some of whom got cookies two and three times!), 12 security guards, and 27 media people.

And during the last three months they had also delivered literature on the Consortium of Light, which they were hoping to have online by the time the Cookie Lobby was ready for retirement. It meant that approximately 900 people in the congressional office buildings knew about the effort they were trying to mount to get people thinking positively and in unison.

One of the last offices Sophie had visited formally was Senator Snailer's. She'd called up and made an appointment to see him. She deliberately did not take Cassie with her for the appointment, leaving her to stay with Adam at the McLean house where he was inputting data on the computer. She did, however, take Ray.

The secretary, Miss Pender, was quite cool. No smiles, no pleasantries. After they'd been waiting in the outer office for over 30 minutes, the phone rang on Miss Pender's desk. They knew as she answered it Snailer himself was on the other end.

"Yes, sir. . . . Yes, sir. . . . I will, sir."

She hung up.

"Senator Snailer regrets he will be unable to keep his appointment with you," she said curtly.

They thanked her politely and left the office. Naturally, they left behind a package of cookies and literature, though in her mind's eye, Sophie envisioned Miss Pender delicately picking up their packets with two reclutant fingers and trashing them as soon as they left the office.

When they were out of earshot, Sophie said to Ray, "My, she was a sweet little number, wasn't she? You'd think we were carrying bubonic plague!"

"Nah," said Ray, "just AIDS."

"So, did you pick up any vibrations from her?"

"Sure did," he said. "She'd just as soon stick her letter opener in our hearts as spit at us. But her animosity is subdued compared to the fear and hostility I've picked up at other times. So there's more to protect Cassie from out in the general populace."

He shrugged as if to say she should let go of her anxiety and continued, "Anyway, we've paid our respects to the senator's office, and he has essentially told us to take our cookies and stuff 'em. So let's put two marks on the side of the people in congress who don't like us, and 1,800 and how many . . . ?"

"Forty," she said.

"And 1,840 on the side of people who were positive and pleasant to us. Look, lady," he said, putting a companionable arm around her shoulder, "you've done more than the average citizen has done to further your cause, and 99.9 percent of the people you talked to were not just polite, but even looked forward to having you drop by. What do you want, for *everybody* to love you?"

"Of course!" she said. "Isn't that what we all really want?"

*****

During early August, Cassie's birthday came and went without much fanfare. Sophie gave her a couple of new video games for her Nintendo system, but Adam had been teaching her the joys of computer hacking on the system he'd installed in the basement office, and somehow just playing a game didn't have the thrill it once did.

Meantime, Ray had contacted the various police departments in Northern Virginia to let them know he believed the Cookie Lobbyists might be in some danger from unknown factions and to ask them to send regular patrols past the McLean house. And he and Sophie decided to share the expense of installing a burglar alarm system which would ring at the local police station.

Sophie had also asked all those people she trusted enough not to think her crazy to visualize Cassie surrounded by a force field of light at all times. This naturally included Cassie herself.

"Always see yourself as protected, honey," she said, "because as good as Ray is at keeping track of you, you need to be actively involved in your own protection as well."

Perhaps this was why there had been no further incidents of negative forces impinging on Ray's sensibilities. In any case, the first public service announcements for the Consortium of Light began being aired the last week of August without his picking up any negative reactions. He even wondered to himself if perhaps he'd been wrong about being followed that day when he and Cassie had gone to the movies; maybe the woman at the theater just didn't like little kids. Or maybe she didn't like little kids who had slightly effeminate male bodyguards! Still, he decided that when school started again, he'd continue to be on hand to escort Cassie to and from it. Just in case.

Response to the public service announcements was immediate and enthusiastic. In just a couple of weeks Adam was totally swamped with requests for more information and with letters from both individuals and groups desiring to sign on to the Consortium's bulletin board. Help came from the distaff side of the Consortium's innovators, with Lucy finding the time to help design some brochures, and Celeste Jacobson—Adonna strapped to her tummy in a Gerry pack—beginning to do volunteer office work, inputting data when Adam was installing the phone system or was otherwise occupied, doing a little bookkeeping, and answering the phones when they finally began to ring.

After she'd been working in the Consortium office for about two weeks, she said to Joe one night at supper, "You know, sugar, all these people—Cassie, Ray, Adam, Lucy, Sophie—they're just as sweet as they can be, warm, friendly, easy to be around. But I've been listening to their conversations, and they all do things people might consider just a little weird or crazy."

"Like what, hon?"

"Well, besides all that stuff about having died and come back, I understand Cassie thinks her cat talks to her. And Ray seems to get what he calls 'negative vibrations' when people are about to commit violent acts in his vicinity. And Adam was telling me Lucy channels a group of spirits, and she also does this sort of laying on of hands healing stuff. I mean, I had an aunt in North Carolina who was a root healer, but I'm just sort of surprised to find a white woman who calls herself a healer. And Sophie, as I understand it, talks to fairies or some such out in her garden. And then Adam was telling me he had to do this sort of physical trial in the wilderness last spring, and since then he's been seeing what he calls people's 'inner lights.' I told him I wasn't sure they all should tell people about these odd things they do or that have happened to them, because they might lose their credibility if people knew about all this."

"Well, hon," said Joe, "you could be right. On the other hand, lots of people who are considered 'visionaries' in history did literally have visions."

"Like who?"

"Like Abe Lincoln, for instance. Sometime when you go by the Lincoln Memorial, stop and really take a look at the eyes on that statue of ol' Abe. In the right light, he looks a little mad. I've often thought maybe to be a true visionary, a true transformer, you'd have to be just a little bit crazy."

Then he told her about his two encounters this last year with Dave Shumacher.

"You were either dreaming or hallucinating," she said firmly.

"Maybe," he said. "In fact, probably. The first time, he even said he was part of me, part of my subconscious. But he also implied he'd always *been* part of me, I mean, that Dave had been part of me when he was alive. There's an extrapolation from quantum physics, you know, that a single human mind is a hologram of a greater collective holographic mind, and thus has the capacity to know everything that any other mind knows. Or maybe has ever known or will ever know. I don't quite understand how it works—maybe there's no way to explain it in three-dimensional terms. But it does, daily, become more clear to me I'm part of you and you're part of me, and we're both part of everybody else. Now that I've been made aware of the possibility and am starting to look for evidence of it, I'm beginning to see how everyone just might have an effect on everything that exists, and how nothing really happens by accident."

"You don't think my having our baby at a restaurant was an accident?"

"No, I don't. Especially since a perfectly good midwife healer was on the premises. Anyway, I just think if they tell you any more stuff about their unusual experiences or perceptions, you should try to keep an open mind."

"Well," she said, "I'll do my best. But if that pot of impatiens in the window starts talking to me, I promise you, mister, I'm going to freak completely out!"

"Freak all you like," he said, "but just don't get impatient with it!"

*****

Another thing which occurred as the autumnal equinox drew near was Georgia's return to town, briefly and in a whirl of activity.

"I'm only here to move things out of my townhouse and lease it," she said to Sophie over the phone. "I've been in the Canary Islands since June, and I've met the *most* attractive man I've ever known, and he has asked me to move in with him. We've been quite an item for the last month! And if the arrangement works, I just may decide to become Mrs. Heinrich Lowenheim! Or perhaps I should say Frau Lowenheim. Heinrich is German."

Since a month was already longer than Sophie'd ever known Georgia to sustain a relationship, she decided this just might be the love of Georgia's life.

"What does he do for a living?" she asked.

"He's a builder—you know, a developer. Right now he's building a hotel complex in Los Christianos on Tenerife. The Germans are *very* big in the Canary Island tourist business, although it really is a kind of crossroads for travelers from all over Europe. I mean, the country's owned by Spain, but it's very global, really, with people from all over. You go into a bar or a restaurant, and you'll hear people speaking Spanish and German and Italian and French and British-accented English. I constantly find myself falling into a strange patois of muddled Spanglish with a little Deutsche sprinkled in for flavoring!

"But, anyway, the Canaries are just beginning to open up to American tourism, and I have this marvelous opportunity to be part of a new business that's going to appeal to conference planners from the States. So, I figured I'd rent out the townhouse for a year. Maybe this time next summer I'll be back to sell it. Especially if Heinrich and I actually get married. So," she said, having exhausted her own news, "what are you and Cassie doing these days? Keeping yourselves busy, I suppose?"

Sophie was amazed Georgia had totally missed all reports of the Cookie Lobby's activities. She filled her in briefly on what had happened in the seven and a half months she and Cassie had been together, leaving out the actual numbers of people they'd visited, as well as any mention of the interesting metaphysical talents of her and Cassie's new friends and fellow workers.

"I guess," she said, "if you're planning to get married, you definitely aren't going to want Cassie back again, am I right?"

"Oh, heavens, no!" said Georgia emphatically. "Well, I suppose you and the child should think about coming to visit me sometime. And, of course, I'll check in from time to time if and when I'm through D.C. But I thought we had sort of settled it already that you'd go on keeping her. You do still want to, don't you?" Georgia asked anxiously.

"Of course I do," said Sophie. "So far as I'm concerned, she and I are as bonded as if she were my own child. But I should mention our lobbying of Congress has stirred up adverse reactions from some fringe elements, and consequently we have a live-in bodyguard these days."

"Ooh," said Georgia, "a man on the premises! Any possibility of a romance for you from that quarter?"

"Hardly," said Sophie. She decided not to mention Ray's sexual persuasion to Georgia either.

"Well," said Georgia, having run out of interest in the subject, "I'm sure you're taking wonderful care of Cassandra. Give her a kiss for me," she offered perfunctorily, "and I'll be in touch with you both with a wedding invite, in the event there's a big event."

*****

The first week after the equinox was designated to be the official first week of Consortium activity across the country, and naturally, the first focus of that week's daily meditations and letter writing campaign was rain forest awareness. The time decided upon for the daily meditations was 4 p.m. EST, chosen out of practicality because it meant across the country most people would be at work in the afternoon, not at lunch, but not yet on their way home for the evening. Options for letter writing included congressmen, the president, and the heads of state of appropriate South American countries.

Adam had arranged for each caller who linked with the system to get information out to note whether and to whom a letter had been written the previous week. If the caller was a group, the Consortium asked for a tabulation of members who had written letters; they were encouraged to split their membership evenly in directing their letters to the possible recipients for the week.

By official count, although it had to be admitted there was no way to really tabulate results, some 7,000 pieces of mail had been sent either to the president or to congressmen, and approximately the same number of letters split among the heads of government of several tropical rainforest countries.

Either by coincidence or perhaps actually as a result of the Consortium's efforts, the following week it was learned that several Central and South American countries had begun actively negotiating with the U.S. and with each other about some solution to rain forest depletion.

Joe immediately put the Consortium in D.C.'s public eye by writing a column about their efforts. At the same time, one of the networks reported on the letter writing campaign's results in their evening news segment. And New Age radio stations around the country began calling to ask for the focus of the coming week, so they could announce it to their listeners, as well as play appropriate meditation music at the time of the focus.

By the end of October, the official mail tally was up to some 23,000 letters for the president and members of Congress. The focus for the week before had been aimed at getting government funding for renewable energy sources. The following week, several members of the House and Senate made statements that legislation on funding for renewable energy sources was to move up to priority status; the president in a press conference indicated he'd been apprised of a groundswell of interest in an energy policy for the country and particularly in the use of renewables and was himself making it a priority issue.

Every day the Consortium was receiving dozens more calls and letters from individuals and organizations wanting to become members. By the end of November, they calculated they had over 120,000 people meditating and generating letters, and the number seemed to be increasing exponentially on a daily basis.

And each day at 4 o'clock, whoever was in the office would gather together in a circle, holding hands, and take turns making a statement about the focus for the week, and just letting the energy flow around and through them as they visualized that focus coming to a positive, healing resolution.

That five minutes every afternoon was the peak point of the day. It was addictive. Adam found himself craving it for at least two hours, and often in the middle of the afternoon he'd catch Celeste looking at her watch, so he knew he wasn't alone. The cue, however, was the opening of the front door as Ray and Cassie came in from the school, usually just before 4:00.

When Adam and Celeste heard their footsteps upstairs, she would look at him, grin, and say, "Let's go get high!"

And then one afternoon, as they stood together in the circle, focusing with all their power on the project for that week, they realized the energy flowing through them was more than just what they were generating themselves, and that those across the country who were joining them had reached some sort of critical mass. For the energy became a tide that was physically palpable, energy you could almost touch, energy you could certainly feel, electrifying energy—powerful balm and benison. They felt as though they were levitating. Maybe they were.

When the meditation was over, Adam looked at Sophie and said, "Hey! I think the 100th sheep just came into our fold!"

*****

One afternoon about two weeks before Christmas, Sophie rang up Joe at the newspaper.

"I just got a call from Alexander Weiskopf, and Celeste thought I should call you right away. Do you know who he is?"

Her voice sounded more excited than Joe had ever heard it. He sifted through his mental Roladex.

"The name sounds familiar, but I'm not quite placing it," he said.

"He's the chairman of the American Alternatives Party. Don't you remember, they ran Arnold Adams for president in 1980 and '84."

"So," said Joe jokingly, "does he want you to run for president next year?"

There was a long silence. Then her voice, filled with awe at the very idea, said softly, "Yes, he does. He wants me to run for president."

"Ohmigod!" said Joe. He really had been just joking, he thought. Of course, he'd joked about it in the past, too. That day he'd first interviewed Sophie and Cassie, he'd joked about it.

"Do you have any idea in how many states the AAP is on the ballot?" he finally asked.

"Yes," she replied. "He told me. They're on the ballot in 32 states. They've actually run somebody in the last five general elections, though Adams is the only one whose candidacy ever made a splash nationally. What he said was, they've always in the past picked somebody who had a solid academic or business background, who they thought was a creative problem solver—somebody with really innovative ideas that might catch fire in the imagination of the American people. And with a carefully coordinated publicity campaign, they've tried to push him into national prominence.

"In the past," she continued, "Weiskopf says the best they've managed to do was get some of their candidate's innovative ideas adopted by one of the major parties, usually the Democrats, in their platform."

"I think I'm getting the picture," said Joe.

"Yes, well, it's obvious, isn't it?" said Sophie. "They want me to run on their ticket because the Cookie Lobby and the Consortium of Light have already put me in the public eye, what with the public service announcements, and all the news stories in national magazines about how well we've done. Actually, we're already offering a lot of the alternatives the AAP supports. And the public has already caught fire to a certain extent. My 15 minutes of fame have been extended to about an hour this last year."

"So what're you going to do?" asked Joe.

"That's why I called you," she said. "I told him I'd have to think about it for a couple of days, weigh the pros and cons, that sort of thing. I don't know if my running for president would help or hurt the Consortium. It would certainly take me away from energizing our venture from this office. I'd have to do a lot of public speaking. And I'd have to do a lot of studying up in order to be able to field questions on all the issues."

"Maybe not as much as you might think," said Joe. "The Consortium is an issue-oriented organization, and you're a pretty quick study, I've noticed, when it comes to remembering facts."

"Yes, well, my gut reaction is that it would be very good for our cause of changing consciousness for me to be in the public eye this way. It would get me platforms all over the country, plus the opportunity to gently encourage the idea of networking and bridging with other networks as the most powerful source of transformation. So I think campaigning is probably a good idea."

"I'm thinking it might be," said Joe. "But what sort of staff will they give you? And what sort of funding does the party have?"

"Weiskopf said the funding was moderate—just a few million in the campaign coffers, which is why they wanted to run somebody who already had a certain amount of name recognition. And they do have a staff of professionals with whom they've worked before, plus some wild-eyed young radical innovators who are eager to try their wings at running a campaign. But he also said they had some money set aside in the event I wanted to appoint people of my own to my staff."

"Who did you have in mind?" asked Joe, trying to think of people he was acquainted with who'd had experience on the campaign trail as advisors, research assistants, speech writers, and so forth.

"Why you, of course!" she replied, as if there were only one logical answer. "And perhaps Lucy. I wouldn't consider batting around the country without some of my family with me. You're my man so far as publicity goes—we all know we'd never have come this far with either the Lobby or the Consortium without your expertise!

"And Lucy's the most accurate judge of people of all of us," Sophie continued. "Adam thinks she would be a good personal secretary, to help whoever the AAP assigns me in the way of secretarial staffing. It would, of course, take her away from her art for the next nine months or so. But frankly, I think her intuitive guidance could be invaluable in helping deal with people." Joe had noticed Sophie often used the word "intuitive" as a euphemism for "psychic."

"What's the pay for a publicity staff job?" asked Joe.

She mentioned a figure more than twice what he was making at the newspaper annually.

"The only problem," she added, "is if you were to join me, it would take you away from your job at the paper, and, of course, the job as head of campaign publicity would only last 'til November. So that's why Celeste wanted me to call you right away. Unless you took a leave of absence in the meantime, you'd be out of a job at the end of the campaign."

"Not necessarily," said Joe. "You might still need a good speech writer or press secretary at the end of the campaign."

"Whatever for?" asked Sophie blankly.

"Because, dear lady, if you run for president, you just might win!"

"Oh, dear," said Sophie softly, the awe slipping back into her voice, "I hadn't really considered that!"

*****

Senator Snailer heard the news about Sophie's candidacy between Christmas and New Year's.

He was fully aware that major shift had been taking place for months in public attitude toward rain forest management. Thousands of ordinary people had been phoning and writing their congressmen, saying they had suddenly realized their opinions mattered, and that they wanted some real action on the part of the federal government in setting up avenues for the marketing of rain forest products. Thousands more had written to the heads of foreign governments, volunteering their support both at home and abroad of any creative initiatives that would curb rain forest destruction. There had in fact been such a groundswell of letter writing from all quarters that even gold mining activity was being affected. Snailer quivered with rage when he thought of what this might mean for U.S. investments, not to mention his own financial commitments.

And the Cookie Lobby's literature had brought to public attention as no information campaign before it had done that the South American rain forests were the only source of certain medicinal plants that would no longer be available on the planet if their species were destroyed. As a result of public awareness of this fact, pharmaceutical companies had begun a campaign of their own to get a piece of the action. Who could tell where this all might end?

Snailer's reaction to Sophie's candidacy therefore was to call together all the members of his staff and get them to contact those who had worked most diligently for him during his recent reelection campaign.

Snailer hadn't gotten elected to four straight terms in the Senate without knowing how to manipulate his constituency with fear tactics related to empowerment of women, minorities, and of course, homosexuals. As it happened, his power base extended well beyond his home state. Indeed, he was part of a strong good ol' boy network himself from years back which consisted of large numbers of politicians and businessmen who would have joined organizations like the KKK if such liaisons hadn't been a threat to their public image.

Among his supporters were men who had grown fat on the status quo and who had also become proficient at foot-dragging, while still appearing to be responsible, forward-thinking citizens. And there were plenty of indoctrinated women among his supporters as well, who still believed a woman's proper place was in the home, not in the boardroom.

These were people who defined their actions by the letter of the law, not necessarily its spirit, and who sought clearly delineated black-and-white issues as moral guideposts. And if they didn't always quite manage to stay on the clean white side of the boundary, they at least tried hard to look as if they did.

Included in the many faces of this reactionary element were power moguls around the country who had found the means to fund Snailer's last campaign. Among them was his good friend Rev. Bobby Buttram, one of the few televangelists whose name had remained unsullied during the '80s, and who still had a popular show originating in Nashville.

"Ya gotta help me do something about this woman's candidacy, Bobby," said Snailer, who fairly sputtered when he had to mention her. "I've been aware of her subtle tactics since early last year when she and the child and that homosexual henchman of theirs were delivering their cookies to Congress. Now, she doesn't use the term much in public, but you're aware, I'm sure, that she's an admitted New Age adherent. She's a servant of Satan, no question about it, sent to lead people astray with her meditating tactics and her talk of a global transformation. Why, I read she's even talked about some sort of plan God has for mankind's evolution, how we're all supposed to become hermaphrodites or some such nonsense! That's what comes from consorting with queers!"

"Now, get calm, Marvin!" urged Buttram. "I've already had two shows this month on the hidden perversions of the New Age, but I can't come right out and condemn her candidacy specifically. I have to be subtle myself, you know."

Snailer almost smiled, for his experience had been that when he got on a roll in front of the cameras, Buttram was about as subtle as a jackhammer.

"You sound as if you already have a plan," he said hopefully.

"I do, I do," said Buttram. "I've been keeping track of this woman and her activities for some time, and you don't have to work to convince me some of her ideas are dangerous. Oh, they sound pretty on the surface, with all the words like 'peace,' and 'love,' and 'healing.' But these New Agers would have you believe the word 'Christ' refers to an office rather than to the person of Jesus, and that anyone can attain to that state of self realization. And that's blasphemy, pure and simple! We all know that man's inner nature isn't sinless or unblemished, and that without the fear of God and His just punishments, we'd all be damned."

Snailer nodded emphatically in agreement.

Buttram went on, "I tell you what I'll do that will show this Nussbaum woman up for what she is. I'll ask all the candidates who are running for president in this election to come on my show early in the campaign to discuss their stands on certain moral and ethical issues. This kind of debate hasn't ever taken place before. They're all likely to decline, of course, but when *she* does, we'll make as much capital out of it as possible, saying she refused because she doesn't want people to know the true hidden agenda behind her organization."

"Suppose she and the others all agree to come on?" asked Snailer.

"Then we'll just have to think about whether we want them all on together or in separate but equal time slots," said Buttram. "But don't you worry; when I have her in front of the cameras,

I'll make hash of her," he added simply. "She won't be able to hold her own in the face of *my* interpretation of the Bible."

*****

It was an interesting idea, inviting the candidates for equal airtime on shows with a reactionary slant, and Snailer's election team had ingratiated themselves years ago with all the *bona fide* backlash elements. And so, much to her surprise, Sophie was informed by her campaign staff that she was being sought as a guest, along with all the other candidates, to appear in a series of shows known to be funded by and directed toward America's Bible belt.

"You can't go!" said Joe emphatically. "They'll do their best to demolish you."

"They'll fail," said Sophie. "I'm a pretty tough bird. Moreover, you need to remember, I'm running to make our positions known. In a way, I'm kind of a fanatic myself, trying to convert as many people as possible to a consciousness that believes a healthy, safe, free, and peaceful planet is possible, especially if we recognize the value and equality and connectivity of everyone and everything on it. And here I have an opportunity to be a bridge between the Biblical 'strict constructionists,' so to speak, and the 'hopeful futurists,' as I like to think of them.

"Maybe it would be nice to win the election. I can't really judge that, since I've never been president before. But we've all agreed it's important for me to run, because it will make our causes known not just in this country but around the globe."

"Yes," said Joe, "but if they make you look really bad this early in your candidacy, it will do more harm than good."

"What do we know about risk-taking?" asked Sophie patiently.

"I know I took a risk signing on as your campaign manager!" said Joe, dramatically slapping his head with the back of his hand as if he had acquired an instantaneous migraine.

Sophie snorted a laugh. "That's not what I mean."

"I know," sang Cassie, who had been doing her homework at Sophie's desk, just to be near her while she was in town for the weekend. "The bigger the stakes the bigger the risk? So the more you risk, the more you stand to gain."

"That's part of it," said Sophie nodding. "What's the other part?"

"That people who don't take risks are acting out of fear."

"Good," said Sophie, slipping into her schoolteacher mode. "And what do we know about fear?"

"That Tolly Burkan, who taught you how to firewalk, says it stands for 'false evidence appearing real'."

"Excellent!" said Sophie.

"The kid's been brainwashed," muttered Joe.

"And what," said Sophie, ignoring him, "are you supposed to listen to *before* you take a risk?"

"Your tummy!" said Cassie.

"Correct!"

"What do I win?" asked Cassie.

"Some chocolate covered raisins and a trip to Peoria," groused Joe.

"Oh, goody! I've never been to Peoria," said Cassie. She looked from Joe to Sophie, recognized the interchange was over, and went back to doing her homework.

"Cassie's right," said Sophie to Joe. "When in doubt about what to do, ask your tummy. Or that little voice inside. Yes, I'm more than a tad nervous about accepting an invitation to go into Bobby Buttram's lion's den. But that little voice inside me says I need to go."

"Are you sure it's not your ego?" asked Joe.

"I don't think so," said Sophie. "As I understand the term 'ego,' it would be encouraging me to do it for self-aggrandizement. Or it would be telling me the *opposition* is too stupid to come off looking good. But neither of those things is true. I certainly don't care at my age what people think of me personally, and I've been around long enough to know Buttram and his ilk pull a lot of weight with certain people in this country.

"But the real truth is, the opposition is only *in* opposition because it is afraid of *my position.* If I can do anything to dissipate that fear, which is really 'false evidence appearing real,' then I have an obligation to do it. At least that's what my tummy is telling me right now."

"Okay," said Joe resignedly. "But I'm going to do everything I can between now and the time you appear on the Buttram show to change your tummy's mind!"

*****

Sophie and Cassie got a letter from Georgia just after the first of the year saying she and the builder were planning to be married in May. For a change, Georgia was tuned in to their activities, and after extending to them an invitation to the wedding, in which she actually volunteered to pay their way to the Canary Islands, she closed her note by asking, "If I had kept Cassie, would I be running for president now?"

Sophie wrote back, "If you want to run for president, come right ahead, provided Cassie and I can move to the Canary Islands and I can marry your builder!"

Sophie's showing in the early primaries where the American Alternatives Party was on the ballot were modest but respectable. Clearly her Cookie Lobby had caught the public's fancy, and the efforts of the Consortium of Light, which continued to gain converts daily, certainly wasn't hurting her candidacy. Polls run early in the year indicated she was favored by 11 percent of those who were planning to vote; by spring, she was favored by 18 percent. Not enough to win, of course, but a good showing for someone in a third party who had no background whatsoever in politics. But of just as much interest was how the rest of the vote split almost equally between candidates of the other two parties.

The incumbent, President Flushing, in fact had 42 percent favoritism in the polls. The three top candidates for the opposition party had a 26, 8, and 6 percent split.

News pundits, who enjoyed predicting the future about as much as do astrologers, but who to Sophie's mind didn't do half as good a job, had fun pointing out Sophie was the monkey wrench of the campaign. Of course, they didn't take Sophie's candidacy any more seriously than Sophie usually took herself.

What they said was that should the major opposition party decide to include some of Sophie's creative solutions to world problems into their platform, and should she and the two less popular opposition candidates drop out of the race, the opposition frontrunner would perhaps garner the majority of the swing votes and thus make a better showing than the incumbent. On the other hand, should the two less popular opposition candidates drop out while Sophie hung on, she just might pick up their following herself, to make a better showing than the opposition frontrunner. In which case the Alternatives Party would supplant the opposition party as the more viable of the two less popular parties. All of which speculation seemed to Sophie very similar to an Abbot and Costello comedy routine. All in all, she was rather enjoying the campaign trail. She'd never minded rubber chicken luncheons even before she'd stopped eating chicken—her Saul must really be laughing, she thought, knowing she hadn't had to cook anything for herself in over three months.

The only thing bothering her was a lack of time with Cassie. She hadn't taken on responsibility for the child to run off and leave her. Of course, Ray was a wonderful mother substitute, and he and Cassie really enjoyed each other's company. But she didn't want a substitute mother for Cassie—she wanted to be with her herself.

Cassie, naturally, was quite firm about *not* being a barrier to Sophie's candidacy.

"It isn't every day one gets to run for president of the United States," she'd said way back at the beginning of the campaign. "And you're the first woman to run, which is a real coup. You simply can't refuse. And if you were to refuse because of me, think what a burden you'd be putting on *me*. I mean, if the country goes down the john, it would be my fault, wouldn't it, for getting in the way of the best possible candidate? That's too heavy a responsibility for you to put on me!" she said, smiling slyly. "After all, I'm just a little kid."

So Sophie pushed down her anxiety at not being on the spot for Cassie at all times and just tried to arrange to be home as many weekends as possible. She was looking forward to Easter vacation, though, more than she ever had before, even when she was teaching, because Cassie was going to be able to spend a whole week traveling with her then.

Since Cassie had stopped making public appearances and since there was a whole new set of public service announcements running for the Consortium which didn't have Cassie in them, Ray had picked up no negative vibrations on her behalf. He occasionally got little niggling negatives when Sophie appeared in the news, but she had her own set of bodyguards out on the campaign trail. And it seemed whatever had been tracking Cassie and later Sophie during the Cookie Lobby's efforts had finally been placated. Nonetheless, he stayed in the McLean house.

"Cassie can't do without your mothering if I'm gone," insisted Sophie, "even if there's no longer a threat to her safety."

He had agreed, for these people had filled the void in his life left by Colin's passing. They were more family than he'd experienced since the death of his mother.

*****

For reasons having nothing to do with Sophie, the Bobby Buttram show had been postponed again and again. As it happened, both the front-running opposition party candidate and the incumbent president had decided they did indeed want to participate, and Buttram and Snailer had discussed whether it would be to their advantage to let Sophie appear at the same time, or to schedule her at a different date. They finally agreed it would do the more conservative president no harm to appear on the same stage where Sophie was likely to meet her philosophical demise at the hands of the fundamentalist Buttram. And the show, usually just a staple for Christian broadcasters, was for this one segment to be picked up by all the commercial networks as well; the more people who saw it, they gloated, the bigger Sophie's fall would be.

Thus, when a firm date was finally scheduled, it turned out it was to be the same weekend in May as Georgia's wedding. Sophie was most distressed, especially since Georgia had already arranged for round trip tickets to the Canary Islands.

"You'll have to go to the wedding in my place, Ray," Sophie insisted. "I can't see having Cassie miss it altogether, just because I'm not going to be able to go."

So Ray and Cassie had gone into D.C. one afternoon and applied for passports.

A couple of places back behind them in the line at the passport office was a middle aged man in dark glasses. He was coatless, but he did have on a tie with his off-white shirt. Cassie had the vague impression she'd seen him before, but the excitement and interest of filing for a passport took her attention when they got up to the window, and she soon forgot even to mention him to Ray. When Cassie and Ray were through at the window and left the office, the man waited a full two minutes longer in the line before getting out of it and leaving himself.

And he didn't follow them, as he actually had done often during the past eight months. Ray had never picked up on him because the man felt no animosity toward him or the child. He was just a watcher, paid to follow, paid to keep track. And so, when he left the passport office, he went to a phone and made his report to the person from whom he received his pay.

When she hung up the phone, Miss Pender smiled. She would find out through a contact in the State Department just where Gonzales and the Allman child were going. The senator was going to be very pleased to learn about the impending trip of these devil's spawn. How wise it had been of the senator, when he'd found out about this Gonzales fellow's ability to feel animosity, to start having them followed by people who had no feeling toward them at all. How wise the senator had been to warn her and the rest of his staff to be cautious about their negative thoughts, so Gonzales would be lulled into complacency.

They had all been careful. They had not indulged in active hatred. And after all, what had they to fear anymore? The senator had implied that when the time was right, he would see to it these evil people were taken care of.

If her sixth sense was correct, she thought as she dialed up her contact at the State Department, the time when all these evil people would be laid low was very soon now. Very soon.

*****

Ray and Cassie had flown from Dulles to JFK on Friday morning and spent a lot of time and money in the east terminal building waiting for Aer Europa to open its ticket desk and take their luggage. Cassie, who'd never been out of the country before, was really excited by the prospect of visiting a place off the coast of Africa but owned by Spain, which catered principally to Germans and British.

"I'm going to have so *much* to write about in my journal when I get back to school!" she'd enthused.

The trip from JFK to Tenerife had been just about six hours; with the six-hour time difference, it made exactly 12 hours difference from the time they had left—3:20 p.m. on Friday afternoon to 3:20 a.m. the next morning. Needless to say, when they arrived, Cassie was no longer enthusiastic, but limp and ready for bed.

"Once we get through the passport check and get our luggage," said Ray, "we're to take a taxi to the villa your aunt Georgia and soon-to-be uncle Heinrich are currently renting in San Miguel," said Ray. "Just hold on a little longer, kiddo."

Cassie had been fantasizing for a couple of weeks about what this trip would be like. She'd been permitted to get out of school, had been shopping with Lucy the previous weekend for an absolutely gorgeous dress to wear to Georgia's wedding, and had a crystal dinner bell carefully wrapped and cushioned in her backpack as a wedding present for her aunt, a gift she'd chosen and paid for herself.

As the plane touched down in the Tenerife airport, some scattered applause indicated a few people were pronouncing the rather choppy landing good. Cassie'd flown a lot around the U.S. and wasn't impressed. Except that maybe, with all the plane crashes that happened regularly around the world, the applause was for getting down at all! She decided she'd think that idea through. When she wasn't quite so tired. Maybe next time, she'd applaud if they just got down, no matter how.

The plane taxied for a while, and she looked up and smiled at Ray. She loved him so much; he was sort of a mom and dad both, with his gentleness and nurturing, and his protectiveness and strength.

She knew she'd been really lucky. A lot of kids who lost their parents—what a strange way to put it, *lost*, as if she'd somehow been careless and misplaced them—might have had to go to an orphanage or a foster home. Or, heaven forbid, to live with a relative like Aunt Georgia fulltime! She was happy to be visiting, but she wouldn't want to live there. No, she'd been so lucky, to have someone like Sophie as her guardian and friend, and Ray as her bodyguard and friend. And Emerson as her pet and friend.

The plane came to a stop, and Ray got up and opened the luggage rack overhead, handing down her Polaroid camera and her backpack. He donned his own backpack and camera bag, then let her out into the aisle in front of him.

Once they were out of the plane, they followed signs and crowds to the passport desks.

"Here," said Ray, "you need to hold your own passport as you go through."

She went through first, watching as the official stamped her passport, and she was examining the stamp when Ray handed his passport to the official at the desk. And then suddenly Ray was surrounded by people in uniforms, and she heard the word "Interpol," and she forgot about the stamp on her passport as she became alarmed for him, and there were four men bigger than Ray surrounding him and pulling at him, and he was saying something in what she was pretty sure was Spanish, and then he shouted to her, "Cassie! Call your Aunt Georgia!" and he was being pulled away down a corridor, and she ran after him, but a tall, heavyset man who had been on the plane with them stepped in her way and said, "Hello, hello, what have we here? A little girl what's got separated from her folks? Well, you just come with me, lass, an' I'll take ya to yer Aunt Georgie."

"You know my aunt?" said Cassie disbelievingly.

"I certainly do," said the man, as he put a huge hand on her shoulder and drew a handkerchief out of his pocket.

"I can't go without Ray," Cassie started to argue, but the man pulled her around, blocking a view of her with his body so no one who might have noticed the furor could see, and he put the handkerchief over her mouth.

"That's it, now. No need to cry. Yes, yes," he said soothingly. "Well, now, the poor little thing is just worn out, she is."

And she smelled the strong smell of bananas, and suddenly she couldn't keep her eyes open.

And then, as had happened only once before, she wasn't in her body anymore, but up above herself, watching as the man stuffed the handkerchief into his pocket, picked up her limp body, slung her backpack over one shoulder, and placed her over the other, in a semblance of tenderness. He went past the customs guard, and though she didn't understand the language he spoke, she knew he was saying they had no other luggage and that his little girl was very tired. And then they were in a taxi, and she was hovering above it, and then inside it, watching as the man dumped her body into a corner and ordered the taxi driver to go to the dock in Los Christianos.

No question about it, thought the astral Cassie. I've been kidnapped!

PART III
The Second Coming

What had come to be known as the "morals and ethics" debate on the Buttram show, but which Sophie had come to refer to privately with her family as the New Inquisition, was scheduled to take place at 8 p.m. Saturday evening, Nashville time. Ray had said he would call to let them know he and Cassie had landed safely sometime that Saturday morning. But by the time the taxi came to drive Sophie and her AAP-assigned bodyguard to Dulles to catch their flight, Ray still hadn't called in.

Sophie tried placing a call to the number she had for Georgia with the overseas operator, but the line was busy, busy, busy, so she left it to Celeste to try to make contact.

"I'm very nervous!" she admitted to Lucy when they met at the airport. "I dreamed about midnight that Cassandra was by the side of the road, and a produce trucker picked her up and lashed her to a stalk of bananas, and said, 'I'm taking you to the Queen of Catalonia'."

"Do you think that means anything?" asked Lucy.

"I've found my dreams always mean something, but I seldom can figure out what until after the fact, when I can interpret the symbols in the light of what really happens to me. It's like seeing 'through a glass darkly.' Needless to say, I couldn't sleep for the rest of the night. Did your Ancestors say anything about Cassie this morning in your meditation?"

"I'm afraid they do not always speak about a subject unless asked. And while they will advise me on my own actions without my going into meditation, they seldom tell me anything about others when I am fully conscious. If you like, I can meditate once we are on the plane and it takes off, and perhaps find something out to soothe your mind."

Later, at 20,000 feet, Lucy closed her eyes and drifted for a few minutes. When she came back to full consciousness, she had a little frown on her face.

"I am told to tell you Cassie is not where she was sent, nor is she currently with Ray, who has been detained. But she is safe, and forces are at work to keep her that way."

Lucy paused, looking very uncomfortable, before continuing, "I am also told to say you will likely receive a message before the day's end that will cause you great fear, unless you hold fast to your faith. Do not be swayed to act foolishly out of fear."

"Is that it?" asked Sophie.

"That's all they broadcast," said Lucy. "I don't feel very good about this, because I know you're worried about Cassie and Ray, and this sounds as though they haven't made it to their destination yet."

Sophie asked the stewardess to make a call to the Consortium office to see if Celeste had yet managed to get through to Georgia.

When she came on the line, Celeste sounded as if she were bordering on hysteria herself.

"We had a lot of trouble getting through to Georgia because she was on the phone trying to get Ray out of police custody. Someone had apparently told Interpol that Ray had a deadly disease and should be quarantined, so she and Heinrich spent all day finding out how to get him sprung. But in the meantime, Cassie has completely disappeared. Ray's still in custody, but he did get to talk to them, and he said the last he saw of her she was standing in a hallway at Tenerife Airport as he was being dragged off to confinement. He told her to call Georgia, but she never did." Celeste was on the verge of tears. "What do we do now?" she moaned.

Sophie, who felt physically ill at the news of Cassie's disappearance, said quietly, "We wait. But you be sure to contact me if there's any update, anything at all."

*****

"I don't feel good about this," said Nelson, "an' *I* ain't gonna be the one who sets the explosives! She's a nice little kid, an' I don't think she's never done nobody no harm, an' I ain't gonna be the one who's responsible for killin' her!"

"Well, ya don't have to be the one responsible, ya dumb ox," said Logan. "I'm the one what's supposed to set the charge. It's what the senator said, now, didn' he? So you jus' make sure she's tied securely when we set her adrift. An' you damn well better make sure that . . . ."

170

The hatch closed on the rest of the sentence, leaving Cassie to wonder what else it was Nelson was supposed to do. She lay immobile on the lower bunk of the cabin, as she had for most of the last 24 hours. Nelson had fed her some soup about mid-day, and he'd untied her hands, though not her feet, long enough to let her go to the toilet.

So she was going to die again, it seemed. Gee, she thought, it had only been a year and a half since the last time. She smiled a little to herself. Maybe if you could do it often enough, you could actually get good at it!

Strange as it felt, she wasn't particularly worried. It was getting dark in the cabin, and as dusk settled in, she could see the angel lights beginning to glow and knew she wasn't alone. If Nelson and Logan blew her up, it should at least be a pretty fast exit out of the body, she thought. After all, there wouldn't be a body there anymore, just lots of little pieces. Probably better than just being dropped over the side to drown, a fate she didn't think she'd much fancy, as she'd read in a Red Cross safety manual at school that it could take a couple of minutes to lose consciousness after breathing in water, and she figured she would automatically struggle rather than just letting go.

In any case, the fizzy bubble angel lights were growing brighter, as they always did whenever she was in the dark. She thought about Emerson, and how the cat had said the lights were always surrounding her, even when she couldn't see them. She missed being able to talk to the cat, but it was comforting to be able to see the lights. Last night, Logan had left a light on all night, even though she'd asked him to turn it off. Maybe he'd left it on *because* she'd asked him to turn it off. In any case, she was glad nobody was paying attention at the moment to the settling darkness.

There would surely be compensations to dying, she thought. She'd get to see Mom and Daddy and Timmy again. Though she was sorry she wouldn't have a chance to say goodbye to Sophie and Ray and Emerson, and Adam and Lucy and Celeste and Joe. And baby Adonna, who would be a year old next week, on Sophie's birthday. It would have been nice to have wished Sophie and Adonna a happy birthday one more time.

And then she heard a voice, not so high pitched as the voice of Emerson when it spoke inside her head, but very like it in quality otherwise. It was something, some creature, and like Emerson so often did, it was trying to soothe her.

"We are here, child. Be peaceful, we will help you."

"Who are you?" she whispered. "And where are you? I can't see you."

"We are outside your ship," said the voice, "in the water. We have followed the ship since you were put on it, for we saw the lights that surround you. You are different from most beings of your kind, because of the brightness of your lights. But we heard your sadness for your friends who are not here. If you can get into the water, we will help you. There are many of us; we can help much."

"Who are you?" asked Cassie, in her mind this time.

"We are the people of the sea, whom you call dolphins. We have helped others of your kind, and we can help you if you can get into the water."

"But I'm all tied up, and this room is locked," thought Cassie.

"We sensed that was so," said the voice. "But we will wait, and perhaps things will change."

"The men have been given orders to blow up the ship with explosives," said Cassie mentally.

"Yes, we have seen in their minds what is intended for you. But they picture putting you in a rowboat, and setting a charge to go off after a time, so the ship you are now on can get away before the boat blows up."

Cassie got this part of what she was being told not in words so much as in concepts.

"What you must do, if you possibly can," the voice continued, "is get out of the rowboat and into the water. We will separate you from the boat before it blows up, and do our best to keep you afloat. Do not be afraid of the water. We will not let you drown."

Yes, thought Cassie, this was really quite an interesting experience, though she hadn't much liked the kidnapping part of it. But if she got out alive after all, would she ever have a story to write for her journal at school!

*****

Ray was finally released from his confinement at about 8 p.m., Tenerife time. During the course of the day he'd been forced to submit to a complete physical and a blood test. But just before 8 o'clock, the doctor who'd been called in to examine him and draw his blood came with some forms for him to sign.

"You read Spanish?" asked the doctor. "You have a Mexican name."

"*Si*," said Ray. "*¿Por que?*"

The doctor explained the forms were merely a formality, a release required by the Spanish government in the event Ray came down with some illness they had not uncovered in their tests.

"You didn't find anything?"

"*Nada*," replied the doctor. "You are as strong as a camel, like they breed here on the islands. Somebody played a joke on you, but one in very bad taste. You know someone who doesn't like you, maybe?"

"Maybe," said Ray noncommittally.

Did this mean he was now testing negative for the HIV virus? Somehow that didn't really matter much at the moment—what had happened to Cassie was uppermost in his mind.

When he had dressed, had been given back his passport and other papers, and finally stepped out into the hall, he found Georgia and Heinrich waiting for him.

"We notified the local police about Cassandra's disappearance early this morning," said Georgia, "but we still haven't word one about what might have happened to her."

"Vell, ve haf *vun* vurd," argued Heinrich in heavily accented English. "Vun of the customs guards remembers seeing a man vith no luggage carrying a sleeping child out of the terminal. But dat iss all ve know."

"We know one other thing," said Ray.

"What's that?" asked Georgia.

"That I've been a prime idiot for believing just because I wasn't picking up any negative vibes the child was safe. I've been thinking about this all day while I twiddled my thumbs in custody. Whoever took Cassie had to know we were on that flight. So we've been followed, possibly for several months, and doubtless by someone or some group that's figured out how to get around my internal warning radar.

"Given that Sophie is now running for president, the most logical reason for kidnapping Cassie is to use her to force Sophie to do or to *not* do something. The most likely suspect is someone with different political views. And the person who keeps coming to my mind is Snailer."

"You mean the senator?" asked Georgia.

"The very one," said Ray. "Let's contact your police and see if Snailer is registered as owning any property here in the islands. Maybe," he said in a tone of voice that almost belied his hopeful words, "we'll find her safe and sound, holed up in a villa somewhere hereabouts."

*****

Joe, who had been informed of Cassie's disappearance by Celeste, met Sophie and Lucy at the door of their Nashville hotel the minute their taxi pulled up and warned them quietly to keep the news from other members of the campaign staff who were meeting Sophie in Nashville, pending receipt of more information. He recommended they stay by the phone in their suite, and he handled the canceling of all Sophie's appointments for the rest of the day until her appearance that evening on the Buttram show. They would not, as yet, notify the press, he said, in case the disappearance was a true kidnapping and the perpetrators were to make some demands.

About every 20 minutes, Lucy made an effort to call Georgia. But it was nearly 4 o'clock Nashville time when Sophie finally made contact with Ray directly.

"Lucy has asked her guides for more information, and we now think Cassie may be in a boat somewhere. The Ancestors say she is on the water. Ray, I don't know if this is going to be any help at all, it may be a blind lead, but see if there are any boats registered having the name of 'The Queen of Catalonia.' Or maybe some banana boats going to Catalonia."

She told Ray about her dream of the previous night, and he promised he'd check all the possible combinations of names for boats currently registered or docked in the area.

As soon as she'd hung up, the red light on her telephone began to blink. Lucy offered to dial the desk.

"Yes, ma'am," said the sweet belle desk clerk who answered. "While y'all were on the phone, someone delivered a letter for Miz Nussbaum. We wanted to know if y'all'd like us to send it up right now?"

"Yes, please."

In less than five minutes a boy appeared at their door with an envelope. He was ushered in by the staff bodyguard, who waited while Lucy gave the kid a tip, then ushered him back out and closed the door. Lucy handed the envelope to Sophie, who opened it carefully, holding it only by its edges.

The message was printed in block letters with a red crayon: "LET BUTTRAM MAKE A FOOL OF YOU TONIGHT. AT THE END OF THE SHOW, ON THE AIR, CANCEL YOUR CAMPAIGN. DO NOT NOTIFY THE POLICE, OR THE CHILD WILL DIE."

"Get Joe quick!" said Sophie. "We have to decide what to do right away!"

*****

From about 5 p.m. on, Lucy spent most of her energy on the phone with the office of the Tenerife police, sometimes talking with the officer assigned to the kidnapping, sometimes with Ray or Georgia or Heinrich. But no breakthrough of any sort came until nearly 7:00, just about the time they were to leave for the television studio, when Ray came on the line with the information that there was indeed a yacht named *Reina de Catalan*, a small sea-going vessel, owned by an American business enterprise, which had docked earlier in the week in Los Christianos. A check indicated the yacht was not presently in the slip it had been assigned. The police were still trying to trace the members of the corporate group that owned the boat.

Which meant it, and Cassie, could be just about anywhere else on the face of the globe.

"The authorities here say they can begin scanning the waters around the islands with helicopters as soon as it starts getting light," said Ray. He was trying to sound hopeful, but Lucy could hear the frustration in his voice when he added, "That's about another four hours."

"If it's any help, Ray," said Lucy consolingly, "I've been told there are other forces at work to keep Cassie safe. At least that's what the Ancestors say."

Neither of them mentioned the kidnapper's note, for they had all agreed not to energize the threat by giving it credibility.

"Just keep affirming she is going to be found safe and whole."

Well, thought Ray as they rang off this time, if I'm no longer HIV positive, any sort of miracle is possible!

When Lucy had hung up, Joe appeared from his room with a pad and a cellular phone like the one he usually carried when he was working, which was most of the time since he had joined Sophie's campaign.

"Under the circumstances, and until we can tell someone else on the staff the situation, you'll need to be our control central. Here's the number for the Nashville police, in the event they need to be informed at some point about events. Use the hotel phone for calling Tenerife; use this phone for calling me at the TV studio."

For the last half hour while Lucy had been on the phone, Sophie and Joe had been agonizing over the pros and cons of calling in the FBI and the CIA. Because Cassie had been kept out of the news for so many months, it appeared the police on Tenerife had not yet tumbled to the connection between the missing child and the American lady who was running for president of her country. What would be the benefits of involving U.S. authorities? What would be the detractions?

They had to assume the kidnap note was real since no one but a handful of people yet knew about Cassie's disappearance. If Sophie agreed on national television to drop out of the campaign, would the kidnappers really return Cassie? What was to keep Sophie from changing her mind as soon as she got Cassie back, saying she had been forced to drop out by a kidnapper's threat? Why, she could pick up her banner and start running again; it was still six months until the election. Surely, whoever had taken the child had something else in mind, and Sophie didn't really want to admit what that might be.

"If Cassie has been taken by one of our old friends who used to send her venomous vibes every time she was on television, then perhaps my campaign is only part of the reason why she's been kidnapped," she said finally. "I mean, it isn't logical for someone to have taken her simply to stop my election, when the election isn't even coming up 'til November. No, I think there's more to it. I can't help thinking someone has a vendetta against Cassie for her own sake, or perhaps against the two of us together. For a while there, she became a kind of focus because of her ingenuousness and candor about her belief that God loves everybody, no matter what. In some circles, like the one I'm going to be in tonight, that sort of belief is anathema."

She looked hard at Joe before continuing, "And then again, maybe it has nothing to do with Cassie per se. In any case, my fear reaction is to think they want to destroy me utterly."

"And how would they go about that?" asked Joe.

Sophie waited a long time before finally answering, "By killing her no matter what I do."

*****

Nelson had come down shortly before midnight and let Cassie go to the head again. When he retied her hands afterward, he started muttering to himself.

"Nobody tol' me when I agreed to run this tub I'd have to be involved in a kidnapping. I don't like it and I don't wanna be part of it. One slip up, and we'll have the FBI an' the CIA an' who knows what other police forces crawlin' all over us."

"If you don't want to be part of it, Mr. Nelson," said Cassie, "then why don't you just tell Mr. Logan he shouldn't have kidnapped me, and you can take me back to land and call my aunt to come get me. I won't tell anybody where I've been. I'll say I ran away!"

"Ya don' unnerstan', kid," said Nelson. "Logan knows some stuff about me, and if I try to cross him, he'll finger me. An' then some night when I least expect it, wham! Somebody'll hit me with a board an' I'll be instant fishbait. An' besides, he's the man with the firearms on this ship. If I don' keep my riggin' taut, he's liable to shoot you an' me both. And on top o' that," he added sadly, "you've seen my face, kid, an' you could I.D. me. Even if ya' said you wouldn't, you would eventually."

"Well, it's okay, Mr. Nelson," said Cassie. "I know you're sorry for what you think you have to do. Maybe not quite so sorry that you won't go ahead and do it, but a little bit sorry. So I forgive you."

"Ah, Jeezus!" whined Nelson. "I don't want you to forgive me, kid. I want you to be a nasty brat so I won't have to feel so bad about what's going to happen to you."

"You mean blowing me up?"

Nelson did a double take. "How did you know that?" he asked incredulously.

"I heard Mr. Logan talking this afternoon."

"Yeah," he said uncomfortably. "I just don't understand why the guy who's paying for this job insisted on blowing you up. I mean, why couldn't we just tie an anchor to you an' drop you over the side?"

Cassie shuddered. "Well, Mr. Nelson, I don't swim very well, although my dad did teach me how to float on my back the summer before he died. But in either case, once I get over the initial shock of dying, I'll be just fine."

Nelson looked at her as if she was crazy. "Wha'd'ya mean, you'll be fine? You'll be dead, kid. An' dead is dead!"

"No, Mr. Nelson," said Cassie. "That's where you're wrong. There's really no such thing as being dead. I died once before, so I know. You can blow me to pieces, or drop me over the side, but as soon as the body quits working, for whatever reason, my consciousness will just be out and on its way to heaven."

"Yeah, sure, kid," said Nelson. "You're crazy, you know that?"

"No, I'm not. And I think I can even prove it," she said. "When Mr. Logan kidnapped me, he put something that smelled like bananas on a handkerchief to knock me out. But while my body was knocked out, my consciousness was out of the body. That happened to me when I died, too, about a year and a half ago. I was in a car wreck, and the rest of my family was killed, all smashed up, but I was in the back seat, and my heart just stopped, so they could bring me back. But before I was resus. . . resuscitated," she said, stumbling over the word, "my mind was out of my body, and with my whole family, I went up to heaven.

"Well, when Mr. Logan kidnapped me, he knocked me out, and I got out of my body then, too. And I was up above, sort of whooshing along both above and then inside it when he put me in a taxi and brought me to the boat. And I even saw a sign with an arrow that said, 'Los Christianos, 6 km,' which I guess means kilometers, right? And you know my body was knocked out when he put me down here in the cabin and had you tie me up, and you know I haven't been out of the cabin since I got on the boat, but I saw the name of the yacht while I was out of my body. We're on the *Reina de Catalan*, aren't we? And I knew, even though I don't know any Spanish, that the name means 'Queen of Catalan,' doesn't it?"

Nelson just sat staring at her as if she were some sort of hitherto unidentified life form, possibly from outside the galaxy.

"Oh. . . my. . . God!" he finally choked in a barely audible whisper.

"So you see," she went on, now that she knew she had clearly rattled him, "there really isn't any death. Whatever you do to me, I'll still be around."

"Does that mean," he asked, "you'll come back to haunt me if you die?" He sounded serious.

Such a thing really hadn't occurred to Cassie, since the idea of haunting anybody was totally alien to her, and she was surprised to find that a big, hulking man like Nelson might be afraid of ghosts. But she suddenly saw a way to achieve what she needed from him.

"Maybe," she said cautiously, not wanting to lie outright. "But I'll tell you what. If you don't actively do anything to make it impossible for me to survive, I promise not to haunt you."

"What do you want me to do, kid?" he asked.

"Just make the ropes, at least on my hands, loose enough so I won't have to die by being blown up. I can get out of the rowboat and into the water."

"You still won't survive, kid," said Nelson. "We're 50 miles from any sort of land. Even if it were light enough for you to see Mount Teide in the distance so you knew which direction to go, you wouldn't make it swimming."

"That doesn't matter," said Cassie. "As long as I can get out of the boat and into the water."

*****

The Bobby Buttram Show generally used an interview format, but for tonight only, the soundstage had been set up with three podiums for the distinguished guests. Buttram was to act as questioner, with matters of ethics and morals as the alleged topics, but matters of religious dogma as his true hidden agenda. Like King Nebuchadnezzar of old, he planned to put his guests through a trial by fire. He would act as the Angel of the Lord to save two of the three. He expected the lady to go up in smoke. If nothing else, he would close the show with a tirade against all the flaws in her thinking; he hadn't been a champion debater for nothing.

As she entered the studio, the Nussbaum woman was gripping her publicist's hand with white knuckles. Buttram had watched her on television many times in the past, and he'd never seen her look as shaken as she did now. "She's terrified," he realized. And then he began to gloat. "She's terrified of me!"

But he was mistaken.

President Flushing was the next to arrive, flanked by his own press staff and corps of secret service personnel. He shook hands with Buttram, then exchanged a handshake and a few words with Sophie and Joe. At that moment, the opposition contender appeared, thus rounding out the guest list for the evening. After more handshakes, Joe pulled Sophie aside.

"Have you decided what to do?" he asked.

She nodded. "The tummy votes to make the appeal the first chance I get," she said.

"Then I'd better slip into the control room," he said, "and be on hand in case somebody tries to cut you off."

Buttram suggested that, since all his guests would be asked to answer—in a sort of debate-style, three-minute oration—the same questions, they should draw lots to see who would go first for the first round of answers. In the next round, whoever had been second would be first, whoever had been third would be second, and the person who had gone first would be last. Sophie won the draw.

"Ah, ladies first," said Buttram. "I hope you won't mind, then, if I introduce you in reverse order from the luck of the draw."

And so, when the cameras began to roll, Buttram announced his guests in turn in the order in which they had lost the draw—the president, the candidate of the major opposition party, and Sophie, and explained to the audience the mechanics of the questioning process, and just why it was Sophie would speak first.

Then Buttram asked the first question. "Mrs. Nussbaum, the issues of abortion and euthanasia are two of the most serious moral issues of our time, dealing as they do with the taking of human life. What is your stand intellectually, spiritually, and morally on these two issues?"

Sophie seemed to be listening thoughtfully as Buttram asked his question. Then she answered, "Normally, Mr. Buttram, I would be willing to answer this, and any other questions on ethics and morals you might wish to ask. I have, in fact, been preparing for this appearance for many days, perhaps indeed for my whole life.

"But I must apologize to you tonight, and to all of you here in the studio, and to those who may be listening at home. For I am here under false pretenses, as I do not plan to answer any questions at all this evening."

There was an audible gasp from the studio audience, and Buttram's mouth dropped open.

At his residence in Great Falls, Virginia, Marvin Snailer sat forward expectantly on the edge of his chair.

"Please believe me," continued Sophie, "I would *not* alter the format of this evening's broadcast but for the gravest of reasons, and I appeal to you, Mr. Buttram, as a man of God and a compassionate human being to allow your viewers across the country to hear me out."

Buttram started to rise from his chair. He tried to motion to the floor director to cut the camera on Sophie, but in the control room Joe nudged the technical director out of the way and took over operation of the switcher in order to maintain the focus on her.

"Yesterday," she said, pulling a glove out of her pocket and putting it on while she spoke, "my ward, Cassandra Allman, was kidnapped, in an apparent plot to make me forfeit my campaign tonight on this show."

Buttram sat back down and motioned for the crew to keep the cameras running. He hadn't known about any plot. And before all else—before his convictions, his principles, his morals, his values—he was, first and foremost, a showman. Whatever was about to happen, he didn't think it could hurt his ratings, and by the end of the show he'd figure out a way to make it help them.

Sophie, having slipped on the glove, reached into the pocket of her blazer and pulled out the kidnapping note.

"Today," she said, "I received this note at my hotel here in Nashville. I am handling it with care so as not to spoil any fingerprints it may be carrying, as I have not yet contacted the police."

She read the note aloud, then turned it so the camera could confirm for the millions of viewers at home that her rendering was accurate, before folding it and putting it back in her pocket.

"This note," she said, "was an attempt to force me, in the most demeaning way possible, to recant the spiritual and humanistic convictions that have caused me to be in a position of candidacy for the presidency in the first place. Please believe me when I say if I thought Cassandra would be spared by my so demeaning myself and dropping out of the race, I would gladly do so. Nothing in life is more important to me than my child.

"But I do not believe the madmen who have taken her will let her come back to me. Logic tells me her kidnappers realize that once I had her safe at home again, I could turn and recant my recantation, and explain to the public why I had willingly made a fool of myself. And so I do not think whoever has her intends to bring her back.

"What I believe is that she and I are being victimized by those who are afraid of us. And why are they afraid of an old woman and a child? Because, my friends, we have together been able to assemble a vast number of people of good will—and quite frankly, I believe the majority of the people of this great country, when they are truly awake, are people of good will. And we have charged these people with a responsibility to join together as healers and peacemakers and asked them to focus just a little of their time and their energy and their good will on issues that, when acted upon in creative ways, will help heal the planet.

"Because of the success of our venture, I have heard it is rumored by those who fear us that we are black magicians, using the powers of evil to do good, in order to subvert the innocent and the righteous. How could we have been so successful in such a short time, they say, if we hadn't been using magic?

182

"The answer is that there is no magic except the power of a clear and unclouded mind. If we are made in the image of God, then why should we not, when we beam the laser light of our mental faculties jointly and in one direction, be able to work miracles? To paraphrase Dr. Margaret Meade, the only power that has ever accomplished anything consisted of the combined effort of a small group of dedicated people. How much more, then, could the concerted effort of a large group of dedicated people accomplish?

"And so I say to you, there is no evil power behind our movement that will try to supplant God. One of our freedoms in this country is that we are free to believe in God in any fashion we choose. We have only asked our friends—those people of good will—to believe in themselves as well, and to become assistants in accomplishing the divine plan God charged us with in giving us dominion over the earth. We were, I believe, to learn to be good stewards, not a wrecking crew.

"I truly believe what I have been preaching to you for the last year and a half. It is said that 'Where your treasure is, there will your heart be also.' My child, Cassandra Allman, is my treasure, for she has had my heart since she came into my life. And the time has come for me to put my treasure where my mouth is."

Sophie's voice began to choke as she realized the magnitude of what she was doing.

"I say to you, therefore, that it doesn't matter what your religion, or how you believe the Second Coming will occur. Perhaps Jesus really will come back, either on a cloud or in a spaceship. But I believe the Second Coming, whatever else it may be, is also us, living out of love rather than fear, focusing together, whatever our religious backgrounds or our ethical principles or our morals—it's us letting each other be whoever we are, just as we are, loving each other without condition, recognizing that every single one of us is a valuable being. Nobody excluded. Nobody in the back of the bus. And when we come from that position of unconditional love toward each other, we have the power to move mountains. We become healers and makers of miracles.

"And so I would ask you, all of you in the viewing audience tonight, to put aside your fears and prejudices, whatever they may be, and join with me in moving a mountain. I do not know if my child is still alive, but my intuition tells me she is. And it also tells me that if all of those watching this show tonight will focus their energy on her safe delivery from her kidnappers, she will be returned unharmed.

"Please, when you turn off your television sets, join hands with those who are there with you, or else go into a quiet place where you can be undisturbed, and focus the healing light of your unconditional love on the safe return of Cassandra Allman. Please keep focusing until it feels right and comfortable for you to stop. Do it together. Do it now!"

Sophie turned from the podium, to the no-sound of awed silence from the audience. She left the soundstage and met Joe and some of the AAP staffers. Together they walked out into the hall, where they linked hands and began to meditate on Cassie's safe return. Soon they were joined by the opposition candidate, the president and his mob of secret service personnel, and two-thirds of both the audience and the Buttram show's crew.

Buttram himself moved to a position in front of the one cameraman who hadn't left the floor and made an effort to sum up what had happened and explain why the show had gone awry, but as the audience continued to exit, he finally gave up. The networks attempted to fill the airspace with commentary, but when no more news was forthcoming they eventually switched to alternative programming.

At his home in Great Falls, Marvin Snailer began shouting obscenities. Fortunately for him, no one of his constituency was around to hear him.

Television ratings for the evening gave the first 15 minutes of the Buttram show 76 percent of the national viewing audience. It was estimated, however, that when Sophie Nussbaum finished her appeal and walked away from the podium, all but about one percent of the people who had been tuned to the show had clicked their television sets off.

Heaven knows what they were doing.

*****

"We haven't got all night, ya know," said Logan. "I want to be back in port by daylight. So go get the kid, an' make sure she's tied up tight."

184

Nelson tried to look angry about being forced to participate in Cassie's murder, but he was frankly feeling rather cheerful. He didn't know why; even if she managed to get out of the rowboat before it blew up, she'd never be able to swim to land. But he somehow didn't feel quite so much like he was damning himself anymore.

He went below to fetch Cassie. He'd retied the rope on her hands at least four times to make sure she knew how to free herself. Externally, the bonds looked perfectly tight, but if she pulled on a little piece that dangled down into one palm, the tie would come loose from the inside out.

Now he came down the ladder, picked the child up, and slung her over his shoulder.

"Good luck, kid," he whispered as he carried her topside.

Logan had already lowered the rowboat by the time Nelson reached the deck.

"I don't understand why you ain't just usin' a rubber lifeboat. It'd be a helluva lot cheaper than a good fiberglass rowboat," observed Nelson.

"Because, dumb ass, I wouldn't have anythin' in a rubber lifeboat to secure the kid to," replied Logan.

"Wha'd'ya mean?" asked Nelson, feeling his stomach sink.

"I mean, I wouldn't be able to tie her into the boat, and she could just roll right out." Logan shouldered his little bag of explosives and picked up a length of rope he had sitting on the deck. "Now put the kid in the boat and come back up here and get this hulk warmed up. We'll have just three minutes after I set the charge to get out of the way."

"I don't know what he's gonna do, kid," said Nelson as he deposited her in the bow. "An' I don't know how I can help you any more, but I'm gonna go toss a lifesaver off the other side of the ship. If you can make it into the water, see if you can spot the lifesaver—it ought to look white in the moonlight."

"Thanks, Mr. Nelson," said Cassie. "You've really tried to help me. I guess whatever happens, I won't haunt you."

Nelson scrambled back onto the yacht, and Logan climbed down.

He took the length of rope and pulled it through the ones that secured both Cassie's hands and feet. Then he wrapped it around the middle seat of the rowboat and tied it securely. He took a flashlight out of the little bag that held the explosives and beamed it on the knots he'd made.

"There," he grunted, satisfied with his work. "If you try to jump out, you won't get very far."

Then he turned around and set up the timed charge in the stern of the boat. In a couple of minutes he stood up and clambered up the ladder.

"Say your prayers, kid," he sneered over his shoulder as he clambered back aboard the yacht. "Let's go, Nelson!" he shouted, and the ship pulled away into the darkness.

"One Mississippi. . . two Mississippi. . .three Mississippi," counted Cassie as she yanked on the length of rope in her palm.

She could feel the bonds give a little, but they didn't just fall off when she wiggled her hands as they had in the earlier drills.

"Oh, dear! Mississippi. . . fifteen Mississippi. . . sixteen Mississippi!"

"Do not panic, little one," came the voice she had heard in her head that afternoon. "Just keep wiggling your hands. You will free yourself soon enough."

Cassie heard a slapping sound as the water broke and a blunt nose appeared on the port side of the little craft. Below the nose, in the moonlight, a liquid black eye stared at her. She stopped counting and started wiggling earnestly.

La Reina de Catalan cut its engines about two minutes away from the rowboat.

"We wait here until we see it blow," said Logan harshly. "Then we head for Tenerife. By my calculations, it should go up in just 30 seconds."

They stood together on the deck. Logan waited smugly, arms crossed. Nelson was surprised to realize he had unconsciously crossed his fingers; he didn't quite know why, and he uncrossed them.

"About 10 seconds more," hissed Logan. "Nine. . . eight. . . seven. . . six . . . five. . . four. . . three. . . two. . . one . . . blast off!"

And nothing happened.

"I must have miscalculated," said Logan in a surly tone. "But it should go up any minute now."

Logan leaned against the rail, searching the darkness. Time stretched on.

And nothing happened.

Ten minutes passed. Then five more minutes. Then yet five more minutes.

And nothing happened.

"Damn!" spat Logan. "Something must have gone wrong with the trigger. We'll have to go back."

Nelson started the engine again and they headed back to where they'd left the rowboat. It took about five minutes before they spotted it in the ship's spotlight.

"God damn it all to hell!" screamed Logan, and Nelson knew what his next words would be before he said them: "The kid's not in the boat!"

Nelson cut the engine and ran to the railing. Throwing out a grappling hook, he snagged the rowboat and brought it alongside. Logan, clearly enraged, glared at him for a long moment, then climbed down into the rowboat.

"Bloody hell!" he shrieked, and held up the three lengths of rope. "She got untied! Who the hell was she, Houdini's daughter?"

As Nelson leaned out to examine the ropes, the charge in the stern of the rowboat finally went off, blasting away the entire forward half of the yacht. The aft portion sank in less than a minute. Needless to say, the explosion instantaneously reduced Logan, Nelson, and the rowboat to globules of flesh and shards of bloodied bone and fiberglass.

Nelson looked down at the floating debris. What was left of his body was flotsam and jetsam. Shark bait.

"The kid was right!" he marveled. "Ya don't need a body to still *be!*"

He felt as if he had expanded, as if the case which had been holding him had really been a too-tight shoe, as if he was many sizes larger than he had been in his body.

Then he saw the thoughtform that had been Logan literally pull itself together out of the floating rubble below and flow up toward him.

"Race ya t' the moon!" laughed Nelson, as he began speeding toward the Light.

*****

At 7:23 a.m., a coastal reconnaissance helicopter searching for the yacht *La Reina de Catalan* spotted an extraordinary sight west of the Canary Islands and radioed it in to headquarters.

"*¡Madre de Dios!* You won't believe what we are seeing! Pods of dolphins, all swimming together and traveling due east. There must be hundreds of them!"

As the helicopter swooped down for a closer look, Cassandra, bobbing along joyfully in a life ring being pulled by its rope by the dolphins, raised her arm and waved.

*****

"A toast," said Adam, when he had filled everyone's champagne glasses with Alpenglow, "to the next president of the United States, Sophie Nussbaum!"

"You're being a little premature, I think," said Sophie. "I still have six more months of hard running against a moderately popular incumbent and an entrenched bipartisan system. So I'm afraid your toast falls into the category of tabulating your domestic fowls before they incubate. But I appreciate the vote of confidence," she added, as they all clinked glasses and sipped.

"Well, I have a toast," said Joe, looking lovingly at Sophie. "To tummies, and those who listen to them."

"Hear, hear!" agreed Sophie as they all clinked glasses again. "I'll drink to that!"

"My tummy says it's time to have the cake," said Cassie.

She'd been hungry ever since her adventure on the high seas. The dolphins were kind hosts, but she'd found their cuisine somewhat lacking.

Little Adonna, who was just beginning to take her first steps alone, was guided by her mother to Sophie's lap, so they could cut the cake together. It was a delightfully decadent artifice of chocolate cake and chocolate mousse, decorated with a golden spider web in the center, connected to rainbow colored webs at the end of each strand.

"For your network of networks, Sophie," said Lucy, who had designed the decoration for the cake. "And because you and Adonna were born in what was once the 13th sign of the Zodiac, the sign of Arachne, the spider goddess who helped create the world. The Indians, too, you know, have a myth that Spider Woman wove the world on rainbow strands."

"I've often felt I needed eight arms and legs," said Sophie. "Now I know why! But before we mangle this cake, I want someone to take a picture of it."

"With black and white film," said Joe, holding up one camera and snapping Sophie and his baby girl, "suitable for the newspapers. And with color," he said, holding up a second camera, "for the scrapbooks."

"I'd like to announce, by the way," said Adam, "while we're on the subject of networking networks, that the Consortium has been financially successful enough that Celeste and I now officially have salaries to go with our job descriptions. We are no longer living off the bounty of our spouses!"

"And speaking of work arrangements," said Sophie, "those involved have talked it over, and we've agreed that Ray and Cassie will take Lucy's place on my traveling staff this summer. This will free Lucy to do some painting, without which she has found she doesn't thrive. And it will permit me to teach Cassie the delights of the campaign trail."

She didn't mention that as valuable as Lucy was in sizing up people and situations, her synesthesia created great stress for her whenever she had to be in large crowds. Which was most of the time while they were campaigning. She knew Lucy would be happier away from the mobs.

Ray spoke up. "Well, I'm looking forward to riding the trail myself. It will permit *me* to exonerate myself for the fiasco in Tenerife Airport," he said. "Both Sophie and Cassie will get up an hour early with me every morning and start practicing Tai Chi, too. I'll have less to worry about when they can handle their own self-protection."

"What happened in the airport wasn't your fault," insisted Cassie, who was sitting next to Ray, stroking Emerson. Smoo, who had come to visit for the birthday celebration, sat at her feet and seemed to be ignoring the cat as long as Cassie rubbed him with her foot. "And besides, if I hadn't been kidnapped, I'd never have swum with the dolphins!"

"Well," said Adam, "the FBI is investigating Snailer's association with the company that owned the yacht the kidnappers used, so we're hoping he'll soon be out of commission, as well as out of the Senate. I just wish we could trace who delivered the kidnapping note."

"I'm told the FBI report indicated there were no fingerprints on the note or the envelope, so all my care in wearing gloves was for nothing," said Sophie. "But we know Snailer wished us ill, so it's important to deflect the negatives in a positive way, and transmute his darkness into light. And maybe we should just visualize a general state of enlightenment for any stragglers who may not yet have tuned in to the shifting global consciousness raising. Let's send light to any little dark spots that are left."

"Yes," said Celeste, who felt she had learned some remarkable lessons working with the Consortium, "it's important to love your enemies, if only because it drives them crazy!"

Cassie thought of Nelson and added, "Well, maybe sometimes it drives them sane."

"Pur-r-p!" exclaimed Emerson.

*****

It had been a good party, thought Sophie, as she got ready for bed that night. Whatever might manifest in the future, she and her new "family," as she liked to think of them, had accomplished much, and she was grateful they were once again all safe and together.

Oh, there would be changes in their roles. It seemed everything was constantly changing! Lucy was going back to her art, for instance. And Adam was talking about writing a metaphysical book in his spare time. And dear Ray wouldn't be living with her and Cassie much longer, she sensed. He was bridging a gap, by being part of the work of the Consortium, helping to change minds in the populace at large about what it meant to be gay. But she thought he would want to go back and work in the gay community again soon. And perhaps he would even find someone else to love. He was still very young.

She looked at the wedding photograph of Saul and herself, as she always did before turning out her lamp.

"Well, dear," she said to him, "it's been nearly six years since you decided to go off without me, and though I'll always miss you, I guess I don't have as much time to *think* about it as I used to. But look how many people it took to fill up the empty space you left behind—practically the whole world!"

And as she turned off the light, lay back, and prepared herself for sleep, she smiled a little, for she thought she heard him laughing.

EPILOGUE

"Only that day dawns to which we are awake. There is more day to dawn. The sun is but a morning star."
—*Henry David Thoreau, Walden*

Cassie dreamed.

It was the summer before her 30th birthday. She and her husband Kwan Lee had decided to take a vacation in their solar terracar with their two children, Nan and Juan. Adonna Jacobson, who had just graduated from high school, had been invited along for the two-month adventure as a part of her graduation present.

In the decade following its inception, the Consortium focused often on long-standing hot spots around the globe—South Africa, the Middle East, Northern Ireland, Alabama, and other places where conflict existed principally because it always had in living memory.

Communities like Farset Farm in Northern Ireland, where Catholics and Protestants worked together, and Neve Shalom-Wahat al Salaam in Israel, where Palestinians and Jews lived in harmony, had already proved people of different religious and political persuasions could discover creative solutions to their conflicts. For it was well known among conflict resolution professionals that peace is not the absence of conflict, but the active pursuit of win-win results.

With the exponentially increased positive energy of the Consortium behind their efforts, the attitudes such communities bred proliferated until there had finally been born a generation of children for whom the ancient conflicts were no longer the norm.

Human rights world-wide were a next necessary concern, but as Sophie had once predicted, when the critical mass of consciousness reached a certain point, all people came to recognize the folly of their prejudices against others. Race, religion, age, gender, and even sexual predisposition were recognized as incidental to a person's worth.

Much credit had to go to Consortium members in the Soviet Union for encouraging the globalization of democratic principles, though they admittedly seemed a necessary adjunct to the global economy which was beginning to develop. The Consortium's toughest nut, from the retrospective of the second decade of the 21st century, had been China, where economic reform had begun in the '70s almost exclusive of the world economy, and where rigid political control was entrenched and seen to be more important than people, but by 2015 the governments of the globe had all become democracies.

With world-wide peaceful coexistence as the standard, it became possible for the world's powers to demilitarize completely. This meant a substantial force of young men and women from countries round the world could consider themselves no longer at war but at peace with each other. The United Nations then requested that each country of its member nations require two years of mandatory service—to one's country or to the planet—from each youth upon graduation from high school. Wages for service were paid by each member country out of the no longer needed military budgets. The model for such service was the volunteer U.S. Peace Corps, which had functioned as a substitute for military service in the latter part of the 20th century.

The program worked well, especially when service assignments to other countries often found youths of 10 or 15 nationalities working together, and especially when an updated variant of Esperanto, known as Terran, became the common medium of communication. It was expected that youth from virtually all countries would be participating in the service program by 2030, when it was predicted the world would finally be perfectly balanced economically. In the meantime, the Planetary Service Corps became so popular that participants often signed on for an extra two years of service. Ultimately, entering the PSC became the true rite of passage to adulthood, and those who had been deprived, for whatever reason, of their period of service at age 18 often requested it in their 20s. Adonna Jacobson was certainly looking forward to her induction into the corps at the end of this vacation trip!

Economically, the rise of the Pacific Rim and the coalescing of the countries of Europe had created two very powerful and creative entities which redefined the tensile strength of the world's markets. And in much the same way that the European Common Market had essentially united the peoples of Europe in the '90s into a borderless economic unit, so the Pan-American Accord a decade later had made all the Americas borderless and open to free trade among the peoples of North, Central, and South America.

Further, it had been recognized within just two years after the Cookie Lobby had completed their canvassing effort that if the rain forests in the southern hemisphere of the Americas were to be salvaged, the people of the northern hemisphere were going to have to assist in upgrading the standard of living of their brothers who had the stewardship of the forests.

The result was the establishment of a Pan-American coalition, the first wave of which allowed United States businesses to lease the rain forests for a period of 25 years in order to co-create with South American countries the appropriate business channels for the non-destructive harvesting of their considerable resources. The second wave was the educational effort, aimed at turning poor peasants into proficient farmers, skilled builders, and trained health-care workers who could effectively tend the needs of their own villages. The efforts of the Consortium of Light and Sophie's bid for the U.S. presidency had of course helped focus attention and consciousness toward the positive value of these efforts.

A long-held theory maintained that population growth would be curtailed once the health and hunger problems of a given nation were solved. This proved to be the case in the South American countries, and birth rates declined. With the assistance of the Planetary Service Corps, Africa, India, and China were finally able to turn their deserts into farmlands through irrigation and crop rotation techniques. It was thus expected that by 2020 all the world's countries would have stable populations.

Of course, environmental and ecological responsibility had increased hand-in-hand with the awakening consciousness of the earth's peoples and their recognition of their interdependence and mutual worth. As global lifestyles and global cuisine came to be appreciated, it was recognized that the consumption of large amounts of animal flesh by human beings was flagrantly wasteful. A balance of grains, legumes, nuts and seeds, and occasionally dairy products provided all the protein essential to sustain life. As populations ate less animal flesh, their incidence of cancers, arthritis, high blood pressure, and atherosclerosis decreased.

And in the same way all human beings had come to be seen as valuable, no matter what, so did all species of plants and animals on the earth come to be seen as worthy of preservation. And the dying out of whole species ceased.

The Consortium also had a hand in finally focusing consciousness on the establishment of a global energy policy that relied principally on renewables. Great solar collectors in the deserts of the American West provided enough energy for the needs of the whole country. Third world countries, which by the late '90s were already relying heavily on wind energy, supplemented that renewable source with solar. Because no one really wanted to deal with the problem of what to do with nuclear wastes, nuclear energy became passe. And with the cessation of use of fossil fuels, the threat of global warming became a thing of the past as well.

As people continued loving and respecting each other and themselves and all life on the planet, it was observed they were living longer by decades. Perhaps because they finally wanted to.

And as the consciousness of the people of the planet had become global and responsible, arbitrary borders no longer made any sense, and everyone wondered why they ever had. And so it was that, with the European and Pan-American models working so effectively, all the countries of Earth were expected to join the Planetary Accord by 2020, thus making the entire planet a family of one people.

It was the western hemisphere of this world without boundaries or borders Cassie and her family were visiting. They drove their solar terracar from Alaska, where they were now living, across Canada, to Washington, D.C., where they picked up Adonna and went south, down Mexico, around the curve of Central America, and into South America, down Peru on the west and back up through Brazil in the east. And they reveled in having no border crossings, and in visiting with the new men and women who truly knew their worth, who lived and worked in harmony with the earth and were rewarded bountifully in return.

One night on the trip, Cassie sat on a stone at the High Gate at Machu Picchu. She looked up at the Pleiades, and she thought, "How lucky I was to have come into the world just when people were ready to wake up after a long and stony sleep. How lucky I was to have died and come back, so I could help tell people not to be afraid of anything anymore. How lucky I was to be a to be afraid of anything anymore. How lucky I was to be a dreamer and a maker of magic, and to be here on this planet when people finally found the consciousness and the will to turn it back into Eden."

And the Seven Sisters of the Pleiades shimmered in the night sky, and she heard a voice inside her head say, "Life and love are both eternal. There are other worlds, not to conquer, but to bless, protect, and transform. But for now, you have done well. Your reward is to enjoy what you have built, for you have truly earned it. Live long in peace and sweetness, little sister."

And as Cassie woke from her dream of Eden, she knew it for a reality that the people of good will everywhere would bring to pass.

ABOUT THE AUTHOR

Honora Finkelstein readily admits to being the model for Sophie Nussbaum in *Magicians*. Like Sophie, she once yearned to be a psychologist, has always loved teaching, talks to nature spirits with pretty good results, and has walked on hot coals without burning her feet. And she has had a long-term love affair with the American Transcendentalists, who offered some practical models over a hundred years ago for loving and preserving the planet and its people. Unlike Sophie, she has no desire to be president of the United States.

In a varied career that spans over 30 years, Honora served as an officer in U.S. Navy intelligence during the Vietnam crisis; has a Ph.D. in English; is the mother of four children; is an ordained minister; is producer and host of a new paradigm television show in the Washington, D.C. area; and is interested in building co-creative communities with other visionaries in all fields.

She firmly believes that ordinary people can make a difference in the world from wherever they are, and that if enough of them were to try to effect change, they could literally turn Earth into Eden.

Books and Tapes Available from SUNWEAVERS,™ Inc.

From SERAPH PRESS:

**MAGICIANS: A Novel of Transformation
and Co-Creation** *by Honora Finkelstein*
ISBN: 1-885776-00-4 (book)
(Softcover, 208 pages; $12.00; available July 1994.)

PIECES OF EIGHT: A Card Set for Co-Creation
by Honora Finkelstein and Susan Smily
ISBN: 1-885776-01-2 (card set)
(Prototype 90-card deck uses archetypes of the hero's journey and symbols of the medicine wheel as they apply to work in relationships; deck comes in cloth pouch with instructional booklet; $15.00; available Fall 1994.)

**BICYCLING TO BYZANTIUM: A Workbook for
Empowerment in Co-Creative Relationships**
by Honora Finkelstein and Susan Smily
ISBN: 1-885776-02-0 (book)
ISBN: 1-885776-03-9 (book with card set)
(3-ring binder: A series of empowerment booklets examining such concepts as the Hero's Journey, Co-Creativity, the Medicine Wheel, Conscious Communication, and much more. 192 pages; $15.00; available Winter 1994. This workbook also comes in combination with the "Pieces of Eight" deck for $25.00.)

From SERAPH MEDIA:

TO YOUR HEALTH: A Whole Foods Cooking Video
*Honora Finkelstein talks to whole-foods educator
Roberta Robinson about everything from soups to desserts.*
ISBN: 1-885776-25-X (video)
(2-hour video tape has a 30-minute interview on the principles behind whole-foods eating, and a 90-minute cooking demonstration. $20.00; available January 1995.)

TO ORDER: Contact SUNWEAVERS, Inc.
2104 Twin Mill Lane
Oakton, VA 22124
Telephone: (703) 264-5033.